Needles Arizona

Bill Coates

For family dogs past and present
Homer, Sammy, Benji and Maggie –
To name a few

Also by Bill Coates

Pug Ugly and Pretty Dead

Rancho Javelina

People, Places and Dogs:
Columns from the Casa Grande Dispatch

Chapter One

Early June 2007
The Cubs still lovable losers
Flip phones still cool

Billy Olsen sized up his chances of stooping under the low-slung police tape. He imagined an elephant doing the limbo.

With a shrug, he cut the ribbon with a pocketknife and watched the yellow ends settle to the dirt.

Then Billy Olsen lumbered up to the hole.

Not a particularly deep hole. But you don't have to dig far to remove, say, a fifteen-foot saguaro cactus. Whoever stole this saguaro knew that. They knew to dig just deep enough to separate the plant from its main tap root, cut the shallow roots and load it on a flatbed. The entire job probably took no more than five, ten minutes tops.

The sun had crested the horizon. A mild orange ball, minding its own business. Give it a few hours. It'll work its way to noon and settle in as the broiler for the urban oven known as greater Phoenix. But Olsen wasn't complaining. At the moment, in early June, it was a good time to be outdoors. Pleasant, almost cool. All that would change by July, where hot was 24/7.

Something moved. Olsen caught the outline of a bat, clocking out after a night of draining nectar from gaudy white saguaro blossoms. The saguaros had greeted it with raised open arms, all bristling with needles. Trumpet-like blooms sprouted from them,

1

as gaudy as flowers on a clown's nose. The sun ticked up slightly and revealed a small puddle, near the hole from the missing saguaro.

Olsen, a large man, shifted his weight slowly, left to right.

"Jesus," he said.

He waved to the Paradise Valley police officer standing some fifteen feet away. Another half dozen stood in a circle, chatting amongst themselves. The one cop had arms the size of a lamppost. His shirt was too tight from all the muscles. Olsen felt a tinge of envy. His shirt was too tight from waffles and beer.

"You might want to see this," Olsen said.

The officer looked up from a clipboard, annoyed. Olsen knew the look. The one that said Olsen was barely worth his time. The one that said Olsen wasn't a real cop. Maybe a step above Captain Kangaroo, and Olsen could almost see his point. Olsen just didn't look the part. He had no shiny badge cast from a half-pound of brass. He didn't wear a crisply pressed dark blue uniform. He went with comfort. A khaki outfit more suited to a Boy Scout troop leader, from the pleated cargo shorts tightly wrapped about big-man thighs to an un-ironed short-sleeved shirt. He was armed with a clamshell phone, clipped to his belt.

But Billy Olsen was, by law, a real cop. Sure, no badge. But he had an arm-patch, a saguaro cactus embroidered in bright-green thread. Below that, another patch read: "Native Plant Enforcement, Arizona Department of Agriculture." Back at the office, his police-academy diploma was framed and on the wall. He even owned a .38-caliber revolver, though he rarely carried it around. He kept it under the seat of his pickup, next to the hamburger wrappers. The bullets locked in the glove compartment, in case it was stolen.

The officer glanced at the puddle. Pointed with his chin. "Yeah, I know," he said. Still annoyed. "Blood. It's in the report." He went back to the clipboard.

"Right," Olsen replied. "Blood."

So maybe it wasn't such a neat job of cactus rustling after all. Somebody got careless. Got perforated. An occupational hazard when working around plants that defend themselves with needles big enough to crucify a cat. Then again, Olsen thought: Looks like an awful lot of blood for a few pinpricks.

Something, he noted, was dragged from the puddle, trailing blood across the tire tracks left by the truck. *Dog prints? And what about the tire tracks?* Yeah, they were big. Big truck. Big tracks. Olsen's followed them with a gaze. The driver had been careful not to crush the flora along the way, coming in or going out. Instead of a straight line, he wove around creosote, prickly pear and cholla. The environmentally sensitive getaway.

Out of character for your average cactus thief. Most didn't care about nature. They pronounced "ecology" like it was some kind of disease. They just drove straight to the scene of the crime. And straight from it. If a few plants got in the way — well, that was their tough luck.

It was not an easy drive to begin with. The cactus haulers had to navigate two steep arroyos, cutting through the back half of Russell Larrabee's twelve-acre lot in Paradise Valley, a well-heeled suburb of Phoenix.

In Larrabee's case, well-heeled also meant well-connected. And few people had the kind of connection Russell Larrabee had to the ninth floor of the State House, the governor's office. Governor Roger Pilt counted on Larrabee for his unwavering support. Of course, this was politics – where support meant ninety-nine percent money and one percent democracy. Larrabee was generous with his support, as generous as the law allowed – and sometimes even more so.

The politically connected Larrabee had the governor's private number. Here's what he told the governor, as Olsen heard it. Larrabee heard a scream, like somebody hurt. It was early morning. Maybe or two or three. He jumped out of bed, tossed on a robe and ran outside. He saw a large flatbed truck pull away, lit by floodlights that dotted the property. He noted the crested was gone, plucked from the ground. He called Paradise Valley police, after calling the governor, who in turn called Olsen's boss. Olsen got the call at five a.m.

Political connections get results.

Larrabee's connections flowed from a personal fortune amassed through a nationwide chain of dollar stores, Under-A-Buck. He had come to dominate the market by slashing his prices to ninety-seven cents. And by TV ads aimed at night owls looking for midnight deals on the shopping channel.

His motto: "Sold! For ninety-seven cents!"

In addition to politics, Larrabee spent his dollar-store fortune on things big and pricey, often without regard to subtlety. His house could have passed for your average Tudor manor, though it probably had a bigger swimming pool. The greenhouse, a short hike to the west, was the size of a Hollywood sound stage. Inside, a jaw-dropping collection of rare plants, as Olsen understood it. He also understood that Larrabee had no real interest in the collection, other than he'd hear a plant was rare and decided he had to have it. He'd put down his money and have it shipped to the desert. It didn't bother Larrabee that he had no idea what the hell it was, only that it was hard to come by. And cost a lot. Olsen himself couldn't tell an elm from an oak tree. But he knew a hell of a lot about the native Arizona species he was paid to protect.

4

That brought him around to the hole. Olsen's boss said the cactus taken from it had been a crested saguaro. Definitely native. And, though not from the greenhouse, definitely rare.

Olsen heard a one-man army. Larrabee marched up out of the arroyo, his head bobbing like a pigeon's. Before him, a twelve-count family of quail darted out from under a creosote, running in panic. Baby birds the size of cherry tomatoes chased after two adults, each crowned with a half-curled feather, a perpetual question mark. Like molecules of hot gas, the baby birds collided with each other and ran around in tight circles. So did the grownups. All appeared lost and confused. But somehow, out of this random motion, they fashioned a sense of direction. Tripping over one another, they lined up and disappeared into the desert. Larrabee kept on coming as the rising sun backlit his bald crown and made it glow. He was a man of extraordinary energy and, at the moment, he appeared to be operating on solar power. Thick in stature, Larrabee had a bulbous head and a thick nose to match, though his lips were thin. And he wore a smile you couldn't slap off. He was, after all, a salesman. And, Olsen guessed, he had to be pretty good to sell that many ninety-seven-cent trinkets to become a multimillionaire. Not to mention company stock that apparently had no ceiling.

Larrabee power-walked toward the half-dozen Paradise Valley officers and technicians who were working the tire tracks like an archaeological dig. Smiling, always smiling, he greeted them like best friends. Even in his bathrobe, Larrabee radiated warmth and sincerity. The officers and technicians smiled and waved back. He could have easily sold them a ninety-seven-cent box of laundry detergent and shoe polish of equal quality, on the spot.

Instead, he asked, "Anybody seen couple of dogs? Golden retriever? Little spaniel?"

Nobody had.

"What the hell! They're around here somewhere, digging holes."

When he got to Olsen, Larrabee grabbed his hand and shook it like a dice tumbler. He had his big smile inches from Olsen's chin, Olsen being the taller of the two.

"Good to meet you, Captain Olaf!"

"Olsen. I'm an investigator, but I don't really have a rank."

"You find that cactus for me, and I'll have the governor promote you to colonel! What do you say to that!"

"Fine." Olsen nodded. He didn't know what to say actually, but if anybody could get Governor Pilt to make him a colonel in native plant enforcement, it was Larrabee. And if anybody could get the governor to bust Olsen down to a private — or worse, fire him — it was Larrabee. He had that kind of pull. Otherwise, the department director himself wouldn't have called so damn early to beg Olsen to find the damn crested. By that time of the morning, Rudy Ossylmeyer was nearly sober. He'd be good until lunch.

Had the cactus been stolen from anybody else, Olsen would have looked into it anyway – at a more reasonable hour. Larrabee's special treatment was only a matter of degree. Saguaros were protected plants, no matter whose land they happened to be on – public or private. Just moving one required a state tag, costing a couple of bucks and the minor inconvenience of paperwork. Cactus rustlers, not known as a highly literate class, nonetheless knew how to fill out the forms.

But the saguaro plucked from Larrabee's estate was different. Also known as cristates, cresteds were rare. And, being freaks of nature, they were easy to spot. Slipping a tag on a stolen crested wouldn't fool anybody. Might as well put dog tags on a polar bear.

Russell Larrabee fished a photograph from the pocket of his bathrobe. It showed him next to the freak of nature.

"Here's what the bastards stole. They don't make them like this anymore, do they, Colonel Olsen?"

"No sir." Olsen apparently got the promotion. But, as far as he knew, Larrabee still outranked him.

"And this one, this crested means more to me than just a damn cactus. I can't explain it. It's got a hidden quality about it."

"May I," Olsen asked.

"Sure." Larrabee handed Olsen the snapshot.

Looks familiar, Olsen thought. Maybe he saw it in the file, among the three hundred or so photos he had of every crested in the state. Well, every *known* crested.

"How did you come by this, Mr. Larrabee?"

"The cactus? It was here when I bought the property. I'd say about five years ago. Damn lucky for a collector of rare plants, wouldn't you say?"

"Damn lucky," Olsen said. "How big is this crested, floor to ceiling?"

"Oh, somewhere between a one- and two-story house. I'd really, really like it back. Something special, you know."

Olsen could see that, if just from a picture.

Unlike your average saguaro, the crested did not look like a prickly ballistic missile. Instead, the trunk was topped by a monstrous fan-shaped structure — five to ten inches thick with a five-foot span. On some cristates, the crests looked like half-formed tumors. But the crest pictured here was regal, majestic – an expanse of tucks and rolls, upholstered in fluted green skin. The Jolly Green Giant could wear it as a headdress.

No doubt. This was one hell of a cristate, notwithstanding the large hole in the middle of the crest. Handiwork of a Gila

7

woodpecker, power drilling its way through needles, cactus ribs and pulp to hollow out a nest.

The cactus dealt with it by sealing it off, creating a cavity of scar tissue. A gourd-shaped enclosure known as a boot. It gave the living tissue a work around and made for a nice nest. The hole looked to be about ten feet off the ground. Two, three feet from the top. It was large for a boot. Big enough to put your fist through, judging by the photo.

Something about the whole thing just struck him as familiar.

"Can I hang on to this picture, Mr. Larrabee?" Olsen asked.

"Sure, captain."

Olsen nodded vaguely, then spotted the state's other cactus cop doing his all for the taxpayers. Joshua Hempf, some fifty feet away, stood over one of tracks left by the truck. With a Paradise Valley cop holding the reel, Hempf stretched a tape measure across the width of the tread mark. He let go the tape end. It shot back into the metal case nestled in the cop's hand.

Hempf smiled, a man who just learned a truth he had known all along. He headed toward Olsen.

"Yep. Firestones all right."

Hempf excelled in any detail that didn't involve blood. Blood made him squeamish. Olsen made a mental note. Keep Hempf at arm's length from the puddle at his feet. Olsen didn't want to lose his partner. The state Division of Native Plant Enforcement was woefully understaffed as it was.

"Really?" Olsen said. "I'da guessed Goodyear."

Olsen followed the tracks away from the puddle, back to where Hempf had stood. He pointed along the way.

"See. Look. Can Firestones do that?"

He went about another fifty feet, to a ridge between two arroyos, pointing to tracks here and there. Hempf followed and –

8

curious about what was going on – so did Russell Larrabee. And with Larrabee, half the Paradise Valley police force tagged along, too. They weren't about to miss out on something important. If only Olsen had something important to add. He only wanted to draw Hempf away from the pool of blood. Now he had a following, all waiting for a revelation on tire-tread evidence. But, when it came to tread marks, Olsen didn't know the difference between a roller skate and a tractor.

Olsen wiped the sweat from his forehead. The sun rose by degrees, and so did the temperature.

"Maybe you're right, Hempf. Might be Firestones."

"Durstan had Firestones when he did his job in oh-three," Hempf said. "According to the trial transcripts, the tread match helped sway the jurors. He got two years for stealing a protected species from state land."

"Randall Durstan? Is he out?" Olsen asked.

"Yeah. Released last year."

"Hmm, that's right. How could I forget? So, you think the tread marks … "

"Point to Durstan. Sure. Well, maybe not conclusively." Hempf pursed his lips, squinted. "In the oh-three job, the tread showed considerable wear on the front driver-side tire. Much more so than the passenger side. I don't see that here. Could be new tires."

That was Hempf, a master of detail. Probably no more than twenty-eight, he had been with Native Plant Enforcement less than a year, yet he knew the modus operandi of just about every cactus thief in the state. He studied department reports and court records going back twenty years. In his five years with the department, the thirty-four-year-old Olsen picked up most of what he knew of cactus thieves on the job. What kinds of trucks

9

and hauling equipment they used. Who they hung out with and where they drank. Who they were married to and who they slept with – sometimes, but not always the same person. Backed by his experience, Olsen worked on educated hunches to solve thefts. His hunch had led to Durstan's arrest on theft of a three-armed saguaro near Lake Pleasant, northwest of Phoenix. It took the testimony of Durstan's girlfriend – former girlfriend now – to convict him. It was a crime Durstan couldn't repeat now. The state had since sold the land to developers. The saguaros had been dug up and sold to nurseries. Houses stood in their place.

"Well, new Firestones or old, you might be right. It could be Durstan's work," Olsen said. "But that can't be his blood back there. He's not that careless." Damn, Olsen thought. Who's careless now?

"There's blood?" Hempf asked, though he didn't want to know.

Olsen laid a big hand on Hempf's fragile shoulder.

"It's nothing."

Hempf managed a smile.

Then the dogfight broke out.

Snarls and yips came from the arroyo, giving voice to a dried-up brittlebush, shaking from the tumult.

"Hey, you two, knock it off!" Larrabee grinned as he shook his large bald head. "Goddamn dogs, always fighting over something."

The dogs went quiet. The golden retriever crashed through the bush and trotted up the arroyo, toward the group. Behind him trailed the other dog – the spaniel, small and brown and hairy. The small dog had something in its mouth.

"What you got there, Toodles, girl?" Larrabee asked.

As Toodles was half hidden by the bigger dog, it was hard to tell what Toodles had – until Toodles loped up ahead, stopped at Larrabee's feet and dropped a book. It was covered in dirt and what appeared to be blood. The muscle-bound cop set down his clipboard, snapped on surgical gloves and picked it up. He fanned the pages. About midway through a piece of skin popped out. As soon as it hit the ground, Toodles gulped it down.

Hempf fainted on the spot. A pair of officers dragged him into a patrol car and revived him with a few sips of water. The muscle-head tore off one of the pages that had pressed the flesh.

"DNA evidence," he said.

"Why bother," Olsen said. "You've got blood enough over there to fill a beer mug."

"Pardon me, sir," the cop said. "I'm team leader on this investigation."

Olsen shrugged.

He asked: "Can I see the book?"

"It's evidence. You'll contaminate it."

Olsen pulled on a pair of leather gloves he kept in his cargo shorts. They came in handy for the kind of evidence he usually handled – cactus. He reached for the book. The cop frowned, but handed it over. The cover pictured a skinny man in a loincloth, standing before a saguaro. His hands were uplifted, like a holy man in prayer. Below the picture was the title: *The Cosmic Cactus: An Upster's Travel Guide to Uppermost Consciousness* by William R. Upchurch. Olsen riffled the pages, stopping at a slip of register paper tucked inside. Sedona Public Library was printed at top. Olsen slid the paper out.

"Somebody's in trouble," Olsen said.

The cop picked up his clipboard, flipped to his report, ready to write. He looked up.

"How so?" he asked.

"This book's a year overdue."

Chapter Two

Olsen held the book open with one hand and forked a syrupy waffle with the other. He had stopped for breakfast at the Waffle Den, conveniently located ten minutes from his office at the Arizona State Capitol complex. Not that it mattered. Olsen would have stopped here if the place were an hour out of the way. They made great waffles. Filling and tasty as hell. It must have been the carbs, abetted by generous portions of butter and syrup. It wasn't all good. His doctor warned him that the things he liked were showing up in his blood sugar. Borderline diabetic. Borderline? File that under close but no cigar, Olsen thought. He forked another bite of waffle.

His Pima grandmother's advice was harder to ignore. She had grown up on a traditional diet of beans and squash and corn. She was built like a grandmother should be, with a generous lap for holding and hugging. But she was not overweight like many of her Pima relatives. They had fallen for the Anglo fare of cheap burgers, bread and French fries, abandoning the food of their ancestors. They paid with obesity, heart problems and diabetes.

Yes, whenever he visited, his grandmother warned him about the white man's food. And it played on his conscience. But he was not fat. OK, clinically overweight. But mostly he was just big. Six-five, 247 pounds. Not all of it excess. And Billy Olsen could carry his weight, if didn't involve more than three flights of stairs.

"Another Belgian special?" the waitress asked as Olsen hit the halfway point on his waffle.

"Not today."

She frowned, disappointed, likely counting on Olsen to pick up a slump that never recovered from the anti-carb craze.

He thumbed to the book's title page and reread the handwritten message he spotted earlier.

To Randall, spirit little brother, may Big Spirit fill your days and guide you to Uppermost Consciousness. Wm. Upchurch

"Hmm." Olsen took another look at the library receipt. Upchurch had checked out his own book and given it to Durstan.

So now, Randall Durstan, New Age desert Upster, traveled the cosmos and channeled spirits from cactus-fueled energy fields. At least that was the thinking. On planet Earth, it didn't fit the Randall Durstan he knew. The Durstan he knew didn't seek oneness with saguaros. He stole them. And, in his day, he the was best. Probably half the saguaros planted in SeniorTown had been stolen by Durstan. Of course, of late, somebody had been stealing them back. Perhaps that was another story. Perhaps it wasn't. Here was Durstan's story, as far as Olsen could figure. He had found the light, and it lit the way to spiritual healing, oneness and the occasional trip to Alpha Centauri. But his new-found spiritual awakening apparently didn't stop him from stealing the occasional cactus.

Well, you'd think two years in prison, and he'd have learned his lesson. But time served probably didn't hurt as much as how he ended up there in the first place. The woman who loved him testified against him in order to save her own skin. Roz Ranker was caught buying a stolen cactus. Durstan was caught selling it to her. Tough luck there. Tough luck now. Only this time around, Durstan left some damn good circumstantial evidence at the scene. An overdue library book with his name on it, and autographed by William Upchurch, founder and spiritual guide of

14

the Worldwide Church of Uppermost Cosmic Consciousness. And then there was the matter of blood and skin, the small fragment the dog didn't eat. Could be Durstan's DNA in that.

How could a pro like Durstan let a cactus get the better of him? Well, Olsen thought, it happens. If there's a struggle involving gravity, the cactus always wins.

Better pay Durstan a visit, Olsen figured. He'd swing by the office, pick up Hempf and head out to Durstan's house, about forty-minutes west of Phoenix. Maybe he'd catch Durstan with the cactus, unless he had promised same-day delivery. Maybe Durstan had showed up at the ER with a cactus-related injury. Olsen had thought of that. He'd called area hospitals to alert him if anybody showed up with puncture wounds. Then again, Durstan probably knew better. It's like going to the autobody shop after a hit-and-run. They'll be waiting for you. Besides, Durstan had a devoted, if somewhat older, wife. What was her name? Babs? Something like that. Anyway, Babs would be only too happy to patch up Durstan and nurse him back to health with a big helping of pork chops. She damn well knew how to fry a pork chop. That came out in his trial. Durstan would never leave her, on account of the pork chops.

All the more reason for his lover to send him up the creek, or in Arizona, up the arroyo.

Olsen turned to the table of contents. *Chapter One: The Emptiness of Life. Chapter Two: Finding Love Everywhere. Chapter Three: The Vast Big Spirit of Nature. Chapter Four: Listen to the Saguaro Spirits. Don't Forget Your Crystal! Chapter Five: Channeling the Truth on the Universal Trunk Line. Chapter Six: We're All One. Like Quarks in a Proton! Chapter Seven: Desert Launch Pad to Cosmic Consciousness! Up Ahead – World Peace and A New Volvo!*

He flipped to a random passage. Page 56.

Through desert consciousness, the Spirit is all in one and one in all, of course, and in this way Big Spirit is the father of the Little Spirit in all of us. Big Spirit invites our Little Spirit to experience Him/Her in totality and commune with Her/Him directly. The Little Spirit then will know the blessed love of Big Spirit ...

Olsen's own spirit soared as the last bite of waffle slipped off the fork. Then, having eaten it, his spirit flagged. Maybe he could use another helping after all, considering how early he got up.

He flipped ahead a few pages: *...lift your arms and invite Saguaro Spirit into your bosom. Feel the warmth? Feel the crystal-fed energy from the Desert's own Saguaro Spirit filling your DNA with Universal oneness, healing, happiness and World Peace. No more pain. No more sadness. No more tired feet. Feel that? Yes! That is the flow of Big Saguaro Spirit flowing through and through, channeling the Universal Spirit of Spirits – whose name is Webster – being injected into your very fiber as if through a giant holy hypodermic. Yes, you have been drugged. You have been drugged by the all-one Big Spirit. You have been drugged with Universal Love. You have been drugged with Universal Knowledge. You have been drugged with Universal Divinity. Some trip, huh?*

Something to ponder, Olsen thought. So was the possibility of another waffle. But no. He was full. And he thought of his late grandmother, and of the one other Pima woman he knew who followed a traditional diet: Anna Stewart. She was smart, political-science professor smart. And pretty, exceptionally pretty. What the hell, he thought. He could never measure up to Anna Stewart anyway.

Maybe if he took a break from waffles. Worked out.

His cellphone rang. Self-improvement would have to wait. He flipped the phone open.

"Olsen here."

"This is Sergeant Spence, Phoenix police."

16

"Yeah."

"We were told to call you if anybody checked into a hospital looking like they'd been attacked by a cactus."

Olsen pushed his plate away, giving the phone center stage.

"Guy named Durstan?"

"No, some old fart, though ER staff said he could be anywhere from forty to a hundred and two. I guess he had a lot sun damage to his skin, like he spent a lot of time outdoors."

"That could be any one of a hundred cactus wranglers."

"He told the ER nurse his name was Reggie Jackson. His driver's license said Lucas Wheaton."

"Hmm, there's only one Lucas Wheaton. And he's a lot closer to a hundred and two than forty. He say anything about Randall Durstan?"

"From what I understand, he's not saying much of anything. He came in with dozens of puncture wounds, a few with saguaro needles still in them. Claimed the cops planted them."

"Planted saguaro needles."

"Yeah, when he wasn't looking."

Chapter Three

Olsen ambled into the hospital lobby. The volunteer at the front desk said Lucas Wheaton was in room 704. It was a hospital of many rooms.

The elevator made several stops on the way, none of them very smooth. Olsen's stomach churned in mild protest. The waffle was fighting back. He could have taken the stairs, though he would have had to stop for oxygen every second landing. His conditioning wasn't what it used to be. In high school, he was a star pitcher. He led the baseball team to a second place in state. Got a minor league contract on the strength of a lefthanded mid-nineties fastball. But his best pitch was his slider. A waist-high large-caliber pitch that bent sharply toward the dirt. Swing and a miss.

Back then, Olsen had a jock's body. Big, muscular – without the steroids. Halfway through his first season with the North Platte Platers, the Dodger's front office began to take notice, as did the girls.

That was before shortstop Oscar Cruse rushed the mound with a bat. Olsen tried to shield the blows with his pitching arm. Reflex really. Cruse shattered it, broke the ulna in two places. Really, the pitch got away. It had nothing to do with Cruse's previous at bat, when he crushed a three-run homer off a mistake, a curveball that hung over the plate like a party balloon. But Cruse had a temper and he took the brush-back personally. And Olsen ended up back home with his mother, Olivia, in Phoenix, getting a degree in criminal justice. Eating the occasional waffle, Big Macs and drinking beer. It was a road-food diet he acquired in the minors. Get off the bus and hit the fast-food joint.

Out of college, Olsen got a job writing parking tickets for the city of Scottsdale. A friend from his baseball days ran the city's traffic division.

Then Olsen's mother died. Lung cancer. Frances smoked. She was forty-nine. Olsen moved back in with Grandma Rosa, on the reservation. The Salt River Pima-Maricopa Indian Community borders Scottsdale. Something on the order of the next town over.

Olsen later found work on the rez. More law enforcement, though a step up from meter maid. He patrolled the boundaries, guarding against cactus thieves who occasionally crossed over to steal from the tribe.

He liked the work. And the experience paid off. When an opening appeared, he hired on as cactus cop for the Arizona Department of Agriculture.

Until the Larrabee matter, he stayed clear of political pressure. And he liked the job. He had an appreciation for the cactus he sought to preserve. Perhaps it was his grandmother's love of nature. She had dozens of stories about the desert and all the creatures in it. Some came from O'odham myth. Some she just made up.

It wasn't just the stories. Olsen simply regarded the Arizona Sonoran Desert as one of a kind. Here, the seasons brought just the rain needed to create a garden landscape. A garden of needles. Plenty of cactus to steal. Plenty to worship.

I enjoy nature. I don't commune with it, Olsen thought. *My Pima ancestors saw spirits in all plants and animals. I see only what's on the surface. The biome of the Arizona Sonoran Desert. Respect it, and maybe it won't kill you.*

19

Stepping off the elevator, Olsen entered a circular walkway built around the nurse's stations. Foot traffic came and went from the rooms like cars in a roundabout. Two doors down, Olsen spun out and approached a bed holding a silver-haired man with a gnarled nose and a face that appeared to have been left in the broiler too long. Dry, wrinkled and the color of Georgia clay. His shoulder and right arm were wrapped in gauze. His eyes were closed and his chest rose and fell in time to a soft snoring sound.

"Old timer, wake up." Olsen said quietly.

The patient opened his eyes halfway, glanced at Olsen, then closed them.

"Damn ya, go away. Bastard cop."

Olsen pulled up a chair.

"You should have stayed retired, Wheaton. You're slowing down. Too slow for cactus now."

Wheaton opened his eyes again, fully. They bored in on Olsen.

"Wasn't me. It was those McFinneys. They're dumber 'an worms."

"Oh, the McFinneys were in on the job?"

"I didn't say anything about any job."

"What happened to your arm?"

"Akseydent."

"A lot of people get hurt when the McFinney brothers are around. And it's rarely by accident."

"All I know is they know squattally shit about haulin' cactus," Wheaton said.

Olsen removed the book from his cargo shorts. He shuffled through the pages.

"What's that?" Wheaton asked.

"Book. Belongs to – well, take your pick – either the Wickenburg Public Library or Randall Durstan. Something of a

20

New Age desert spirit bible. Did you know Durstan was a follower of Upchurch? An Upster?"

Wheaton snatched at the book with his good arm, the one closest to Olsen. He missed and paid the price. Pain shot through the other arm.

"Oh, damn, that hurts. That hurts. It's like gettin' attacked with a nail gun." Between breaths, Wheaton got off another question. "Where'd you get that?"

"You know where. Russell Larrabee's Paradise Valley estate. You, Durstan and the McFinney's stole a highly protected saguaro, a crested. Now, as I recall, you've already done two stretches for stealing cactus off federal land. Third time anything federal is probably nothing less than twenty years."

"There ain't going to be no third time. Paradise Valley ain't no federal land. And I wasn't there in the first place, and you can't prove I was."

With the left arm, the good one, Wheaton reached above his head and pushed a red button. A woman's voice came over the intercom.

"Can I help you?" she asked.

"Yeah, I got an unwanted visitor, and I want you to throw the bastard out. Oh, and you better bring some muscle. The son-of-a-bitch is pretty big."

"I'll be right there, Mr. Wheaton."

The nurse came in, and she didn't need to bring the muscle. She *was* the muscle, built like a gold medalist from 1956 Russian Olympic team. Olsen wasn't easily intimidated, until now.

"You heard the patient. He wants to be left alone," she said.

Olsen didn't want to start a fight he'd be sure to lose. But he had to talk to Wheaton. He pointed to the patch on his shirtsleeve.

21

"Billy Olsen, level two native plant investigator for the Arizona Department of Agriculture."

"Is this man under arrest?" the nurse asked.

"Not yet, but ..."

"Look, I don't want any trouble, but this poor guy's got about a hundred holes and a good piece of skin missing."

"Yeah, we got some of it, at the crime scene. Well, what the dog didn't eat."

"Crime scene?"

"A protected cactus was stolen from the estate of Russell Larrabee ..."

"The dollar-store millionaire?"

"Right."

"And you're here to drag an old man out of a hospital bed because of a cactus?"

Wheaton stirred beneath his bandages. "Where the hell do you get off feedin' my skin to a dog! What do think I am, leftovers?"

Olsen stepped back, to get the nurse and Wheaton in the same frame of reference.

"Look, let me lay it out for you both. Real simple. A rare and expensive saguaro was stolen from Russell Larrabee's estate. This is a protected plant, and that makes it my business. Lucas Wheaton, in a long and misguided career, has been twice convicted of stealing cactus from federal land. He did federal time. If he had any part in this last theft, he could still do federal time. Doesn't matter if the cactus was stolen off private property. If it ends up in Las Vegas, and a lot of them do, it's a federal crime when it crosses the state line. Now we found what appeared to be somebody's skin, inside the pages of a book, for some reason ..."

"I was saving it for transplantation," Wheaton volunteered.

"But you dropped the book."

"I ain't sayin."

"Anyway, you couldn't save your own skin."

"Tain't funny."

"Well," Olsen said, "what the dog didn't get went to an FBI crime lab, for DNA analysis. Now, if it is your skin, Wheaton, you're a three-time loser."

"Nurse, get this bastard cop out of here. He's raisin' my blood pressure." Wheaton's head flopped back on the pillow. He grimaced. "More morphine. I'm a hurtin'."

The nurse pulled Olsen toward the door and whispered, through clenched teeth.

"Look, cactus cop, You get five minutes. After that, nobody comes near this guy for a week. Right now, he's already got so much morphine in him, nothing he says is going to hold up in any court."

"I'm not looking for a confession. Just some information that might help me."

"Five minutes. And no rough stuff."

Five minutes hardly seemed adequate for milking information from a salty old cactus thief who wasn't going to admit to anything, without getting something in return. Olsen had that base covered. He went to his other cargo pocket and pulled out a can of beer.

"How about a cerveza?"

Wheaton sat up in bed, his arm reflexively extended to receive the offering. He smiled a like a six-year-old getting a Tootsie Roll.

"I ain't had a beer since, since ... yesterday."

"Has it been that long?"

Olsen the yanked the can away, out of reach. He popped the top. The fizz had the aroma of a cheap beer, which it was. Wheaton appeared to be hyperventilating. He struggled to lean out

23

over the hospital bed, grabbing at the can like his life depended on it. And maybe it did. The can, however, proved elusive. Wheaton collapsed back into bed.

"I'll give you the beer. And I'll put in a good word for you, as somebody who likes to cooperate. Might save you some jail time."

"Screw all that. Just gimme the beer. I'll talk."

"Here."

Wheaton raised the bed and grabbed the beer. The bottom of the can went skyward and Wheaton made glugging sounds as his Adam's apple bobbed like a cork. Half the beer was gone in a matter of seconds. Wheaton paused to catch his breath.

"Well?" Olsen asked.

"Well, what, you son of a bitch?"

"Who took the crested? Where is it?"

Wheaton drank about half of the half he had left, then settled his head softly on the pillow. He appeared to defy gravity. He was as light as a moonbeam, a grinning contented moonbeam. Credit the beer. Credit the morphine.

"Ah, the crested. OK, so Durstan called me Tuesday, asked if I wanted to work a job, and, first I said no I ain't doing that no more. I'm retired. But he said I'd be richly rewarded for a couple hours work. He smooth talked me into it. I said, 'Sure.' I went out in his haulin' truck middle of the night Tuesday. Well, by then, it was early Wednesday. After midnight, you know. The McFinneys came, too – one perv, one maniac, two idiots."

"Perv? You mean the cross-dresser?"

"Same thing."

"Not really … some people have …" Olsen caught himself. He was all for diversity, but he hesitated coming to the defense of the McFinneys, regarded as loathsome by even hardcore cactus

24

thieves. "You needed four people? Sounds like a two-person job to me."

"Durstan's wife, Babs, she made him hire the McFinneys for the job. Her own blood, you know. Nephews. Oh, he sure as hell didn't want them worthless bums working for him. But she told Durstan if he didn't take them, she'd go on strike. No more fried pork chops on Sunday. She left him no choice. He'd already gone through that once, after it came out – in that last trial he had, I think – that he'd had a thing goin' with that nursery gal, Ranker. Babs refused to make him pork chops, even after he got sprang from prison. Not until he stopped sharin' his pecker. He like to have killed himself. He told me, 'No more foolin' around, Lucas. I'm being faithful to Babs, here on out. I am co-dependent on her pork chops.'

"Anyway, Durstan told her the job promised big dividends, and she said her nephews needed the work. Needed the work, my scrawny butt. They didn't do no work, anyway. They're too lazy to work. They just stood around and acted stupid. Except it weren't no act."

"OK, we've established they're stupid, but they were there – at Larrabee's and had a hand in stealing the crested?"

"Damn straight."

With a last gulp, Wheaton polished off his beer.

"Big dividends?" Olsen said. "Who'd pay for a stolen cactus that stood out like a zebra in a mule train?"

"Like a what?"

"You know. Hard to hide. Hard to resale."

"Ain't no dividends. Ain't no money. I got the idea as soon as we loaded up that freak-a-nature. Durstan muttered something about the job being its own reward. Liberatin' the cactus for all the spirit-channelin' Upsters. It's all a bunch a' kooks. See, they

25

believe these spirits they come to earth in these gortex fields, somewhere's out in the desert – and all these cactuses, they're like flashlight batteries … or something like that. Like I said, it's all a bunch a' kooks. And Durstan, he went after that big crested for the main kook. Upchurch. I hear he has a high-gortex hideout ways out in the desert."

"I think you mean vortex."

"Who cares. It's all a bunch a' kooks."

"Who swear by this." Olsen held up the book by William Upchurch – with a personal message from him to Randall Durstan.

"Where'd you get that?"

"At the Larrabee estate, in the dirt."

"Shit. Durstan carried that with him everywhere. Must have fallen out of the truck."

"So Durstan's an Upster." Olsen said, more statement than question.

"Some people get Jesus in prison. He saw some kind of cactus spirit."

Wheaton spoke at barely a whisper now as his eyelids sagged halfway to shut.

"So where's this hideout?"

"Don't know. Ask Durstan. Maybe he'll …"

And with that, Wheaton slipped into a cognitive deep freeze. His arm flopped out like a seal flipper and the beer can popped from his hand and rolled toward the door. Olsen went to pick it up, but it had settled against the nurse's white running shoe. She crushed it underfoot.

"Visiting hours are over."

"I was just on my way out."

Chapter Four

Before heading out to Durstan's, Olsen swung by the office to swap out his truck for a motor-pool vehicle. He didn't want the taxpayers to think he looked down on the free trucks they provided him. Plus, he had figured to ask Hempf along. Olsen could use an extra hand, if he had to make an arrest.

He fetched his revolver from beneath the seat and the bullets from the glove compartment. He holstered the revolver and stuffed the bullets in his pocket. He crossed the north lot to the Agriculture Building. Pulling open a heavy brass-plated door, Billy Olsen entered, turned right and plodded up the stairs. His goal was the third floor. He made it to the second landing before taking a breather. So not totally out of shape. Just leaning that way. Good exercise. And more his size than the elevator, recently refurbished to its original 1930 specs, which apparently called for a capacity of three – two skinny people and a midget. But he wouldn't change it. He had respect for a building that came of age during the New Deal. So maybe the elevator was a tight fit. But aesthetically, it was spot on. He caught his breath and made for the third floor.

The entire renovation, in his book, was money well spent. The old office complex had been lovingly restored, without the asbestos. The mahogany-veneer wainscoting was dark and richly polished. Ceiling lamps — covered with a glazed, etched glass — bathed the halls with the diffused light of an old Greta Garbo movie. The terrazzo floor, smooth and polished — and slightly uneven — collected the lamplight in a series of reflecting pools. Footfalls came in authoritative shoe-tapping strides, except for Olsen's. His New Balance cross-trainers just squeaked.

At the third floor landing, he took another breather, then headed toward his office. As he passed the elevator, the doors parted and out stepped his other reason for taking the stairs – Rudy Ossylmeyer, director of the Department of Agriculture. This wasn't out of sensitivity for Ossylmeyer's personal space. Olsen simply dreaded the idea of getting trapped with a man who was governed by the fear of drowning in his own incompetence. All in all, Olsen would rather be tortured by North Koreans with Vise-Grips.

Though only fifty-one, Ossylmeyer probably had the liver of a man three times his age. And it didn't help he struggled to keep his grip on a department he little understood. Well, at least he dressed well. He wore nice suits. He combed his hair. He flossed. He bathed. But he couldn't hide the fact that he spent his waking hours swimming in bourbon or drying out from bourbon. For the moment, a brief moment, he was dry. His eyes, for the moment, were clear – if somewhat rheumy. As usual, he wore a half-smile, always prepared for things to get worse or better. If they got worse, he drank. If they got better, he drank. But frankly, they rarely got better. Ossylmeyer just wasn't up to the job of running a state agency, and he knew it. Just five years ago, he was running a lawn-mower repair business. Three years ago, he won a seat in the state Senate after campaigning on the slogan, "The system's broke, and I got a big wrench." Two years ago, he switched a vote to give the governor authority to buy state office supplies from "any retailer promoting ninety-seven cent prices." That meant Larrabee, of course. As a consequence, every state agency had pens that

28

never wrote, staplers that couldn't staple and surplus eye-gouging paper spindles outlawed by OSHA years ago.

At first, Ossylmeyer balked, picturing hundreds of state workers in eye patches.

But he was sold, he says, by the governor's words, "This will teach people to spindle responsibly."

And by the governor's promise to give Ossylmeyer an entire agency to fix up. And who better to fix it up than a repairman? Besides, Ossylmeyer knew he had the qualifications for the job. Why, it's the Agriculture Department that oversees the sale of grass seed. And since lawnmowers cut grass, and since Ossylmeyer knew everything there was to know about lawnmowers, he was the man for the job. A stretch perhaps, but Ossylmeyer's friends in the Senate quickly confirmed the appointment, perhaps mindful that they might, too, get called into public service – that is, handed a good paying state job as a political favor.

Exiting the elevator, Ossylmeyer signaled for Olsen to stop, then wrapped his arm around Olsen's shoulder. The arm shook like a cold Chihuahua.

"Billy, the governor would like this crested investigation to be ... um, discreet."

"Well, that won't be hard. Nobody pays any attention to us anyway."

"But I hear the cactus libbers might be behind this."

"Could be ..."

"I'd hate for that to get out. You know, weird cult group sharing headlines with the governor's biggest donor. He wouldn't like that."

"No, I guess he wouldn't."

"Of course, the quicker you find the thieves, the less likely it will fall into the wrong hands," Ossylmeyer said. "Russell Larrabee has a ... a special attachment to this cactus. A treasure."

"What treasure?"

"I don't know. He wouldn't say. Must be something valuable. Gold, diamonds, money. Just in case."

"In case of what?"

"Don't know. Divorce, indictment ...?"

"Bad economy?"

"Huh? No, It's too solid," Ossylmeyer said. "That'll never happen."

"So small fortune in a cactus."

"In the woodpecker hole."

"The boot."

"Boot? What boot?"

Olsen blinked. Said nothing. The hum of the air conditioner filled the silence.

He glanced at his watch. He didn't care about the time. It was a signal. He had to go. He freed himself of Ossylmeyer's arm and made for his office. Ossylmeyer didn't seem to mind. By now, he'd have a gnawing need for a drink.

Three doors past the elevator, Olsen turned left into his office. The room seemed to shrink. His desk became too small when he sat behind it. His phone looked like a toy when he picked it up. For a man Olsen's size, everything was small – except his problems.

His biggest problem now was in the hands of the Salt River Tribal Council, which had all but condemned his reservation home to the wrecking ball. OK, the wrecking ball went out with fifty-cent-a-gallon gas. The tribe would tear down Olsen's home the easy way. With a bulldozer. The house that belonged to

Grandma Rosa. The house Olsen lived in now. It happened to be where the tribe wanted additional parking for a museum expansion. Olsen favored the expansion. He favored telling the fuller story of the Akimel O'odham and the Piipaash, better known as the Pima and Maricopa – the two Native peoples that made up the community.

He even favored more parking. But the house was something of a museum all its own. Built-in shelves displayed the baskets Grandma Rosa had made, a craft handed down from her mother. Made with natural fibers. Tinted with dyes from native plants. The porch was a place where you sat, had a beer and watched the traffic. Mainly busloads of retirees headed for the casino.

For the past three years, this had been home. He had moved in shortly before Grandma Rosa died. He was settled in now, comfortable. Everything he owned was here. And it came mortgage free. The tribe had plenty of options for parking. This wasn't the only space good for an extra acre of asphalt.

The house and land had been part of an allotment. It was kind of like private property for tribal members, each allotment passed down generation to generation. Heirs often got equal shares. After a few generations, some family members were left with a piece of dirt the size of a postage stamp.

Grandma Rosa had one living heir. Billy Olsen. He was lucky. Or so he thought.

All Olsen wanted was to keep his home. He'd even hired a tribal lawyer, Ronnie Clark. Clark was truthful. Olsen likely didn't stand a chance, he said. They last met over coffee at the casino.

"What about an appeal?" Olsen asked.

"The council's decided. The tribal judge has decided. And Grandma Rosa decided."

"What do you mean?"

"Grandma Rosa gave the property to the tribe, before she died."

"Nobody told me."

"Nobody knew about it before this turned up, buried in the in-pile in the tribal records office."

Olsen nodded.

"You've got two months. So take your time. But not too much time."

So there was that to look forward to.

And now? It was back to work.

Olsen pulled the crested file from the cabinet. It was medium thick, with pictures and descriptions of every known cristate in Arizona. By chance, he flipped to one that had been stolen in the early Nineties, from the desert west of Phoenix, near the California border. Wally Jackson had loaded the cactus on his truck and hauled it to Vegas in search of a buyer. No luck. Nobody would touch it. The feds had already put out a bulletin, with a complete description and a photo. Somebody turned Jackson in, for the five-hundred dollar reward. Jackson got two years. The cactus was replanted on state land. In the file, it was number 133. All 312 cresteds on file had a number. Olsen flipped through a few more pages, skimming and browsing. He stopped and shuffled backward. Then he flipped forward, then backward again. One was missing. There was no number forty-three.

He reached in his pocket and rummaged through the bullets for the picture he got from Larrabee. Maybe that was number forty-three. He couldn't find it elsewhere in the file and – damn – if that cactus didn't look familiar.

"Hey, Billy." Olsen looked up. Joshua Hempf had invited himself in. "Going out to Durstan's, aren't you?"

Olsen checked his watch. Nearly eleven o'clock.

"Yeah, I was just about to give you call. I might need your help," he said, getting up and pushing back a somewhat unruly head of hair. Not quite black. Not quite straight. Not quite curly. A bit Norwegian. A bit Pima..

"Glad to help."

"Routine stuff," Olsen said. "Have a look around. A few questions for Durstan. But … it's nice to have a backup, just in case."

"Right, right. Long as there's no blood."

"Not so much as a nose bleed. Promise."

Chapter Five

Durstan made his home in Wittman, an unincorporated dustbowl about a half-hour's drive past the Gray Belt of Sun City and Sun City West. Billy Olsen drove, heading up Highway 89. Joshua Hempf gazed out the window.

The temperature crept upward. Mirages shimmered on the two-lane asphalt, disappearing as the truck closed in on them. Olsen drove just above the speed limit. They were about ten minutes shy of Wittman. On the right, a freight train fell behind as they slowly overtook it. On the left, emergency crews gathered around an overturned pickup truck.

The accident scene passed by in a blur. But not before Joshua Hempf caught sight of it.

"Jeesh!" Hempf said, almost in a wail. It was as close as he came to cursing, and only when something really disturbed him. Hempf happened to be sensitive to blood, open wounds, broken bones and just about anything else that got him to reflect on his own mortality. Other than that, Hempf struck Olsen as a dedicated officer who had a genuine interest in saving what was left of the desert.

"Jeesh, that was bad."

"Yeah, pretty bad," Billy Olsen said, nodding slightly. *Driver must have been reckless,* he thought. Olsen knew about reckless. Every time he had ridden with Uncle Ivan he sensed he was going to die. Uncle Ivan, his mother's half brother, thought nothing about taking risks. He ran lights. He ran stop signs. He passed cars doing a hundred. For some reason, Olsen's mother trusted him with Uncle Ivan. He drank, but always managed to make it back alive. Up until about about five years ago. He'd pulled his Chevy onto a railroad crossing and passed out. The train didn't stop in time.

Hempf collected himself.

"I hear you're some kind of Swede, but I'm betting you're Samoan. Anyway, you look Samoan."

"Not Swede, not Samoan. My father was Norwegian. My mother was Akimel O'odham. Pima to most people. I don't remember my father. Very little of him anyway. I lived with my grandmother, off and on, until I was five. He never bothered to visit. Just as well. He drank too much. The day before my mother took me back, he went back to Norway, to catch whales or something. I haven't heard from him since."

"You sure look Samoan. Bet you were an all-star defensive lineman, you know, with all that weight."

Olsen took that as compliment, mostly.

"I played baseball, in the pros, well Single-A. I was a pitcher."

"Oh," Hempf said, unimpressed. He seemed unable to accept the fact that Olsen never played football. What else would a big Samoan do?

"I did play football half a season, when I was a kid, about eleven years old. You know, Pop Warner," Olsen said. "Coach had me as a blocker. I was the big offensive lineman. My last game, our quarterback fumbled the ball, and all I saw was a ball bouncing past me, so I went for it. Only the quarterback beat me to it, kind of came in low and covered the ball. I just fell right on top of him. I was told you could hear the bone snap from the sidelines. Compound fracture, his throwing arm. I don't know if I felt his pain, but I was very upset. I ran off the field just shouting 'I'm sorry' over and over. Never played football again."

Billy Olsen glanced over at Hempf and noted the blood draining from his face. Olsen might have said too much.

He changed the subject.

"So, uh, you made a lateral move in the department to become a cactus cop. What did you do, monitor aphids or something?"

Hempf nodded, taking deep breaths. The color in his cheeks appeared to be returning. He stared out the window thoughtfully as he spoke.

"No, I was a fruit inspector. Made sure all fruit grown here or trucked in for sale met state standards. All those watermelons in the produce aisle, they've all been pre-thumped."

"All of them?"

"Well, no, a randomly selected sample."

Hempf dabbed beads of sweat from a high forehead. Olsen stole a glance. Maybe it just looked high, thanks to the buzz cut. A style popularized by Gomer Pyle and George Goebel.

"When this job came along," Hempf said, "I jumped at the chance. And so far, it's been great."

"It's no secret your father's chief of police in Gilbert," Olsen said. "You could have gotten a real police job. And here you are guarding cactus."

"I'm a deputized law enforcement officer," Hempf replied. Sensing – correctly – that it didn't quite answer the question, he added: "I'm doing police work without all the ... the ... you know ... the blood and ... the bodies. It's not question of ... of ... using a weapon. I don't mind shooting things. I love guns. I'm not a Communist or anything. But I'd have to investigate accident scenes, and the mangled ... bloody bodies ... I just couldn't..."

36

Hempf was beginning to hyperventilate. The blood, once again, had drained from his face.

Though not given to squeamishness, Olsen could see Hempf's point. Olsen, too, had no desire to immerse himself in the grisly world of real police work. Homicide, for example. There was a line of work best avoided by the sensitive types.

"I'm with you on that score, Hempf. The last thing I want to do is help a coroner count stab wounds on a body."

Within sight of Wittman, Hempf rolled down his window and threw up.

Olsen went silent and turned his thoughts to the scene before him: Wittman, a shabby, unsightly burg of aging, creaky houses, mongrel dogs and cactus thieves. It was an outcast of a village, but until recently, nobody seemed to mind — or at least notice. Until recently, Wittman sat on a bleak stretch of desert, far from the scenic saguaro-studded hillsides pictured on Arizona Highways. Scrub plants like creosote and tumbleweed dominated the landscape. For years, Wittman was an isolated, forgettable halfway point of a forty-five minute drive west from the fringes of Phoenix to the upland deserts of Wickenburg. Now the fringes stood at Wittman's doorstep, poised to swallow it whole.

Olsen finally cleared the last leapfrog subdivision. The houses that had slipped past had one thing in common, which is that they had everything in common. You couldn't tell them apart. Repeating forms of caramel-colored stucco blown on styrofoam and chicken wire. One after the other, with no variation in sight. And that suited the residents just fine. They took pride in their sameness and brought the homeowners association down on anyone who dared put up awning that clashed with the covenants. Or didn't have the shrubbery properly aligned.

Wittman, just down the road, must have grated on these fine people. They must have groused about the brown, unwatered yards littered with the rusting shells of junked automobiles.

Let them bitch, Olsen told himself. He'd take Wittman over Cloned Groves – Olsen's name for them – anytime. Wittman had character, however seedy. He thought of his own little house on the Salt River reservation. It too was old and falling down. But it, too, had character. The large ironwood tree that shaded it gave it character. The crazed yellow blooms of the brittlebush gave it character. The drooping porch where young Billy hung out gave it character. Memories of sitting there and listening to his grandmother's stories gave it character.

Now, years later, he felt at home there. Comfortably at home. And he thought he would remain there, in comfort, for years to come. Well, months to come anyway.

Turning off the highway, Olsen eased the pickup over a railroad crossing into Wittman proper. He hadn't been here for some years, not since he last stopped by Durstan's. He couldn't remember which street his house was on. But there couldn't have been more than ten blocks to the whole town anyway. He'd just cruise around. He'd know Durstan's house when he saw it.

A pack of stray dogs trotted across the street, heading for nowhere in particular.

"Must be in the commercial district," Olsen said, pointing to his left while he drove at a crawl.

A sign held by chains swung from the porch of a cramped whitewashed house. It said: "Law Offices," as though the building had room for more than one. The yard in front was piled high with porcelain bathroom fixtures: tubs, sinks and toilets. A balding man sat reclined on the porch, reading a newspaper. He wore a yellow tie and a crisply pressed white shirt. Managing partner,

Olsen thought. A dog stopped to sniff a toilet bowl, then lifted his leg.

At the next street, Olsen made a right.

The street looked familiar. Three houses down he recognized Durstan's. It was an aging green clapboard job with steps leading up to a heavily cracked concrete stoop, circa 1940. A chain held up one half a porch swing. The other half had fallen to the concrete, the broken and rusted chain draped over it. Cobwebs underneath had trapped a quivering assortment of dried leaves and dead bugs.

Olsen pulled onto a gravel drive. They shouldn't be long, he thought. Still, he took the key out of the ignition. He always took the key out. Ever since his truck was stolen from a 7-Eleven. He had stopped for a Slurpee.

He climbed the steps and rapped on the frame of a battered screen door. No answer. The main door had been left open. Olsen could feel on his face a slow-moving current of stale-dry air, pushed through the screen by the lazy spin of a poorly maintained swamp cooler. A tattered section of screen fluttered like a dying butterfly. The air smelled of old furniture, bacon grease and bad potatoes. Olsen pulled on the handle, but the door didn't budge. It had been latched from inside. Durstan's stab at security.

Olsen peered through the screen door, but couldn't see much. The windows were covered with aluminum foil, sealing in the darkness. A bat could get a good day's sleep.

"Durstan!" Olsen shouted through the screen. "It's Olsen, Billy Olsen, Arizona native plant enforcement!"

No answer. No sound but the churning of the swamp cooler and an indistinct hum. Something electric. Hempf stood back, on the bottom step. He looked on with an air of tentative caution, unsure if he should lose the fear response.

"What if he's in there, waiting for us?" Hempf asked.

"Let's check out back," Olsen replied.

Hempf nodded, pursed his lips.

Olsen patted his right back pocket, feeling the outline of his .38 revolver, now fully loaded. Hempf had a 9 mm. Ruger in a holster. Like Olsen, he was officially checked out on firearms. Realistically, Olsen wouldn't trust Hempf with a slingshot. Around the side, a gravel drive led to a stand-alone garage. A big garage. Big enough to accommodate the oversized flatbed Durstan used to haul cactus.

Olsen tried the garage door. From the bottom, he gave it a tug. Locked. He drew a breath and looked around. The only thing with wheels was a 1980s-vintage Ford LTD with a broken passenger window and a crumpled fender. Olsen gave the door another tug. Still locked.

If the truck was in the garage, Durstan might be in the house. He just wasn't answering the door. Or maybe he didn't stay or didn't come home. Maybe he's driving around with a stolen crested looking for a buyer. Maybe he had a buyer, though Olsen had no idea who that might be. Who'd touch a cactus that stood out like a rabbi in Mecca?

Sure, you couldn't underestimate Durstan. If anybody could sell a hot crested, he could. He wasn't just a cactus thief. The man was a smooth talker, a gifted salesman. He'd invite you over for dinner, take your coat and – when it came time to go – he'd sell it back to you. And you'd think you got a good deal. Then, again, old man Wheaton said Durstan had found religion and that he had stolen the cactus as a gift for William Upchurch, high priest of the holy cactus. Farfetched, maybe. Maybe not.

Olsen returned to the house. He'd try the back door. His shoes ground into oil-stained pebbles laid over a bed of greasy dirt.

40

Taking a deep breath, he glanced back at the garage. He spotted a side door. Could try that. He exhaled. Well, he was closer to the house now. Check it one more time. If Durstan wasn't in, maybe he left some clues. Clues about where he was headed. Where Upchurch was, if that's what he had in mind. Maybe he had other prospects. Circled their names in a phone book.

Two steps up led to the back door. Olsen climbed them. The back door looked a lot like the front door – a screen of ratty, torn mesh. As he reached for the handle, he glimpsed a smattering of spots on the concrete stoop – dime-sized and dark. They formed a ragged line, like a graph. You could follow them from the gravel, up the stoop and to the door.

Blood? Could be, Olsen thought. Maybe the crested left its mark on Durstan. Maybe … no, that wasn't it. Nobody dragged a body up here. Something that big would have disturbed the gravel. There was no disturbance, just a faint dribble of a stain.

"I'll take a look inside. You wait here," Olsen told Hempf.

The screen door was unlatched and swung open at Olsen's tug. Perhaps Durstan never used the front door, and kept it latched, coming and going by the back. Perhaps Durstan was not such a stickler for security after all. Olsen stepped inside and let the screen door slap shut. He stopped to listen. There was nothing but the spinning rattle of the swamp cooler. And the hum.

Hempf shouted from outside the door. Olsen jumped slightly, startled.

"I'll check out the garage!"

"It's locked!" Olsen shouted.

"I'll try the side door."

"Wait!" Olsen replied, holding his hands up, in a "don't move" gesture. Hempf didn't hear him, see him or – more likely – simply ignored him. Hempf headed for the garage.

Olsen paused to get his bearings. The place was like a cave. Durstan must have gone through three rolls of Reynolds wrap covering his windows, blotting out the sun. The hum was louder, a pitch above the rattle on the swamp cooler. It sounded more like door buzzers powered by weak batteries. Olsen's eyes adjusted. The dim surroundings came into view. He was in the kitchen. On the sink, to his right, stood a pile of unwashed dishes. Two or three flies circled lazily around them, almost indifferent. An insult to the chef, Olsen thought.

He spotted a light switch to his left, flipped it on. He followed the stain, a dribble of spots, past the kitchen. Down the hall.

The damn buzzing. It was constant. Maybe a short in a light fixture. As he followed the trail, the noise grew. At the first door on the right, louder still. The bathroom. The stain turned and entered. Olsen followed. The room was narrow. The sink was on his right. A small window was broken, the occasional fly inviting itself in. Air from the evaporative cooler blew through a vent over the door. It did not blow away the foul odor – the bad-potato smell. The noise, the smell, the spots. They all led to the toilet. The lid was down. Olsen stared at it, thinking he had seen enough. He had smelled enough. But the noise. What the hell was that? It sounded like a million volts running through a power line. He touched the lid. No shock. He lifted it. Flies by the dozen, flies by the hundreds, boiled out. Olsen froze. By layers, the flies streamed out. Olsen could barely make out the image at first, like bad TV reception. Then it became sharper. A large fleshy face. Gray tangle of hair half afloat, half bonded to the porcelain. The nose, large and meaty, sticking out of the water like a fat shark fin. And a lingering expression of shock and anger on the face behind it, belonging to Randall J. Durstan.

Holy Christ, Olsen thought, as he stumbled into the hallway and ran toward the backdoor. Outside, on the stoop, he met Hempf running the other way – from the garage. His face a whiter shade of pale. Hempf froze, looked up at Olsen. He pointed to the garage, then held out a folded scrap of yellow paper.

"I found this ... and ... and ... then ..." He shoved the scrap into Olsen's shirt pocket.

"And what."

"A body! ... With no head! ... Oh, god, I've gotta find a bathroom! I'm gonna be sick!"

Hempf brushed past Olsen, threw open the screen door and scrambled through the kitchen, down the hall, in search of a bathroom.

"Wait!" Olsen screamed. "Don't go in there!"

He couldn't stop Hempf. All he could do now was wait, as his heart pounded in his ears. Three beats, four.

Hempf screamed. "Oh my god, no!"

Olsen heard him fall to the bathroom floor. Damn, Olsen thought, I don't want to do this. And he didn't know if he could. He was shaking like five cups of coffee, but he had no choice. He turned to go back in and get Hempf, just as an old Buick pulled into the driveway. A stout woman in her late forties got out. Olsen recognized her. Durstan's wife, Babs. Startled to see Olsen, she snapped, "You would like to tell me what the hell's goin' on here?"

Olsen let go of the door, bent forward and rested his hands on knees.

"I'd rather not, Mrs. Durstan."

"Out of my way."

She pushed him aside. It was easy. He was too busy hyperventilating, and having second thoughts about the waffles.

43

Chapter Six

Olsen settled behind his desk and thought about – nothing. But that never lasted long. First, came thoughts about his mother, Olivia. Pretty. Naive. Taken in by a blond alcoholic from Trondheim. Tigor, the father he never knew. The father who left him as soon as his mother took him back from Grandma Rosa. Tigor didn't want to share Olivia, and wanted nothing to do with him. Olsen couldn't say why that was. It just was. His thoughts drifted some more and settled on a more immediate problem. How to find the crested. And maybe find it or get fired. Certainly, the job was complicated by political pressure, coming from the governor himself. On other the hand, Olsen had reason to believe that the well-connected person who claimed the cactus really had no right to it.

OK, so where's the cactus? Durstan stole the cactus, but then what happened to it? It wasn't in the garage, where Hempf found the body – *sans* head. Perhaps Durstan had already delivered it to the buyer. He must have had somebody lined up. Upchurch, most likely. But where was the truck used to haul the thing? Had he made a delivery, the hauling truck still would have been parked at the house. You dropped off the cactus but kept the truck. That's the way it was done.

Well, here was a thought: Whoever murdered Durstan also stole the truck and took the cactus. And who else but the McFinneys? According to Wheaton, there were only three people besides Durstan in on the job – Wheaton himself and the

McFinneys. And, as any cactus hauler would tell you, the McFinneys had one hell of a mean streak. Their job resume read like a rap sheet, with a lot of experience in aggravated assault. And it's not a big step from that to murder. Just an extra blow to head, although the McFinneys apparently skipped that step and went right to removing it. Still, decapitation seemed a little out of their league.

Olsen's phone rang.

"Olsen here."

"Ossylmeyer wants to see you." It was the boss's gatekeeper, Sylvia Mendoza.

Olsen checked his watch. Two-thirty.

"I haven't had lunch yet."

"How could you think about lunch?"

"Well, I can't, actually."

"Good, he's waiting."

And so he went. Sylvia sat at her computer, clicking through the Internet. She seemed to be online-shopping for new shoes. She had come over to the Agriculture Department with Ossylmeyer from the state Senate, and before that, worked on his campaign. Her biggest asset was giving Ossylmeyer large blocks of drinking time, making sure no one disturbed him, either personally or by phone. The only exceptions – the governor or the governor's friends.

Reaching beneath her desk, Sylvia pushed a button, unlocking the inner-office door.

Olsen stepped inside. Ossylmeyer waved him to a chair before a large mahogany desk. Olsen lowered himself into it, gently. He was like poppa bear taking baby bear's chair, trying not to break it. Behind Ossylmeyer a big window offered a view of the Capitol Mall, a tree-lined grassy walk of monuments and statues.

45

"Do you have it?" Ossylmeyer asked.

"Have what?"

"The cristate, man. The crested. Have you got the cristate?" Some spittle popped out on the second "cristate."

"No." Olsen said the word in two syllables. "I just got back from a murder scene."

"So I heard."

"The murder complicates my investigation."

"How so?"

"It brings in the county sheriff."

"Not the Wittman police?"

"Wittman's unincorporated. There are no Wittman police."

"Well," Ossylmeyer's voice cracked. The normal pressure of heading an agency he was unfit to run usually drove him to drink. The added pressure to get back a cactus for the governor's friend – clearly, it was getting to him. His hands shook while they mangled a paper clip. He forced a grin, the kind of grin found on a man facing a firing squad and trying to make the best out of it.

"Well," he began again. "This is one case that needs to be closed. Has to be. So whatever it takes. Even if you have to work with the county sheriff."

Olsen looked stoic, meaning he wanted nothing to do with the sheriff and his gang of brown shirts. This sheriff billed himself as the "baddest sheriff in America." He was a publicity seeker without parallel. Olsen hadn't heard of a major case he had cracked, leaving unsolved a string of murders where bodies had turned up in irrigation canals in groups of three and four. The murders didn't bother the God-fearing citizens of Maricopa County in any case. In their collective mind, the victims were mostly illegal immigrants and weren't supposed to be here anyway.

Here's where Sheriff Morris Ring – Sheriff Mo or the Mo-Man – got his reputation as a crime-fighter: Three years ago, he arrested a political rival just as the man showed up for work. John Bustamante was former cop turned airline pilot, and the Mo Man's deputies put him in cuffs just outside the security gate, charging him with trying to fly under the influence. It was Sunday, and the sheriff received a tip that Bustamonte had gotten hammered on communion wine. The county attorney later let him go on learning the Bustamonte was a Baptist. Bustamante lost the election but retired on the $5 million settlement he received from the county.

"You and the sheriff, you both want the same guys, don't you? The McFoonies."

"McFinneys," Olsen said.

"That was an awful thing they did. Awful. Like a jihad. You think they were on a jihad?" Ossylmeyer's hand shook like it was wired to a car battery.

"No. The McFinneys aren't that religious."

"Have you talked to the sheriff's office at all about what happened this morning?"

"Not yet. After I dragged Hempf, then Mrs. Durstan out of the house, I wasn't much for talking."

"No sweat," Ossylmeyer said. "I'll fix you up."

He hit the intercom button.

"Sylvia, call the sheriff's office. Tell them I want to work with them on the Durstan case. I'm sending Olsen over to meet their lead investigator. Thanks."

Inwardly, Olsen cursed. To Ossylmeyer, he said: "Sir, that's really not necessary. I can work the cristate theft without the sheriff's ..." He was about to say "help."

Instead, he let it drop. Ossylmeyer had no idea what he was doing, but anyone who placed a premium on job security never argued with the man. He had fired three deputy directors since his appointment two years ago. They either stood up to him or tried to intervene behind his back – and that was a mistake. Ossylmeyer knew that everybody knew he was incompetent, and that just made him paranoid. Through Sylvia, he spied on his deputy directors and if word got back that they had tried to undermine him, he fired them. He thus secured the Agriculture Department's status as worst-run agency in the state. The governor voiced concern, but if Ossylmeyer could get that valued crested back in the hands of the governor's valued supporter, all would be forgiven. Or so Ossylmeyer believed.

"By the way, how's Hempf doing?" Ossylmeyer asked. He *was* very concerned – not about Hempf, but for himself.

"I hope his father doesn't raise a stink," Ossylmeyer said. "I promised the chief his boy wouldn't see anything worse than a goose bump from a cactus needle. I can't face Chief Hempf now. Damn, I won't even take his calls. It's bad enough I have to meet with the governor tomorrow. I'll probably get an earful about poor Hempf. Poor Hempf? What about me. I'm the guy who signs his paychecks. I need to warm up my coffee."

Ossylmeyer's hand began its customary crawl toward a small stack of styrofoam cups. He pulled one off the top and held it behind the desk, out of Olsen's sight. Olsen heard a drawer slide open, and something being poured. Shutting the drawer, Ossylmeyer put the cup to his lips, tipped his head back and drained the contents. His eyes shone like marbles in Karo syrup.

"So ... how is Hempf?"

"The doctor said he'll need a couple of months of therapy. He'll be OK, eventually."

"And Durstan's wife?"

"She came to just as the paramedics and sheriff deputies arrived. She seemed to like the attention. Invited them all over for pork chops once she got the place the cleaned up."

"Hmm."

Silence followed, as Olsen and Ossylmeyer appeared to run out of things to say, which was fine with Olsen. He pushed down on the armrests, the first act of removing a large object from a small chair.

"So, find Durstan's nephews …."

"His wife's nephews," Olsen interrupted.

"All right, find his wife's nephews, and you find the cactus," Ossylmeyer said, covering old ground, but this time under the influence. "How hard can it be? Two guys hauling a crested around in a large flatbed registered to Randall Durstan."

Olsen eased himself back into the chair. It creaked with the sort of stress heard before a building collapses. The chair held.

"Unless they switch trucks. But, I don't see it. Too much work for the McFinneys."

"Uh huh. Uh huh."

"The working theory is Durstan stole the cristate as a gift for William Upchurch. I'm thinking the McFinneys wouldn't give anything away for free. Not a cristate they murdered for. So Upchurch is out of the picture. So, the McFinneys are probably out making cold calls, looking for a buyer. I don't know who the hell would touch it."

Ossylmeyer made a face. Not a happy face.

"Right," Olsen said. "I'll start with the nurseries in my 'bad apple' file."

Ossylmeyer nodded an increasingly heavy head.

"We have to have that cristate," Osslymeyer said. "It's a state treasure."

"If it is, I have no record of it, though I could have sworn it looked familiar after seeing the picture Larrabee showed me. Who knows? I've three hundred cristates on file. Maybe I just confused it with another crested. I just can't figure out what happened to number forty-three."

"I don't care about the number. What matters is that we find the damn cactus."

Olsen said nothing. Ossylmeyer was breathing heavily and his hand, with an apparent mind of its own, reached for the special drawer. "Excuse me, I have to ... my coffee." That was as far as he got. His head bowed and his chin came to a rest on his sternum. He began to snore. Olsen saw himself out the door.

He hurried through the outer office, where Sylvia was clicking the mouse on a fifty-dollar pair of shoes. In the hall, he could feel the sweat on his forehead. He reached for a tissue in his pocket. He didn't remember putting one there, but he felt one now. The tissue unfolded in his hand, but it was no tissue. It was a yellow page torn from the phone book – the same sheet of paper Hempf had stuffed in Olsen's pocket. It had a listing of plant nurseries. Somebody had circled the entry: "Needles Arizona – You want cactus? We got cactus."

"Good place to start," Olsen thought.

Chapter Seven

Three-thirty. The thermometer began to peak at 107. Olsen crossed the steamy asphalt and got into the hot cab of his own pickup. The steering wheel felt like a blistering coil on a stove top. He looked out across the street at the covered parking for the Department of Health Services. Shade for cars. No burning steering wheels there. Olsen filed that away under "life ain't fair," turned the air conditioning to full blast and pondered stopping off at the Lower House, a beer and peanut joint on Nineteenth Avenue – before heading home to the rez. He was tired. He'd been up since four and it was nearly quitting time for bureaucrats anyway, at least unofficially.

Needles Arizona could wait until morning. Nurseries didn't pick up roots and move overnight.

Olsen backed up, slipped the truck into drive and nearly hit the SUV blocking the exit. Cop car, Maricopa County Sheriff's Office. What the hell? Olsen spread his arms out in a gesture of disbelief, then jumped out of the truck, nearly twisting an ankle under his own weight. Hitching his shorts, he went to have a word with the inconsiderate jerk behind the wheel. The inconsiderate jerk got out of the patrol car and met him halfway.

She grabbed Olsen's hand and shook it like a tumbler.

"Billy Olsen? The receptionist told me, look for a big Samoan. Glad to meet you. I'm Deputy Sheriff Fillmore. Jane Fillmore. I'm investigating the Durstan murder and I was told to work with you on this."

"So soon?" Olsen got his hand back.

"I get right on things. We're not all fat and lazy ... not that there's anything wrong with fat."

Olsen managed a smile that said he took it personally. As for Deputy Sheriff Fillmore, there was no fat hidden by her uniform, which was khaki like Olsen's, if a shade darker. She was slender top to bottom, with the kind of legs found on swimsuit models – though much whiter. Shorts apparently weren't a regular part of her routine.

"I figured as long as we're going to be chasing cactus rustlers across the desert, I might as well dress the part," Fillmore said.

"I not chasing anybody across the desert. I'm going ..."

"I'm way ahead of you. Needles Arizona, a cactus nursery on the north side."

"No, but ..."

"Phoenix PD forwarded a call to us. Seems the suspects just paid the owner a visit."

"Roz Ranker?"

"You know her," Fillmore said.

"She used to be Randall Durstan's secret flame, only it wasn't so secret. She testified against him and put him in prison for two years, to save her own skin."

"Wow. Well, anyway, they tried to sell her some kind of a special cactus. A Christ cactus of some kind."

"Cristate."

"That's it!"

"And?"

"She told them to shove off, and they did. She persuaded them with a large gun."

Olsen folded his arms as he listened. He tried, in part, to hide his stomach, which in recent years had begun to swell and droop over his belt. Waffles. Sugar. Beer. Burritos. His diet would have shamed his Grandma Rosa. Standing in front of the fit and fine figure of Deputy Fillmore, he felt – if not shame – something on the order of embarrassment.

"It would have been nice if she could have stalled them," Fillmore said. She took a breath. "We need to pay her a visit."

"No argument here," Olsen replied. "Might as well take your car. Mine's trapped."

Billy Olsen parked his truck and worked his way into the SUV's front seat, just behind the computer, shotgun and radio. It was a tight fit. Fillmore cranked the engine, jammed the stick into drive and tore down the side street that passed behind the Agriculture Building – while giving Olsen a long once over.

"I bet you were an athlete, at one time."

"Baseball. Wild Man Pitching they called me. I wasn't that wild. Maybe some control issues with my curveball." As he spoke, Olsen squeezed the door handle as though it would save him in the likely event of a crash. Fillmore turned right, Olsen was flung left. Fillmore turned left, Olsen was thrown against the door.

"Really. You know, if you worked out a little, cut back on the junk food, I bet you could lose some of the ..."

"I'm losing it now. Can't you slow down?"

"Hey, you don't solve crimes by going the speed limit."

"Hadn't heard that one," Olsen said, trying to avoid eye-contact with any pedestrians. He didn't want them to see the terror on his face.

"So what's the big deal about this cactus? It must have some religious significance. Jesus Christ cactus."

"Cristate, it's another word for crested. But, yeah, that's the origin of the word. Hey, watch that bus!"

Fillmore jerked the wheel and swerved around a city bus parked to load passengers.

"I got it, OK? Now about the cactus."

"Cristate, um, it's a saguaro whose growth cells have gone haywire."

Fillmore braked hard for a light, sending Olsen against the seatbelt.

"Saguaros. They're beautiful. They're big, mean and green. Growth cells?"

"Saguaros grow at the tip," Olsen said, smoothing his brown hair back into place with a swipe of his hand. It fell back over his ears and the back of his neck. "If that dies off, the cactus doesn't grow, though they'll sometimes sprout another arm from near the tip. And that'll grow at the tip."

The light turned green. Fillmore stomped on the gas pedal, driving Olsen into the seat back. He felt like an astronaut training on a rocket sled.

"And cristates?"

Billy Olsen fished Larrabee's photograph out of his pocket, handed it to Fillmore. She gazed at it, looking up on occasion to swing around cars, buses, motorcycles, stray dogs, mothers with baby strollers and merging onto a freeway just ahead of a semi tractor-trailer going eighty-five.

Big mistake, Olsen thought. *I'm going to die now.*

"Wow!" Jane Fillmore said. "This is some cactus. It looks like it's wearing a giant green headdress."

"That's the crest. Something happened to interfere with normal growth. But just what that is is something of a mystery. Mutation. Lightning strike. Those are just guesses. Saguaros are so slow-growing it's a tough phenomenon to observe."

54

Fillmore swerved around a slower school bus and charged into the car-pool lane, speeding past homebound commuters in their SUVs. If anybody pulled out in front of them, it was all over. Closing his eyes, Olsen crossed his fingers. It was how atheists prayed.

"So this is a big deal? A mutant cactus?"

"Well, they're attractive, and they're rare. Very rare. Probably fewer than one in a million saguaro seeds dispersed in nature ever grow to maturity. And you get only one crested for every 200,000 mature saguaros."

"Not great odds."

"Better than mine."

The patrol car crossed three lanes, threaded through a stream of traffic and flew onto the Cave Creek Road exit. A minute later, Olsen said: "Turn here."

She made a sharp right onto a dirt road, another right and followed an asphalt drive up to a parking lot and squealed to a stop in a spot reserved for the handicapped. The smell of burning brakes blew in through the air conditioning vents. Olsen sat wordless for the moment, thankful he made it here alive, then dreading the ride back. He opened the door, then hesitated.

"This is a handicapped spot."

"It's police business, right?"

With a shrug, Olsen got out, hitched his shorts again and headed for the entry, marked by the boughs of overlapping mesquite trees. He was greeted by a 103-pound sprite with rust-red hair, untamed by a John Deere ball cap. Her face was a deeply freckled burnt umber. A lifetime of Arizona sun.

"Hey, what the hell you think you're doing parking there? You blind?" Roz Ranker snapped.

"Sheriff's business, ma'am," Fillmore said.

55

"Screw the ma'am crap. You can't park there. I'm calling the city accessible enforcement, if you don't move your damn car."

"OK, OK." Fillmore put her hand out, the universal "hold-on there" gesture. She went to move the car as Olsen approached Ranker.

"A few questions," Olsen said.

"McFinneys? I shooed them away. Excuse me, I've got a customer."

Roz Ranker strode under the boughs into the nursery, Olsen lumbering close at hand. The entrance opened up to fifteen acres of cactus and succulents. Rows of potted barrel cactus gave way to rows of prickly pear, followed by rows of small bare-root saguaros – stretched out flat like wounded soldiers. Behind them were larger saguaros, some with arms, planted in the ground and supported by two-by-fours angled into their sides.

Ranker stopped and turned to Olsen: "Don't ride me, cactus cop. They all got proper tags."

Before he could say anything, she took off again. Olsen glanced back at the cactus, then continued to take stock of the inventory. Toward the back stood potted desert trees: mesquite, paloverde and ironwood. A denim-clad worker with shoulder-length blond hair stood atop a ladder and busied himself lopping limbs off a mesquite with pruning sheers. Working a different side of the tree, a Hispanic man severed larger branches with a hand saw. Pausing in his work, the blond stared across the nursery at Roz, then climbed down the ladder, making his way past all the plants Olsen had noted – in reverse order.

Ranker meanwhile went up to a young upwardly mobile couple who appeared to be looking over a bundle of dead sticks. They probably had a new house forty miles from the center of town and a yard full of rocks that passed for desert landscaping. That was Olsen's guess, anyway.

"What is this?" asked the woman. "Some kind of cactus skeleton?"

She fixed her gaze on Roz as she asked her question. She couldn't seem to look away. Ranker couldn't care less. She just answered the questions.

"Not a cactus anything. It's an ocotillo. After you plant it, give it a little water – not too much – it'll leaf out."

The woman, a model for tank tops and tight jeans, nodded – and kept staring. The man, a model for hairstyling and hundred-fifty dollar athletic shoes, frowned.

"That plant's dead. You're trying to sell us a dead plant."

"No sir," Roz Ranker replied, rankled. "That's just the way it is with ocotillos and a lot of desert plants. They go dormant when it's dry out, but this isn't dead. It's not a parrot."

The man noticed his wife staring at Roz Ranker. He followed her gaze and saw what she saw.

"Your neck. Looks like a tattoo of a cactus on it. What's that all about?"

"It means I pray to my inner cactus. I'm an Upster."

The wife stuttered: "Is … is … is that some of kind of cult?"

"Not to me, it isn't."

"Does this involve children?"

"Why. You got any?"

"No … I."

The woman backed up. She looked worried.

The blond cowboy, having crossed the nursery, stepped in. He had a big easy-going smile. It was big smile on a big man – nearly as tall as Olsen, but with broad shoulders and a tapered waist.

Nothing tapered on Olsen. From top to bottom, he went from large to very large.

"Ma'am, my wife, here, she loves to kid."

He put a big arm around her, and she didn't seem to mind. He turned to Olsen, now joined by Fillmore, back from the parking lot.

"Hey, aren't you that cactus detective?"

"Billy Olsen, field agent for the Arizona Department of Agriculture."

"I thought I recognized you from across the nursery. I'm Ted Ranker, Roz's husband."

"I know," Olsen said.

"Shit, at first, I thought you were just another Upster. Like that guy they found dead in Wittman."

Ted Ranker put on his serious face, wrinkles lining his weather-beaten forehead. It was a good look, on him anyway. Ranker was Hollywood star weather-beaten. Paul Newman weather-beaten.

"You heard?" Olsen asked.

"On the radio when I went out for a Big Gulp."

Olsen turned to Roz. Her eyes were red. Olsen noted it, in passing.

"Allergies," Ranker said.

"You knew about Durstan?" Olsen asked.

"Knew it and got over it, about as long it takes to exhale."

"That fast?"

"I find solace in nature."

Olsen looked at his watch. Already it was six, and here he was on the job, when he should been well into his second beer. He felt extremely sober.

"Yeah," Ted said. "She's an Upster. Durstan was an Upster. Comes right out of prison rejecting our savior Jesus Christ, for

58

some crap about spirits shacking up in a cactus. I tell you, you wonder what they're doing with our tax dollars. Anyway, his first week as a free man, he looks Roz up, behind my back. Maybe he intends to tell her, 'No hard feelings.' She did, after all, rat on him. But no. He tells her about the cactus spirit and all about Upsterism. And, right in front of me an' God, she buys into it. Now she bows down to Saguaros. Sees God in a prickly pear. It's been rough, on both of us. We're working on it, though, me and Roz. You know, counseling with the pastor, that kind of thing."

The woman he loved, her arms folded, looked at Ted like he had been talking about somebody else altogether. Ted dropped the subject.

"So," he said to Olsen, "What brings you out here – again?"

"The usual, Ted. Somebody stole a cactus."

"Hell, we're clean, ain't we Roz, honey?"

"Always have been," she said, without a hint of irony. "Although you look cleaner than usual, yourself."

"Oh, just thought it would be nice to wear a clean shirt for once."

The glam couple, tiring of the chitchat, began to shuffle off, headed toward the exit. Roz made a quick head jerk toward them, a gesture meant for Ted. He knew just what to do. When she was bad cop, he was good cop. He caught up to the couple.

"Hey, forget the ocotillo. I can tell it's not right for your garden. Let me show you something that will go perfect with the new desert landscape. It's new, right? In need of lots of drought tolerant plants."

The young couple nodded in tandem.

"I've got these trees, called Chilean mesquite. They're from Chile. Ha, ain't that rich! Anyway, I believe God made these trees to grow fast because he knows life is short. Follow me!"

59

And they followed, as Ted weaved through the cactus to the far corner of the nursery, past a small tool shed and an adjoining greenhouse. They reached a stand of mesquite trees in large wooden boxes, ready for transplant. Unlike native mesquite, they had no thorns. That made them popular. Personally, Olsen preferred the native plants. Like half his ancestors, they were here first.

He turned back around, trying not to stare at Roz, but doing so anyway. She had a face of New Age desert spirit. The glow of the universal oneness that flows through the air from a million cactus needles – like sparks flying off a science-class generator. It was a glow not found in people who spent every moment in fear for their eternal salvation.

Despite counseling, she remained a practicing Upster.

"Why don't you just tell people you see God in a tortilla." Olsen said.

"And let them think I'm crazy? … Hey! What are you lookin' at?"

Olsen glanced over at Fillmore. She was looking at Ranker as someone to be pitied. And pity was the last thing Roz Ranker wanted. Fillmore cleared her throat and pulled a pen and pad from her pocket.

"We're investigating a murder," Fillmore said.

"Don't look at me. And I mean it."

Olsen bit his lip, and decided to move matters along. He just wanted to get back to the rez, and grab a beer and a Hungry-Man TV dinner. He had given up the idea of stopping off at the bar. It was too late now.

"The McFinneys. When were they here?"

"Oh, about three, maybe three-thirty. Said they had a cactus I might like. Wanted five grand for it. Worth that? Not if it was hot."

"They say anything about Durstan? You know ... " Fillmore asked.

"About murdering him? No. But *I* could kill the son-of-a-bitch. He comes out of prison all lovey-dovey and abandons me after my conversion. Puts me on the path to enlightenment, then goes back to his pork chops."

"Conversion?" Fillmore put her hands on her holster belt, a move to show she was serious. Serious about conversions, Olsen thought.

"Haven't you heard? I'm an Upster. I subscribe to the teachings of William Upchurch, founder of the Worldwide Church of Uppermost Cosmic Consciousness through Succulents."

"Upster, huh?" Fillmore said. "Better than a Downster."

"Hey don't knock it. He's working on world peace, as we speak."

Olsen steered back to the matter at hand: "What kind of cactus?"

Roz Ranker rolled her eyes, green peas in a tight orbit.

"The cristate, you know! The cristate!"

"A cristate stolen from the Paradise Valley estate of Russell Larrabee, dollar-store tycoon. That cristate," Olsen said.

"Look, it wasn't the McFinneys to sell, but it didn't belong to some pompous ass in Paradise Valley."

"Who does it belong to?"

"The Master, the Holy High One. Durstan promised him a cactus with an energy field so powerful he could talk to Rilukku. And he's pretty damn hard to get a hold of."

"I have a question," Olsen said.

"Why stop now?"

He took out the yellow scrap, the one from Durstan's garage. It had been torn from a phone book.

"What's this?" Olsen asked.

"Don't have a clue," Ranker said. She snatched it from his hand, balled it up and tossed it into a nearby pile of uprooted prickly pear cactus.

Hempf went through a lot of trouble for that, Olsen thought. He left it in the pile.

Fillmore adjusted her khaki cap, to fit the ponytail pushing out above the adjustment strap. A bead of sweat of rolled down her temple. Otherwise, the heat did little to dampen her appearance. Olsen dared not check his own uniform. He felt the sweat spreading from his armpits like coffee spilled on a napkin.

"Holy High One?" Fillmore asked.

"You know, Upchurch," Olsen answered. He pulled the paperback from his back pocket. Handed it to Fillmore. "The cult leader."

"Not a cult," Ranker said. "Any more than praying to Jesus. I do that, too."

"Got your bases covered," Fillmore said.

Olsen didn't join the theological debate. Instead, he thought back to the rash of cactus-theft reports piling up on his desk. And wondered if Durstan might be behind them, stealing saguaros for Upster rituals. It was, as Upchurch had written, a win-win. Freeing plump overwatered saguaros from highway medians and front yards and returning them to nature, the open desert, where they can get better reception.

Olsen would look into it later. At the moment, he had a bigger fish. Find a rare crested and, with any luck, Durstan's killer. Or killers.

Ranker ignored Fillmore. She turned to Olsen. "I told the two goons the cactus belonged to Upchurch. I told them to leave it here. I'll make sure he gets it. They asked me where they could find him – Upchurch, that is.."

"The goons, the McFinneys," Olsen said.

"Of course, the McFinneys. One had the brains of a chickpea. The other was dressed in a mini-skirt."

Fillmore gave Olsen the book back, then flipped open her notebook.

"You remember what color?"

"I don't know, red or blue or something."

"Upchurch has a desert hideout?" Olsen asked. "Known only to his followers?"

"His retreat. It has a high concentration of spiritual energy. Good for healing, and erasing bad relationships, bad karma, bad backs – that sort of thing," Ranker said.

"Durstan must have known, if he was stealing for Upchurch. But he didn't let his nephews in on it."

"Maybe Randall wouldn't tell them, so they .... they ... Oh, Randall... "

Roz Ranker's eyes grew teary and red. Her emotional shell had slipped off, if only partly.

"So why not direct them to Upchurch," Olsen said. "He'd get his hot cristate, for a price anyway."

"I'm not letting those two goons get anywhere near him."

"Right."

"Look, I really don't know where the hell Upchurch is. And I told them that. And they said they'd have to soften me up a bit.

Especially the one who wears the pants. He's one mean son of a bitch. He pulled out a big handgun. Ted hadn't got back from getting his Big Gulp, so I pulled out ol' number twelve from behind the big rock – gave it a pump and told them to get the hell out of here."

"You couldn't stall them?" Fillmore asked

"Are listening to anything I say? I told you they pulled a gun on me, and threatened to work me over. So I pulled out my twelve gauge and threatened them back. So they left. But not before I told them if anything happened to that cactus, I'd have their balls for breakfast."

"Sound appetizing," Fillmore said.

"I'm not talking to you. Anyway, they got the hell out of here, maybe a half-hour ago. In Randall's truck."

Olsen nodded, not in agreement. He was just acknowledging he knew of Roz Ranker's way of handling trouble. Get a bigger gun. As he rubbed the back of his neck with a big left hand, the glam couple strolled past, wheeling a four-foot Chilean mesquite on a little red wagon. Ted Ranker came up from behind and wrapped his big muscular arm around the wiry frame of his wife. He smiled. It didn't seem to bother him that his teeth could have passed for moon rocks.

"I did it. I sold them a tree. All because I love you. Everything I do, I do for you Rozzie."

"I know, I know."

He gazed down on her, shaking his head, if only so slightly.

"I sure wish Durstan hadn't shown you the wrong path. It ain't Christian to be worshipping product."

"I don't. This place has no spirit. No immanence. Besides, I'm still a Christian, with a side gig."

"Well, you're praying to things that got roots. I can tell. You got the karma orifice about you."

"That's aura. And you're wrong."

He caught sight of the book, clasped in Olsen's left hand, hanging by his side. Ted Ranker grabbed the book and brought it to his wife's face. He kept his other arm around her, except more tightly.

"This yours? You been cheatin' on Jesus?"

Olsen reached out and firmly – but without force – took the book back.

"It's mine," Olsen said.

"You? You don't look Upster."

"Research."

Roz Ranker pushed Ted's arm away. She cut through two rows of agave to reach the Needles Arizona office, a bare wooden shack on a concrete pad. Looking back, she yelled: "I got to check out the receipts, Ted. You'd better get back to trimmin' that tree. It's takin' over the nursery. Maybe you're not using the right tools."

Ted Ranker held his hands out, palms up, cocked his head.

"I'd do anything for her."

Chapter Eight

As the late-afternoon sun lingered over the horizon, Olsen settled into the broiling interior of the patrol car. Fillmore fished for her keys, then – startled by a deep rumbling sound – dropped them. Like fans at a tennis match, she and Olsen turned their heads to the left in a single synchronized motion. A truck sped toward them. It was a flatbed truck, a big one, cutting across the now-empty parking lot. The flat grill on the red cab appeared to get bigger – as it moved from the background to the foreground. Now Olsen could make out two men in the cab. The driver was grinning like a maniac. The passenger was busy filing his – *OK*, Olsen thought, *her* – flaming-red nails with an emery board. She wore matching lipstick, had teased hair and a five-o'clock shadow.

The McFinney brothers, an image embedded in a fraction of a second. And, Olsen thought: Likely his last.

"Don't look now," was all he could think to say.

Fillmore glanced out the window.

"God damn!" She made a desperate stab for the keys on the floorboard. "Where the hell are ..."

The truck hit the patrol car and carried it halfway across the parking lot. The only thing stopping them was a lamppost. It tried to come through the back door, twisting the SUV into a half a pretzel. Olsen blacked out for a minute, maybe less, before coming to his senses. Fillmore had been knocked sideways, ending up on his lap. At least in part. She was out cold, but breathing. Then came the screaming, from outside.

Through the shattered windshield, Olsen saw the McFinneys dragging Roz Ranker across the parking lot.

"Let go of me, you pervert! If my husband catches you ..."

"Let him try. We'll just beat the shit out him."

The McFinney who wasn't wearing the skirt spoke. He was the grimacing menace. He had her by the hair. The skirted McFinney had an arm. He handed the arm off to his brother.

"Hold this for a sec, Hector."

"Yes, Edweena."

Reaching under her tank top, she pulled a sock out from under a bra, deflating her right breast. She pushed the sock into Ranker's mouth, then cocked her head to admire her work.

"Yes, it's so you! And, frankly, I'm through with socks. They don't give me that full-figured look. I'm thinking softballs."

Roz Ranker spit out the sock.

"You want soft balls?" she asked. "Here!"

And she kicked Edweena square in the crotch. Edweena grabbed the afflicted area, lifting the hem of her skirt up past her hairy thighs, and shuffled around in tight circles. Hector ran over to his brother, and danced along.

"Oh, Jesus, I bet that hurt, Edweena."

"Let's go," Edweena whispered. "I need to freshen up."

"Good idea, good idea. But first I'm going to hogtie that bitch and toss her into …"

But Roz Ranker had other ideas. She reached behind a rock and pulled out what looked to be a gargantuan semi-automatic .45. She must have had guns stashed everywhere.

"I'm counting to five. When I reach five, I'll killing you both, if you're not gone. One…two…"

Edweena hobbled to the truck as fast as her condition allowed. Hector helped her into the passenger side, then raced around, climbed in and took the wheel.

"We're not through here!" Hector yelled.

In seconds, the truck was halfway across the parking lot.

Olsen eased himself out from under Fillmore and smashed out the windshield with a flashlight. Adrenalin masked the beating he had taken. He'd be sore later. Arms extended, he squeezed through the opening with the all the ease of working the first pickle out of the jar. Olsen tumbled onto the searing griddle that passed for asphalt.

"Ow! Fuck!"

He pulled himself up on the fender, then turned to see the truck – McKinneys, crested and all – speeding into traffic. Drivers swerved. Three cars collided.

Ranker looked Olsen up and down, assessing the damage.

"I've seen worse."

She headed back to the nursery.

Olsen took a breath. It hurt to breathe. He was one big bruise. Every muscle and joint had reason to complain. The burns from the asphalt weren't too bad. Second degree, mostly. Fillmore was largely conscious and groaning. Olsen reached in and eased her out through the broken windshield.

He wrapped an arm around her and led her to the nursery office.

They both collapsed on a pair of plastic chairs. They moaned in harmony.

"What hit us?" she asked. "A Mack truck?"

"I didn't get the name."

Chapter Nine

Olsen rolled over to check his alarm clock. It was a slow and painful roll. The dial came into view with the speed of a sunrise.

One o'clock, p.m.

He thought: *Four days of stiff muscles and a sore back, and still no word on the whereabouts of the McFinneys. A cross-dresser and his idiot brother driving around in a stolen flatbed housing a one-of-a-kind saguaro – also stolen – had somehow eluded the cops.*

Maybe the cops didn't care. There was a murder, but the victim wasn't exactly a model citizen. The sheriff's office had assigned just one investigator, and she had taken the week off, too. That's to be expected when you're hit by an oversized flatbed truck. Fillmore did call a few times to tell Olsen how sore she was. Olsen replied by groaning.

Today, however, he was going to ask some questions. And, if anybody had answers, it'd be the crowd at the One More Round Bar and Grill, a good hour's drive from his home on the rez. Olsen did a quick calculation. On the Sabbath, after church, the place should be flowing with beer and maybe a few loose lips.

Olsen swung his feet to the floor and sat for a moment, absorbing the shock of movement. He stood, then by degrees worked the stiffness out of his muscles as he went through the routine of preparing breakfast, showering and dressing.

The pickup was parked outside beneath an ironwood tree. A spread of thorny branches provided partial shade. The small leaves couldn't catch all the sun. Dust kicked from under Olsen's shoes, not at all like Durstan's driveway – which crunched with gravel greased with decades of oil-leaking junkers. Swinging into the cab, he scraped his shoes by accident on the doorframe. A pebble popped loose and settled on the floor mat. Olsen stared at it, absentmindedly, as he jiggled the shifter into reverse and backed the truck onto a long stretch of reservation blacktop. A car passed by maybe once an hour. This one happened to be a Volkswagen. It screeched to a stop – a half-foot short of Olsen's truck.

Olsen jumped out and ran over to the Beetle, circa 1963.

"Hey, sorry, I wasn't paying attention. You OK?"

The driver gazed up at Olsen, a big grin on her on wide, round face.

"Heyyy, Billy! You're just trying to get my attention, huh, big man."

"Hi, Mary. I was just, uh, going out..."

Mary Martinez shook her head and laughed. Mary laughed a lot, and it wasn't forced. She got a kick out of just about everything life threw at her, even near collisions. Maybe she was the jolly fat woman, but Olsen liked to believe her good cheer came from her heart – not her girth.

Squeezing out of the car, Mary stood and slapped Billy Olsen on the back. Nothing about Mary was petite. A very plus-size body drove the hand that delivered the slap. Olsen felt a new bruise forming on top of the old ones.

"Going out? How about going out with me? I'll show you a real good time, Billy. Your grandmother always said you took yourself too seriously. Come over to my place, and we'll have some fun. Heyy, how about it."

"Fun is my middle name, but..."

"It is? I thought it was Horseman, you know, you're mother's last name."

"No, Mary, I was.."

"Heyy, making a joke, huh? Me, too," Mary said, laughing and slapping Olsen again. He wanted to get back to his truck, but she moved in front of him. Getting around her would be like going around the block. "Say, you still got a thing for that rez smarty, Anna Stewart?"

"Well, I haven't..."

"I'd forget about her, big man. I heard she's going to Brazil, one of the Fulbright deals."

"Oh?" It was all Olsen could think to say. This was the first he had heard Anna Stewart would be away. Of course, he wasn't going to hear it from Anna. She had called him once since his grandmother died, and that was to say she was sorry. Anna Stewart had spoken to his grandmother often, writing down her many stories about the old days – all stored in her memory. Now, Anna never called. She was wrapped up in too many other things. And, of course, Olsen never called her either. He was too intimidated.

"Heyy, big man, cheer up. There's plenty of other girls on the rez – you know? I know one who'd really like to check out those Swedish meatballs."

"Norwegian."

That got him another backslap.

"Heyy, Billy Olsen, you're too funny."

No, Mary was the funny one. And Billy Olsen laughed, though it hurt. Mary, as usual, had broken through the Buster Keaton facade common to cops, Norwegians and a few Pimas.

He was glad for the laughs, in any case. After hearing about Anna Stewart, he needed a bit of laughter therapy.

71

Mary moved back to her car, working her away around Olsen.

"Hey, big man, what's going on with your grandmother's house? I hear the tribe's trying to get it torn down, put a casino there."

"Parking lot. I hired a lawyer, Ronnie Clark."

"Ah, that's that Navajo, eh?"

"His father's Navajo. His mother's O'odham. Anyway, he's licensed to practice on the rez. One thing I can say, he told it to me straight. The tribe's got me on this one."

"Yeah, and he's up against Mike Farley. He's a pretty tough cookie. But, hey, maybe I can soften him up for you, big man. He's got a thing for me."

Maybe he did have a thing for Mary, but Mike was the straightest arrow in the tribal quiver. He couldn't be bought with money or favors. The tribe paid him very well to watch out for its bottom line.

Billy Olsen smiled.

"If anyone can get through to Mike Farley, it's you, Mary."

"Heyyy," Mary said. She cranked over her Volkswagen and backed up enough to clear Olsen's truck, then took off.

Olsen climbed into the cab and headed west across greater Phoenix. He stayed off the freeways – too nerve-racking – and slipped past endless blocks of strip malls, shabby storefronts and fast-food joints; past old houses of painted block, new houses of sprayed-on stucco and the outer fringe of rusted mobile homes. Beyond the fringe sat the bar. The fringe would all be gone in five years, absorbed into that spreading oil slick of a city.

It looked like the usual Sunday crowd to Olsen, judging by the cars. Old Cadillacs, old Chevy pickups and newly minted, heavily financed Ford F-150s. Driven by old men drinking away their Social Security checks, middle-aged men drinking away their failed marriages and young men just drinking. Most of them had this in common: They were – at least at one time – in the cactus-hauling business. Some stole cactus. Some collected them the honest way. The line between the dishonest and the honest haulers, however, was permeable, and many of them just drifted from one side to the other depending on their circumstances. And their circumstances were usually close to desperate. They took work where they could find it. Most of those new trucks would be repossessed in six months.

Olsen circled around to the outer edge of the lot, a half-acre of hard-packed dirt. He pulled to a stop. The dust kicked up by the tires continued to drift past. As it cleared, Olsen stepped out into the June heat. He counted the months. June. July. August. September. October. Not too bad. In other five months, things would start to cool down. He made his way between the trucks and cars toward a sprawling wood-frame building that looked to be specially treated to burn down in two minutes. The neon sign over the front, now switched off, read: One More Round Bar and Grill. It was a lot more bar than grill. Its first owner, Lucky King, had lived through a heart attack. His prayer had been answered. Just one more round.

It was also his last. His second heart attack killed him.

His wife, Eva, now ran the joint – along with her son, Darby.

Olsen entered and waited. The door swung shut, cutting off the bar's only access to sunlight. With no windows and three low-watt incandescent bulbs, the place went dark. He did not move, as he could not see. He knew the bar was straight ahead. There was no missing it. It ran the length of the building. But he had no idea what or who stood in his way. Eva was always rearranging the tables and chairs, just to keep things interesting for fresh arrivals. And the drunks, stumbling all around, took great offense at anybody who bumped them in passing. Accident or no accident. It called for a fistfight.

In a minute or so, Olsen's eyes adjusted. He cast about for familiar faces. All he saw were the backs of heads, all lined up along the bar. Then he recognized one, a carpet of shag hair circling a bald spot.

Olsen rested an elbow on the bar.

"What's good today, Hank, Bud or Bud Light?"

"I don't drink that shit," Hank said, turning to Olsen. His face – elongated and craggy with large grayish-brown spots – looked like it had been overdone in the microwave. He had a nose that bent right, then left. Typical cactus hauler, Hank Tregubov was a man of too much sun and too many fights.

"What shit do you drink?" Olsen asked.

"Miller ... Miller Lite."

Olsen ordered a Dos Equis. Eva popped the cap and slid the bottle to him like a puck on ice. He grabbed it and leaned in Hank's direction.

"How's Margie?" Olsen asked, hoping he'd gotten the wife's name right.

"Oh, she hasn't been same since that meat thermometer got lodged in her brain."

Olsen nodded slightly. Took a sip from his bottle.

"Hadn't heard about that."

"Yeah, big gas explosion, maybe three months ago. She went to check on the pot roast. I told her not to smoke around the oven, but – you know – women. Anyway, doctors said they couldn't remove the darn thing. Might kill her. So, she sleeps on her side now. And oh, she's still got a temper, but now you got some warnin'. Just watch out when she's gets up around lamb and veal."

74

"I see," Olsen said, lifting his bottle again.

Hank could be bullshitting. He could be stating a fact. You never knew. Well, so much for the small talk. Olsen needed some information. Though Hank had officially retired some three years ago, he was still a walking who's who of cactus haulers. He wouldn't snitch on anybody, and just about everybody trusted him not to. Chatting up a cactus cop wasn't snitching in itself. Olsen often hung out here, and made a point to talk to just everybody – at one time or another. And any offer of information held to certain widely understood rules. Rarely did haulers name names. But when somebody's bad behavior went beyond mere livelihood and brought too much unwelcome attention, well, it was OK to drop a hint. And the McFinneys took unwelcome attention to a whole new level. Nobody, Olsen figured, was going to stick up for the McFinneys. They were always regarded as trouble. Bad for business. And now they were wanted for murdering the most respected hauler in the business – even if he had gone New Age on them.

"Too bad about Durstan," Olsen said.

"Goddamn them McFinneys." Hank shook his head mechanically, downed half his beer. "Ain't nobody could steal, uh, haul cactus like Randall Durstan."

"You don't have to hide what he did. I can't arrest him now. But I would like to find the two who did him in."

"I wish I could help, you, big guy. I ain't heard a thing. Nobody else has either. They vanished, it looks like."

Olsen turned from Hank, studied the label on his bottle and thought: Dead end. If anybody at all had heard anything about the McFinneys, it would have gotten back to Hank. He knew everybody: The inner circle of haulers. The outer circle, and every circle in between. The thieves, the legitimate haulers, the fences

75

and legitimate native-plant dealers. Still, nothing. The McFinneys had not approached anybody about buying the crested. Not since showing up at Ranker's nursery.

Of course, nobody would touch it anyway. Too hot. Too conspicuous.

Just maybe the McFinneys weren't as stupid as he thought. And he had to admit, he thought they were pretty stupid.

Slipping four bucks on the counter, Olsen took a final gulp. He heard clicking, like an exposed nail in a boot scraping the floor. He looked down as a pair of work boots on sturdy legs headed his way. No nails, there, he thought. The boots were held together by glue. They stepped up to the bar, next to Olsen. The person inside them was Ted Ranker. He needed a beer to cry in. The tears had already started to flow.

"Eva, draft, please."

"What kind?" Eva shouted from twenty feet away.

"What would Jesus drink?"

"Bud Light."

Ranker looked around, apparently unable to make anybody out yet. He had skipped the usual courtesies and bellied up the bar before he could even see it. He squinted right at Olsen, then smiled through the tears. The smile didn't quite go with the purple lump rising out of his forehead.

"Hey, Billy, what'dya know. Here we are worshiping at the church of the blessed beer," Ted Ranker smiled and slapped Billy Olsen on the back, on top of the same bruise rebruised by Mary Martinez. Ranker was a big man. Nearly as tall as Olsen, and built like a redwood. The slap hit Olsen like a two-by-four. But Olsen took it as Ranker intended it, a good-natured greeting from a good-natured – if occasionally emotional – man.

Ranker sobbed a bit, then winced. His hand shook like it was full of bees.

"Damn, can't slap like I used to," he said. "Cactus needles. I've hauled so much cactus, I've got broken needles embedded in my hands."

Staring at the hand, Ranker noticed something.

"Knocked one loose," he said.

Ranker reached for some tweezers in his pocket. Pinching a small shaft poking out of the back of his hand, he slid out a half-inch needle in an eruption of puss and blood.

"It happens," Ranker said. He wiped the mess off on his shirt. Eva set his Bud Light on the bar, unmoved. She'd seen it all before. Ranker hunched over his beer, cried some more. Olsen couldn't see what he had to cry about. He had great hair. Blond locks that fell over his ears and collar in perfect curls. A face that looked like something chiseled by Michelangelo, except with a better tan. Outside of bad teeth, the man was perfect.

Well, Olsen thought, even near-perfect people have feelings.

"Haven't seen the McFinneys since … what was it, Wednesday?" Olsen asked. Part conversation. Part fishing.

"No. Haven't seen them. They just better not come around again. They upset my Roz, and I just hate for anything to upset my Roz." Ranker drained his bottle, ordered round two. Round three soon followed.

"Seems like she can stand up for herself."

Ted Ranker smiled, then sniffed. "She can stand up for the both of us, that's for sure. But she couldn't stand up to Randall Durstan." Then, hunched over his beer, Ranker sobbed and shook. "He poisoned her with all that aneemistic spirits in the cactus rigmarole … maybe now, maybe now she'll come back to

Jesus. Crap, she hasn't really left him. But, you know, she's making him mad."

Ranker shook his head. A slow sad motion.

"That's between her and Jesus. I know one thing. Roz never loved Durstan. I'm sure of it. Damn sure. Didn't happen. Hell, she ratted him out, sent him to prison. Still ..."

Lifting his beer, Ranker polished off what was left in one grand motion. He set the bottle down hard and shifted his weight, his shoe scraping the concrete floor. The noise grated on Ranker. His raised his left foot, then felt around the bottom of his shoe. He worked at something with his fingertips, nearly losing his balance. He got it eventually.

"There." Ranker dropped a pea-size pebble on the bar. It dribbled to a stop in front of Olsen.

"Present for you," Ranker said, then smiled and cried some more. Eva set another beer before him and he downed half of it in a blink. His eyes were red, moist. He wiped them with the back of his hand.

"Ow, damn!" Ted Ranker shut his right eye tight, like he had gotten something in it. Squinting, he eyed the back of his hand and plucked out a needle.

"Son of a bitch. That smarts. Damn cactus. I can't understand why anybody would want to worship the damn things."

Then he sobbed, loud quaking sobs and drank more beer. And got drunker and became more emotionally distraught.

"She never loved him. Never."

Ranker shook his head. "God, I just love that woman. If anything ever happened to her ... anybody ever tried to take her from me and Jesus, I'd ... I'd..."

Ted Ranker slammed his fist down on the bar. Cactus needles flew out with explosive force. One hit Olsen's cheek like a small dart. He removed it and dropped it to the floor.

No doubt about it, Ted Ranker was a man on edge. Too much beer and too much pain. A powder keg just one match short of exploding.

Olsen's cellphone rang.

"Hello?"

It was Jane Fillmore. "Hi, Billy. New development."

"What?"

"Phoenix PD just got a call from Victor Rodriguez, the gardener at Ranker's nursery, Needles Arizona."

"Uh huh."

"Roz has been kidnapped. The two guys in a flatbed. You know, one wearing a dress."

"Uh huh." With a red-eyed, sniffling Ted Ranker looking on, Olsen forced a smile as he kept his answers non-committal, neutral. He did not want to be around when Ranker got the news. He'd leave that to mental-health professionals.

Another cellphone rang. It was clipped to Ranker's belt.

Ted Ranker, annoyed, yanked the phone from the belt and read the number on the screen.

"It's Victor," he said in a slur. "What the hell could he want?"

Chapter Ten

"I better go." Olsen flipped his phone shut and dived for the floor as Ted Ranker reacted to the news by picking up a barstool and hurling it toward a bank of tables. It shattered a half-full pitcher of beer, soaking the grizzled patron who had downed the other half.

"Jesus!" Ranker wailed. "I'll kill that fairy and his goddamn brother. Fairies are an abomination in the eyes of Jesus! And now one's got my Roz!"

Ranker began to pound his fists on the bar with enough force to send needles flying like bits from a fragmentary bomb. Olsen covered his head, fending off a spray of barbs. He thought: Somebody's got to stop this guy. Struggling against the inertia of his own mass, Olsen rolled toward Ranker, got to his knees and drove his shoulder into Ranker while holding onto his legs. The man fell like a tree, then kicked and swung wildly. Olsen fought off the body blows and wrestled across the floor with Ranker. Bruises atop a previous bruising.

"Settle down, we'll find her!" Olsen shouted.

"The hell you will! The Lord wants me to kill those assholes!"

Olsen heard a distinct metallic click. It came from the .45 semi-automatic now pressed against Ted Ranker's forehead. He looked cross-eyed up the barrel and froze. Slowly, Olsen rolled over and saw Eva bent down and shaking her head. Eva was a thick woman, dressed in loose-fitting slacks and a polo shirt. She was somewhere north of seventy. Her hair was white, and the skin hung loose below her upper arm – the same arm that held the gun.

"Teddy, you've got a nursery to run," Eva said. Her voice was the no-nonsense but caring voice of everybody's grandmother. "What will Roz say when she gets back and the whole thing has just gone to hell – because you went off on and did something stupid."

Olsen got to his feet, pulling himself up on the bar's edge. He looked back down at Ted, who nodded in agreement with Eva, the gun muzzle moving up and down with his head.

"You're right, Eva. I got to stay with the nursery. That's what Roz would want. Can I...?"

"Come on, I'll give you a hand."

Eva helped him to his feet.

"I'll have Darby give you a ride home. You can pick your truck up tomorrow, when you're sober."

"Thanks," Ted said. Maybe it was Eva's good advice. Maybe it was the gun in his face. Either way, he seemed to have come to his senses. So ... Olsen thought. The McFinneys have Roz Ranker, and for what? Maybe Fillmore had a theory. Olsen decided he wouldn't find any answers here, and made his way outside and into the blinding light of the sun. He squinted and shaded his eyes until he could get some sense of where he had parked his truck.

As he headed toward it, his cellphone rang again. It was Fillmore.

"We've really got to find the McFinneys now," she said. "Now they've got a hostage."

"But why?"

"I don't know. Nobody's heard from them. No ransom demands. Maybe ... oh, I don't know. But we have to find them."

81

"Shouldn't be too hard," Olsen said. "A cross-dresser and a cretin driving a flatbed hauling a one-of-a-kind cactus."

"With a hostage," Fillmore added.

"A loud hostage," Olsen said, feeling weary and achy. "Look, I'll call you first thing tomorrow."

"Police might find them by then."

"One would hope."

He hung up and dug out his truck keys. He climbed behind the wheel, slowly and deliberately. It hurt to move. Another week off work sounded good, but that wasn't going to happen – not until he got back the crested for the governor's biggest campaign contributor. Who may or may not have come by it legally. Couldn't prove it either way.

He took off for points east. It was a long haul.

Olsen pulled up to his driveway about four o'clock, the hottest part of a summer day. Sunlight glared from the picture window of a reservation house across the field. It was big, new stucco job, one that could have passed for any house in a high-end subdivision. The owners came into money by leasing a family allotment to a strip-mall developer. With Walmarts on the rez, Olsen couldn't tell where Indian land ended or began anymore. Not many tribal members got rich on shopping centers, though. Most of them lived in decidedly more modest reservation-style block homes, based on some kind of universal BIA floor plan. A few clung to the traditional ways, preferring – or compelled – to live in shacks of timber-reinforced mud walls.

As for Olsen's house, left by grandma Rosa, it fell in between the BIA block look and Pima primitive. The ironwood and overgrown mesquite trees hid it from the street, and the walk from the driveway meant ducking beneath the prickly claws of low-lying branches. At the doorknob, Olsen freed a rolled-up handbill secured with a rubber band. Unsolicited fliers rarely made it to reservation homes. Number one, it was trespassing. Number two, it was trespassing.

Olsen unrolled the sheet. It read: "By order of the Tribal Council, you must vacate the premises within 30 days. Your cooperation is appreciated. Ernest Chiago, Tribal Manager."

"It's the thought that counts," Olsen muttered. He wadded up the paper and carried it into the house. He went to the refrigerator and got the makings for dinners. A beer, bacon, cheese, bologna and three slices of bread. He microwaved the bacon and layered it between the bread slices, along with the cheese and bologna. The middle slice of bread held the sandwich together like a load-bearing column. In front of the television, he ate his sandwich in large bites, choking it down with beer.

The sandwich disappeared. Olsen flattened out the eviction notice, then called his attorney, Ronnie Clark..

"Ronnie, this is Olsen. I need some ..."

"You got coffee? Fresh?"

"I got coffee."

"Good enough. I'll be right over to discuss business."

Ronnie lived a half-mile away, three houses down. His car came to a dusty stop behind the truck. Olsen greeted him with a mug of hot coffee. He settled into a leather chair next to the big sofa Olsen had parked himself in.

Ronnie Clark didn't take himself too seriously, though he could if he wanted. He was, after all, a lawyer. And he was a stickler for sticking to the traditional diet favored by Grandma Rosa. Melon, squash, tepary beans. It showed. Ronnie Clark was as fit as the Pima warriors of old, warriors who once traded blows with the fiercest Apaches.

He was thin and handsome, his dark hair gathered into a shoulder-length ponytail.

Ronnie Clark took a sip from his mug.

"Microwaved?"

"Coffee made in a pinch," Olsen said.

"It'll do," Clark said.

Olsen showed the wrinkled paper.

"I got an eviction notice. One month. I thought I had two."

"Seems like the tribe decided to fast track this."

"I can't fast track it. I'm working a case that's eating up my time. Can't you do something? Reset the clock to two months."

"I can probably file an appeal of some kind. Buy some time. Now, my time is ninety dollars an hour."

Olsen blanched at the fee. But he figured Ronnie Clark was worth it. He knew the maze of tribal bureaucracy better than anybody. He often joked that the tribal seal itself was symbolic of the way the Salt River government worked. The ancient pictograph, appropriately called the Man in the Maze, shows a human figure about to enter a circle of many paths. One path leads to enlightenment. The others to dead-ends. Olsen sought the path to an extra month in his house.

Ronnie Clark glanced around. He put a hand behind his neck under his ponytail and the white collar held partly in place by a loosened red tie. He was raised Pima, but he dressed lawyer.

"I'll admit. I hate to see it go. Your house has a quaintness about it, and I'll never forget your grandmother's stories on the front porch, not to mention the fresh-cooked corn and the bowls of hot tepary beans. Ah, the little tepary – native food packed with protein, fiber and complex carbs."

"You remember her stories?"

"Sure. She'd invite all the kids over. You were with her. You must have been five. I was about eight or nine. She never served fry bread. She said that made you sick. She meant diabetes. And I remember the stories she told of Coyote and Turtle. She was a library of traditional Pima lore. Grandma Rosa liked to tease us, too. She made up her own stories, like Tepary Bean Girl. She always told us which came from our fathers and which came from her. Sometimes she'd make us guess. They all sounded good to me."

"I never grew tired of hearing them," Olsen said. "Even after I moved away, I came back often. And she'd tell the stories, and I remember the hot bowls of beans. They were very good. You don't see tepary beans anymore."

"Specialty stores," Clark said.

Ronnie Clark leaned back in the chair, passing a hand over his mouth in thought.

"You're the Man in the Maze, Olsen. But I'll see what I can do." Ronnie Clark looked at his watch. "Twelve minutes, eighteen bucks. Hey, gotta go. I'm meeting Professor Stewart for dinner. She's written a lot on Indian law, so it's strictly business. Otherwise, my wife might get upset."

"I thought she was in Brazil."

"She leaves next week."

"Oh, right."

"Thanks for the coffee."

Ronnie Clark stood up and went to meet a scholar as smart as she was pretty – or was it the other way around?

Olsen opened another beer, then began to feel sick. He sweated, was out of breath and extremely tired. He thought about dialing 911, but the phone was in the kitchen – and he didn't think he could make it that far. His cellphone was on the dresser. Even farther. So Olsen closed his eyes and struggled to rest through the discomfort. Eventually, he dozed off, unsure if he'd wake up.

But he did, all too soon. The phone he couldn't reach rang. And it wouldn't stop. Olsen pushed his hard-to-manage frame up from the sofa and stumbled into the kitchen.

Picking up the receiver, he managed: "Lo."

"Hey, Billy, things are happening." It was Fillmore. Almost cheerful for ... Olsen checked his watch ... 9 a.m. He had slept through the night.

"Yeah? Picked up the McFinneys? With Ranker, and the cactus?"

"No, I got a call from Phoenix police. I'm told them to call me on anything related to cactus."

"Yeah?"

"We got a bad one."

"Bad what?"

"One badly banged up Upster, at the temple. Male, Thirty-two."

Olsen yawned.

"Temple?"

"The Phoenix branch of the Worldwide Church of Uppermost Cosmic Consciousness."

"How many branches does it have?"

"This is it."

Chapter Eleven

Olsen nosed the truck up to Fillmore's patrol car on West Garfield in Phoenix. At one time, Garfield had been a place of quaint 1940-style houses, where landscaping meant neatly pruned rose bushes and trellises overgrown with bougainvillea. But their time had passed. Half the houses had become run-down rentals. The other half torn down for industrial warehouses or rendered into storefronts that had become, in turn, past their prime. There just wasn't much use for typewriter repair anymore. Olsen double-checked the address on the slumping block storefront. This was it. Somebody had made a halfhearted attempt to paint out the old name: "The Typewriter Fix." Below, stenciled on a picture window, was the current name: "Chapel of the Cactus Spirit: Worldwide Church of Uppermost Cosmic Consciousness." Worldwide? Olsen thought. There couldn't have been more than a hundred Upsters on the planet, and most of them were in Arizona. Because that's where the cactus was. In substance. And in spirit.

Olsen saw Fillmore on the other side of the glass, waving him on in. Then he caught his own reflection – and wished he hadn't. He didn't look good. Overweight, and by all appearances, headed for a one-man crisis in healthcare. Maybe last night's episode was a warning. Maybe he should have steered clear of the Waffle Den.

Olsen went in. Fillmore was talking to a Phoenix cop, another muscle-bound beef-cake in uniform. Cops used to look like most people, except for the guns and uniforms. Now they all had pecks and biceps bulging through shirts two sizes too small. Olsen felt a sense of resentment and embarrassment standing next to Charles Atlas of the badge-and-gun set. Still, when Fillmore turned to him, her face brightened.

"Hi, Billy. We were just talking fitness clubs. Jake has a primo abs trainer."

"Really? What does he train them to do?"

Fillmore laughed and Olsen took a look around. A single bookrack with a bent post leaned up against the wall. It carried a dozen or so copies of one book, Upchurch's *The Cosmic Cactus*. A glass case held displays of souvenirs. They varied in size from half-foot to a few inches in height. All were quartz-crystal saguaros, with etched-in happy faces. On every base, the inscription: "Feel the Energy!" The bigger souvenirs went for seventeen-fifty. The smallest were priced at three-fifty.

"This way," Fillmore said. She showed Olsen through a door into what he thought would be a dimly lit temple. But he was wrong. The place had a skylight you could launch a cruise missile through. A bright summer morning washed over a circle of stones at the center of a large open room. Inside the circle, more stones had been arranged to resemble a two-armed saguaro. Meditation rugs surrounded the rocks, in inner and outer concentric circles. Olsen wondered if the inner mats meant better seating, put you closer to the universal desert spirit.

Then he noticed the woman, a blonde, on a mat in the inner circle. She wasn't seeking higher consciousness. She had her face buried in her hands. She shook. The half-dozen or so cops in the place left her alone.

Two circles up, Olsen spotted a mat saturated in blood.

He glanced at Fillmore.

"Not good, deputy."

"No, it's not," Fillmore said. "This guy was worked over like a piñata."

"And he's ..."

"In the hospital. He'll recover but it'll be a while before the swelling goes down. Right now, he's got a bruised spleen and a half-dozen broken bones. And, as you can see, he lost some blood."

"And the cactus. Is there a connection between him and the stolen cristate?"

"The McFinneys," Fillmore said. "They were here."

"Looks like it. Any witnesses?"

"Her," Fillmore said, eyes shifting toward to the blonde. "Described them to a T. She said they came around, demanding to see Upchurch. Said they had a cactus for him."

"And?"

"And, well, they confronted Quinn."

"Quinn?"

"The young man, an acolyte. Quinn Moody. He said he couldn't help. And they started punching him."

"Hmm, can I talk to her?"

"Well, she's a bit distraught."

"I'll be tactful."

Olsen stepped her way. He blocked the skylight. A shadow fell over her. She looked up. Her face was delicately chiseled. Her skin the glaze of fine porcelain. Extraordinary beauty accented with a tattoo on a long slender neck. It was a little green saguaro. It went well with the large purple bruise on her cheek.

"Hi. My name's Billy Olsen. I'm not a real cop."

"I can tell."

"Oh, well, I'm certifi .. I work for the Arizona Department of Agriculture. I recover stolen cactuses."

"You mean cacti?"

"Sure, I mean cacti. Can you tell me what happened?"

"Well, These two men drove up in a big truck, about a half-hour before we opened for public worship. They said they had a cactus the master would pay dearly for."

"Upchurch."

"That's his earth name. His Uppermost Cosmic name is known only to the world of transcendent bliss. We just call him Master."

"Master Upster?"

90

"No, just Master."

"And what is your name?"

"PureLove. When I meditate, I seek to achieve a state of pure love, for all mankind."

"I see, and, uh, what about these two men?"

"They started banging on the front door. It was about, oh, seven-thirty. I unlocked the door just to tell them to come back at eight, but then they forced their way in. One of them was a man dressed up like a woman. She wore a flower print dress and cowboy boots, but she wasn't very convincing."

"Why do you say that?"

"She didn't bother to shave her legs. They were very hairy. And she had a couple of Olympic-size softballs for breasts. I mean real softballs. If she was going for a transgender look, she fell way short."

"But good enough to call him a she."

"I'm giving her the benefit of the doubt." PureLove said, slightly irritated.

"And the other guy?" Olsen asked.

"He had a ball cap and wore jeans and a white T-shirt. He swore a lot and threatened to hurt me if I didn't tell them where Master was. They said they had the cactus he ordered, the sacred one, from the Master's cactus-thief friend."

"Durstan," Olsen said.

"Yes. Anyway, I said I didn't know where Master was, only that he had gone to his desert sanctuary to pray for peace throughout the universe. That's not just talk. We are not alone. There are other planets, you know, where inhabitants fight and kill each other, as on Earth, but – and this a little known secret – through prayer, channeling and upper consciousness, Master has achieved world peace on twelve of them."

91

"That's a start," Olsen said.

"Yes, just a start," PureLove said. "In his retreat, he has a created a concentrated energy zone by liberating spirits once captive."

"You mean stolen saguaros."

"They had already been stolen. Now they have been liberated. The sacred one would create a cosmic energy field of such strength, only the Master could channel it without harm. And then he'd find Uppermost Upper Consciousness and learn the answer."

"What answer?"

"How to bring about peace on the most warlike planet in the universe."

"Earth."

"No, Wardonia. Earth is next."

"So he wants the cristate. Why didn't you offer to buy it?" Olsen asked.

"It is not theirs to sell. It belongs to the Master."

"Not really, but … you really don't know where Upchurch is? Where his retreat is?"

"I told you, I don't. And … that's what I told the mean one. He slapped me and said he didn't want to do it again. He said I was too pretty to beat up, then ..." PureLove touched her bruised cheek ... "he slapped me again. I told them, over and over, I didn't know. I told them to talk to Quinn."

"The poor follow in the hospital."

"Yes. Quinn Moody."

PureLove let go a burst of tears, then continued.

"The one in the dress, he led the mean one into the energy chapel, even after I told them the place was sacred and for believers only. 'We're believers,' the mean one said. 'We believe Quinn better tell us how to find Upchurch or he's a dead man.'

"They stormed into the chapel. I was afraid to follow. I heard them yelling at Quinn, and I heard him say, 'No, you can't make me.' And then, then I guess they just began to ... to ... then I heard the mean one laugh like a seal bark. Then they came out of the sanctuary. I was frozen in fear, against the wall. The one in the dress said to me, 'See, it wasn't so hard. We just had to reason with him.' "

"And he told them where Upchurch is?" Fillmore asked.

"I don't think so. They are negative spirits. And Quinn wouldn't even tell me. He said he only knew the half of it."

"Who knew the other half?" Olsen asked.

"The cactus lady, the one with the red hair. She's been in here."

"Roz Ranker."

"Yeah, that's her name."

Chapter Twelve

The light went yellow and Olsen slowed. The SUV behind him, following too closely, made a hard stop in a fog of rubber and brake particulates. Olsen drew a breath, grimaced at Fillmore through the rearview mirror, then fished the book from his pocket. He carried the damn thing everywhere, in case he found a hidden clue in it. He had nothing so far.

Nothing in the book suggested what Quinn knew or didn't know, except for a line of numbers in the upper corner of the title page. They went 32.085217. There might have been other numbers written above them, but what? The page's corner had been torn off.

The other half? Olsen thought.

Half of what? Maybe one was latitude. And the missing number of longitude. Coordinates leading to Upchurch. Maybe. One thing was sure: The McFinneys were driving all around town, apparently invisible to law-enforcement agencies, even with a loud-mouthed kidnapping victim. They now seemed bent on finding the one guy who, in their mind, would buy a hot crested – Upchurch.

Olsen pulled into the Ag-building parking lot. Fillmore's patrol car came squealing in behind him and stopped in the parking spot reserved for the director.

She hopped out. Olsen squirmed out.

"You can't park there!" he said, somewhat panicked, somewhat annoyed.

"Police business."

Olsen looked at his watch. Ossylmeyer would show up in about fifteen minutes. Barely time enough.

"Uh, I stopped off for a quick document search," he said. "Then I have an errand."

"A quick bite at Pan-Cake-a-Rama?"

"Heyyy, I don't criticize your driving, do I?"

"What? Is something the matter with my driving?"

Olsen smiled. It was a smile of incredulity.

"No, your driving's perfect. I'll meet you at the sheriff's office about ten o'clock. I can get in there?"

"I'll see to it."

"Good, good. I have some bookkeeping to do."

"Gotcha, Slim."

Fillmore smiled. The morning sun lit up her hair from behind. She radiated from inside as well. For a cop, she was warm, friendly and informal. And a lot different than Anna Stewart, who was cool, book-smart and a bit stiff. Pretty would describe Fillmore. Beauty would describe Anna Stewart. Unobtainable would describe both. Olsen gave himself a mental slap in the face. He had known Fillmore for less than a week. She was a cop he had to work with, not something to be obtained. Not an object. An unobtainable object.

The unobtainable deputy drove off in a cloud of burning rubber.

Olsen took the stairs to the third floor, then a left toward Ossylmeyer's office, not a right, toward his. He caught a brief glimpse of Ossylmeyer's secretary, Sylvia, guarding the perimeter before he ducked into the side hall leading to the bathrooms. She probably saw him. People his size don't sneak around much and get away with it. But he didn't go into the bathroom. He just stood in the side hall and glanced at his watch. Nine-Ten, and there she was, zipping by, on her way to the lunch room to start Ossylmeyer's coffee. He liked it fresh when he came in, so he could be wide awake, at least until his first drink.

Sylvia turned a corner, out of view. Olsen slipped into her office and buzzed himself into Ossylmeyer's inner chamber.

The boss kept the place neat. One file folder was on his desk. A three-drawer filing cabinet stood in a corner across from the window. Olsen checked his watch. Three minutes before Sylvia returned with the coffee. And five minutes before Ossylmeyer himself showed up. Olsen had a rule against overlooking the obvious. He went over to the desk. The file tab read: Drinking Memo. Olsen flipped the folder open. The first page was indeed a memo. But it seemed a thick file for a memo reminding employees it was illegal to drink alcohol in a state office building. Olsen flipped to the next page. It was a photograph labeled "43," an eight-by-ten of a saguaro topped with a magnificent gnarl of rolls and tucks. It was an enlargement of the same photograph of the same crested stolen from Larrabee's estate. The next page had a map of the plant's original location – a remote highland desert about sixty miles east of Phoenix. Mazatzal Wilderness. That was a long way from Larrabee's Paradise Valley estate. The page's corner was stamped with the date filed. A knowledgeable hiker had reported it stolen, pointing out a hole where a regal crested once stood. Olsen must have noted it.

Filed and forgotten, Larrabee didn't forget. He wanted to make sure there was no record of the original theft. That the investigation didn't lead to him. He just needed somebody he could trust. More the point, somebody the governor could trust. A total toady. That turned out to be one Rudy Ossylmeyer. On orders, Ossymeyer nabbed the file. Easy enough. The governor likely told him to destroy it. But here it was, in one piece. Apparently, even for Ossylmeyer, shredding it was a step too far. Or he had to wait until he was sober enough.

Hell, Durstan probably stole the crested for Larrabee in the first place. He knew where to get just what Upchuch wanted.

Or so Olsen had it figured.

Olsen tapped the photo. Yep, that was it, he thought. Number forty-three.

Heels tapping the terrazzo echoed off the walls. *Sylvia?* Olsen checked his watch. Now what? He picked up the desk phone, then thought better of it. She'd know the call was coming from Ossylmeyer's office.

He unclipped his cellphone from his belt and punched in Sylvia's number. It rang just as the heels hit the carpet of the outer office.

"Hello?" she asked.

"Hi, uh, Olsen here. I'm, I'm ... I just pulled in, heading to my office, but I ... I thought I saw somebody passed out on the sidewalk. Might be the chief. I think ..."

"Why didn't you check on him!"

"Well, he looked like he was comfortable and I didn't want to, you know, disturb ..."

"Damn!"

Olsen heard the phone slam down and the heels hitting the terrazzo. He heard the ping of the elevator arriving and the doors opening. When he heard them close, he slapped the folder back on the table and slipped out, with a lumbering dash down the hall. He ducked into his office.

Somebody from livestock inspection might have seen him through an open door. He wasn't sure. He didn't stop to find out. He really didn't know any cow people, and they didn't know him.

Olsen's window overlooked the parking lot. He saw Sylvia step out and look around, just as Ossylmeyer's late-model Cadillac pulled into his reserved spot. He got out, and they exchanged a few words. She gesticulated toward Olsen's office, turning and staring right at him. Maybe she saw him, but he couldn't tell. He knew this: He had a lot of questions for Ossylmeyer. And given Olsen's bogus cell-phone call to Sylvia, Ossylmeyer probably had a few questions for him. Things could get uncomfortable, for both of them. And Olsen avoided discomfort. As they entered the building, he eased himself down two flights of stairs and left by a side door, circling back around to his state-owned pickup. A hardy, four-wheel drive model, it probably got eight miles to the gallon. Olsen stopped at the motor-pool gas pumps and turned off his cellphone, as directed by a sign. He didn't want to spark a fire. And he especially didn't want to hear Ossylmeyer rant.

Tank filled, Olsen made his way to St. Joseph's Medical Center, north of downtown. What began as a small sanitarium for tuberculosis patients – run by divinely guided nuns – had grown into a major city hospital. It was still run by nuns, but now they were guided by highly paid professionals. In front stood a large statute of St. Joseph, greeting everybody who had proof of insurance. But the front was not the entry. Olsen entered through the side, off the parking garage across the street.

At the main desk, a volunteer somewhere in her eighth decade volunteered that Quinn Moody could be found in room 647.

Up the elevator and a left turn, a long walk down a hall, another left, then a right and another left brought Olsen to Moody's room. There were two beds, both with heavily bandaged patients, and Olsen couldn't tell one from the other. The attendants went by some kind of electronic tag. A man and woman in hospital-white entered the room. The woman held a small plastic box, with a screen. She waved a wand over the patient closest the door. She checked the screen.

"Evan del Rios, train wreck," she said.

The man said: "All right, Mr. del Rios, it's time for your physical therapy."

They lifted Mr. del Rios onto a gurney. Olsen worked his way around to the other bed to talk to Quinn Moody, who probably had a few screws knocked loose himself. The McFinneys had worked him over pretty good. Every inch of skin was bandaged. Leaning in, Olsen began to ask about the number scribbled in the book. But before he spoke, the patient on the gurney – halfway out the door – muttered: "Thirty-two zero eighty-five. You're halfway there."

"What's that, Mr. del Rios? The number of the train that hit you?" the woman said.

"I don't think he can hear you, Marge," the male aid said.

"Whatever you say, Randy."

"Wait!" Olsen said. He worked his way back to the gurney's side, tugging at the official patch on his shirt-sleeve and directing it to heir attention. "I'm an investigator with the Arizona Department of Agriculture. You've got the wrong man. That's not del Rio."

The male aide stiffened and narrowed his eyes.

"We don't make mistakes anymore. The new technology is mistake-proof. Marge?"

Marge held up the plastic box with the wand. She waved the wand over the presumed del Rio's left upper arm.

"Look it's all right here on the screen. Except you can't see it. Confidential patient information."

"You mind if I ask him something?"

"I don't know," Randy said. "He's got to save his energy for the treadmill."

Olsen asked anyway: "Quinn, what about the other half. Who has the other half?"

"Roz. Roz has the other half."

"You gave the McFinneys your half?"

The head inside the bandages shook side to side.

"They made me. I don't know why they ... bothered. Durstan already had both halves, so he could find the Master."

"Hey, mister plant cop, this chat has gone far enough," Randy said. "We've got to get this patient to therapy and loosen up all that fresh scar tissue, so he can heal properly. Now if you'll excuse us. These rooms weren't designed to work gurneys around people your size."

Olsen bit his lip and sidled free of the space between the wall and the gurney. Then, more out of reflex than thought, he glanced down at the chart hanging off the foot of the now-empty bed. It read: "Quinn Alfred Moody." Following the gurney out the door, he called to the aids. They made a point to ignore him. Olsen tried to catch up to them. They picked up their pace.

"Look!" Olsen shouted. "That's not del Rio. He's Quinn Moody. Somebody entered the wrong information on the computer!"

The attendants by now were humming loudly, drowning out the man chasing them down the hall and pointing back to the chart on the bed. Like a scene of out a hospital drama, they slammed the gurney through a pair of swinging doors into a restricted area. A security guard blocked Olsen's way.

Olsen shouted: "Go easy with him! He's badly bruised!"

As the door swung shut, he heard Ronnie: "Let's start with the medicine ball."

100

Chapter Thirteen

The space was reserved for police, so Olsen pulled in. A Phoenix police cruiser stopped alongside as he got out.

The officer behind the wheel shouted. "Hey, that's for police!"

"It's OK. I got a gun. And an arm patch."

Olsen walked on, as the cop screamed at him. He'll just have to find another place to park, Olsen figured. He was just one of many cops with a reason to park on Madison. Across the street was the county jail complex. Nothing fancy. Just a lot of concrete and bricks. And, on the inside, a lot of iron bars. East of the Madison jail rose a new copper-plated twelve-story court tower. It had more glass than the old tower. But, inside, it worked the same way. Justice was not some abstract ideal served up by Plato. It was the end product of a massive and constant movement of paperwork, even in the era of computers. Olsen knew the inner workings well. He had testified dozens of times against cactus thieves he had caught in the act, including Durstan. He could breathe easy now knowing he didn't have to make his way up to some courtroom on the ninth floor. His business today was strictly ground level – past the metal detectors and down a long corridor to the sheriff's office.

At the entry, he asked a woman behind bulletproof glass for Deputy Jane Fillmore.

A moment later, the woman buzzed Olsen into the secured area. Fillmore took him to her desk, one of a dozen in a large open space. Still dressed in her desert-duty khakis, she motioned Olsen to take a seat while she finished some paperwork.

He remained standing. Sure, sitting sounded good. But getting back up didn't. He didn't plan on staying long anyway.

"Uh, Durstan's body, over at the morgue?"

"Yes, top and bottom." Fillmore said, looking up from a report.

"The clothes he wore, they over there too?"

"Maybe. Probably. Why?"

"I have a hunch."

"It looks like you want to play it right now."

"You know me too well. I got a truck right outside."

Olsen would make sure he drove. He didn't want to ride with Fillmore until he got a handle on his blood pressure. It was borderline high. Damn. One more borderline medical condition. He couldn't keep track of them. And so far he resisted any effort to bring them under control. He never bothered filling prescriptions from the doctor. He continued to eat just about anything with syrup – and salt. If he had changed, it wasn't for the better.

Still, he had to draw the line somewhere. Riding with Fillmore was a one-way ticket to a heart attack.

"I'll drive," Olsen said. He made it sound like there's no arguing the point. Or tried to.

He walked briskly to the Madison Street exit, and did a quick shuffle to the truck. Fillmore followed. Before getting in, he slipped the parking ticket from under the wiper and threw it on the floor. As Fillmore closed the passenger door, he cranked the engine. He took Washington Street, a one-way thoroughfare that led to the state Capitol, but Olsen wasn't going that far. About halfway, he turned off at the morgue. This was the new morgue.

The old morgue had been housed in a hunched down block building with all the pizzazz of a produce warehouse. It was low-key and didn't announce itself. The new morgue had no shame. It was at three-story modern-looking place with a big sign out front that said: Maricopa County Forensic Science Center. This was the public entrance. The dead went in through the back.

So did Fillmore. Olsen followed. The medical examiner greeted them in his office. He looked to be a fit forty. He wore a nice polo shirt and a pair of jeans and had a grinning, casual manner about him. His degree from the University of Arizona College of Medicine hung on the wall behind him. Olsen noted the name: Daniel Phillip Highland. The white coat he wore for his job hung on a rack in the corner.

"Hi, Jane," he rose from his desk. "You look good in shorts." Olsen thought that was a bit too personal. Perhaps they dated. Fillmore ignored the compliment.

"On assignment, Dan. Working with investigator Olsen on a murder. Billy Olsen."

"Nice to know you, Mr. Olsen. And just what sort of investigator are you?"

"Native plant enforcement, Department of Agriculture," Olsen replied.

"Cactus cop."

"Some say cactus cop, some say cacti cop. But, yeah, that's about it."

Highland sat down at his desk. "So, Jane, if it's a murder. There must be a body."

"Randall Durstan," she said. "He was decapitated."

"Yeah, we've got him. Unusual. Around here, heads and limbs are usually removed to make it easier to hide the body. The victim's already dead. Not so for Durstan. Decapitation was the cause of death. It has the hallmarks of Middle East terrorism."

"More likely homegrown homicide," Olsen said. "Anyway, I don't want to see the body. I just want to check the clothes Durstan had on."

"Well, they're in storage, ready to be used as evidence, if necessary."

"I'd like to see them," Olsen said.

"This sounds a little far removed from tracking down a stolen prickly pear."

Highland leaned back in his chair, rested his right hand on the desk. It was the pose of a man in no hurry to let Olsen anywhere near the inner sanctum of bodies and the clothes they wore. Fillmore stepped forward and placed her hand atop his.

"Investigator Olsen is a duly sworn law officer and we've teamed up to solve a murder and find a rare saguaro cactus, a crested. Dan, I need your help."

Deputy Fillmore ran her fingers up and down the hand. Olsen noted how light and nimble they were. Maybe he should place his own hand atop the desk, he thought. Maybe her fingers would find his. Maybe ... he took a deep breath and let it out.

So did Dr. Dan.

"Follow me," he said. Highland led them to a room of baskets that pulled out like drawers. Near the door a computer sat on a high counter, apparently to be used standing up. Highland typed in Durstan and came up with a number for the basket. Pulling the basket, he set it on the counter and slid it toward Olsen.

"Before you touch anything." Highland yanked out a pair of surgical gloves from a wall dispenser. "Put these on. One size fits all," he said, casting a glance at Olsen's hands. "Usually."

All gloved up, Olsen reached for his back pocket and got the book – Upchurch's book, *The Cosmic Cactus: An Upster's Travel Guide to Universal Consciousness*. After flipping to the title page, he placed the book face down on the counter, then turned to the basket. A pair of underwear and a sleeveless undershirt lay on top. Thankful for the gloves, he lifted out the undergarments and set them aside. A short-sleeve plaid shirt was next. Stiff and stained, it must have soaked up most of the blood. Olsen pulled out the shirt, unfolded it and reached into the pocket and pulled out a small wad of lint. He examined then lint carefully, then placed it and the shirt on the counter. Then came the pants – well worn, blood- and dirt-crusted Lee jeans. Digging around the left pocket, he came up with more lint. The right pocket, same thing along with a bb-sized wad of paper.

"Um, Mr. Olsen, we empty the pockets and put the contents in a safe, for evidence or to be claimed by relatives," Highland said. "There's nothing in them."

"I think I found it."

With pen from his pocket, Olsen smoothed out the wad. It wasn't much. A triangle-shaped thumb-size scrap. He picked up the book and matched the scrap to the corner of a torn page. From whence it came.

"Look," Olsen said, showing how scrap and book belonged together.

The medical examiner forced a smile. "Good job, I guess ..."

"Quiet, he's got more," Fillmore said. She looked at Olsen, expecting more.

Highland glanced at Fillmore, annoyed.

Olsen nodded, smiled almost sheepishly. "Well, it's not much. The torn scrap has numbers, scribbled in."

He held up the scrap. Fillmore and Highland closed in on him and stared down at a shred of paper with a line of figures – 113.23800 … The last digit looked like a partial 4. He placed it back down on the torn page. The bottom half of the "4" matched the top half. Just below that, on the page, was another long number – 32.085217.

"They don't mean anything to me," Highland said.

"GPS coordinates," Fillmore said. Olsen nodded.

"Where the numbers line up, stick a pin on a map and we'll find William Upchurch," Olsen said. "Find him and wait for the McFinneys, if they don't find him first."

"Upchurch. Spiritual leader of the Upsters," Highland offered. "They seek uppermost consciousness … well, meditating on cactus. We had one in here, oh, last month. Automobile accident. Had a small saguaro tattooed on his neck. Anyway, what's that have to do with Randall Durstan?"

Olsen folded the clothes as well as anybody without professional laundry experience and placed them in the basket. He stripped off the gloves and tossed them into a can for medical waste.

"Durstan was an Upster, not just a cactus thief. Upchurch hired him, or rather tasked him, with stealing the crested. Upchurch believed it had, um, special powers."

"Hmm, didn't see any tattoos on his neck."

"Probably where the cut was made," Fillmore said.

Highland nodded.

"I think Durstan planned to give the crested to Upchurch free and clear," Olsen said. "But the McFinneys probably have a different business model. Buy or die."

"The McFinneys?" Highland asked.

"Couple of brothers who inflict pain and suffering as a way to win friends and influence people," Olsen said. "Anyway, Durstan must have torn out the half the GPS coordinates he had written on the page of Upchurch's book, to keep them separate, as a safeguard. Maybe he thought the book would fall into the wrong hands – like his wife's nephews."

"What nephews?" Highland asked.

"The McFinneys."

"I should have guessed."

Highland reshelved the basket, then led them back to his office. He took his working smock from a coat rack and slipped it on. The white cotton fabric had few stains on it. Highland was neat in all aspects, even autopsies.

"So the McFinneys killed Durstan for the cactus?" Highland asked.

"That's what it looks like, Dan," Fillmore said.

Olsen nodded. He agreed, though – he had to admit – this was a new level of violence for brothers best known for assault in all its legal definitions – from simple all the way to aggravated.

"You found the murder weapon?"

"You mean a knife?" Olsen asked. "No."

"Saw, more likely," Highland said. "Chainsaw."

"Um, no. No chainsaw."

"Well, if you find the McFinneys, look for a saw," Highland said. "Or ask them what they did with it."

Olsen nodded again, biting his lower lip slightly. And considered the murder weapon, something he hadn't really done before. The McFinneys were not saw people. They were not knife people. They loved to use their fist, and if they moved beyond that, they went right to guns. He recalled a desert encounter with the McFinneys last year. He had tracked them down on a tip and caught them loading an six-foot saguaro onto the back of a rented pickup. The plant had a tag, and even if it had probably been placed there illegally, Olsen couldn't prove anything on the spot. He couldn't hold them. But he could talk to them, let them know he had their address.

So Olsen talked. And glanced inside the cab. He noted the daily output of a small-arms factory, a dozen rifles, shotguns and handguns littering the floorboards and stacked up behind the seats. Olsen blinked, then smiled gamely as they finished tying down the saguaro.

"I see you like guns," he said.

"We're protected by the Second Amendment, you know," said Edwin McFinney, just beginning to experiment with his emerging femininity. His thickly applied mascara had partially melted in the August heat.

But thick mascara was not foremost on Olsen's mind. It was the sight of all those guns. The McFinneys loved guns. They just didn't strike him as a saw-loving crowd. When it came to Durstan, they had the motive. And maybe they just stumbled upon the means.

"I guess you know the next step," Fillmore said, bringing Olsen back to the matter at hand.

"Hmm?"

She slipped the book out of Olsen's grip. Opening the front cover, she removed the torn corner and, pinching it between thumb and forefinger, waved it in front of Olsen.

"We've got to find Upchurch before the McFinneys, or he's dead, too."

"Well, my job is to find the cristate. But it's a good guess the McFinneys have the coordinates. They got to Moody. And, by now, they've probably gotten to Ranker."

"Each knew the half of it," Fillmore said.

"Excuse me?" It was Highland. Olsen looked down. Highland stood about a head below him, trying to get through the doorway Olsen now blocked. "I've got work to do. Bodies are slowly but surely piling up."

"Right," Olsen said.

He stepped back into the hallway, joining Fillmore. Highland eased down the corridor toward the morgue, then he stopped and turned.

"Jane, how about lunch tomorrow? I'll make room." The smile was infectious. Olsen wanted to go along.

Fillmore shrugged, smiled back.

"Can't. Investigator Olsen and I have to track down a couple of murderers and a cactus, somewhere out in the desert."

Highland shook his head, apparently unable to grasp the ways of the world, and of women. He pivoted and headed for his next autopsy. Olsen and Fillmore found the exit. Olsen pushed open the door and stepped into the afternoon sun. The asphalt radiated solar heat like bricks in a kiln. The whole of Phoenix, with tens of thousands acres of concrete and asphalt, had become one big kiln. Just now, it wasn't so bad. One-oh-five at the most, Olsen thought. As he neared the truck, he dug out the keys.

"We'd better get on our way.," Fillmore said. "We'll go back by the sheriff's office, I'll fetch the GPS device and we'll pick up the SUV. We might need it."

Olsen could feel the acid flowing into his stomach. He felt flush, then cold.

"GPS? I've got a map."

Fillmore pushed a finger into his chest as she looked up at him. "We need the GPS for the coordinates. Map won't cut it. We can pick it up with my gear, along with the SUV."

"I can't ride with you. I have a heart condition."

"Are you saying that I drive ..."

"You're a maniac."

"No, I'm punctual. I've seen you drive. You're a turtle. You drive like a turtle. You inch along with a train of PO-ed drivers behind you. With you behind the wheel, the McFinneys could crawl away, and we still wouldn't catch them. You couldn't catch them if their truck broke down and they got out and carried the damn cactus on their shoulders."

"Turtle? Funny you should say Turtle. You know Turtle is part of O'odham lore. See, one day, Turtle went hunting for food, but stopped to rest in the shade. Soon, he realized he was resting on the trail that the antelope take. So Turtle came up with a plan to trick the antelope into getting food for him and his family."

"What does that have to do with anything?"

"I don't know. My grandmother told me the story when I was five, but .... ah, I don't remember it all. And, oh, at dinner she liked to tell the story of Tepary Bean Girl. You see, Tepary Bean Girl ..."

"I'm still driving," Fillmore said.

"Well, get in, and I'll take you back to the sheriff's office. We'll pick up your gear."

Fillmore belted herself in and flipped open Upchurch's book as Olsen navigated the parking garage and turned south on Seventh Avenue.

"Hey, listen to this," Fillmore said, reading:

"The spirit of harmony and happiness can be reached only through uppermost consciousness. The desert sentinels channel consciousness from the universal cosmic being that flows through all. It is there for all who seek to find the highest energy fields, in the desert far from negative force. Concentrated, divine energy, lifting us to the uppermost consciousness, where we

110

can channel the one true answer from the uppermost cosmic good – Rilukku! But we must start humble and work up. Follow me! You will find Uppermost bliss in Rilukku. You will find true love, and – if Rilukku really likes you – a year's supply of Upster herbal tea.

Olsen pulled up to the sheriff's office. Fillmore rushed in and returned with a backpack.

"Just a few essentials, ready-packed. GPS included. We need to go by the supply depot and the motor pool. I'll pick up some camping gear and a desert-dog SUV. What about you?"

"I got everything we need in back." Olsen motioned to the pickup bed.

Fillmore jumped in the cab, tossed the backpack behind the seat. Olsen headed toward Washington Street, went left. And kept going.

"Hey, where you going? The motor pool's that way."

Olsen went south on Nineteenth Avenue, then right on Buckeye Road, a four-lane trough bordered by mountains of wrecked cars and trucks. Soon the salvage yards gave way to warehouses, followed by new subdivisions – houses shoulder to shoulder, all some variety of beige and all built almost overnight on freshly scraped earth.

"We have to go back!" Fillmore said. Somewhat pleading. Somewhat yelling.

"Well, like you said. We have no time to lose. You're worried about Upchurch. I'm worried the McFinneys won't find him at all and just decide to dump the cactus. They have to know by now, if there's no Upchurch, it's too hot to keep."

"But my gear. The rest of my gear."

"I told you. I got everything we need."

"But ... I'm driving ... remember?"

"Well, of course, you can't drive this. You know, insurance issues and all."

Olsen's cellphone rang. He pried it off his belt.

"Hello."

"Hi, Olsen?"

Hell, it was Ossylmeyer.

"Director Ossylmeyer, how are you feeling?" He had to keep up the fiction of spotting Ossylmeyer face down in the Ag parking lot.

"What? Is there something wrong with me ... that I don't know about?"

"No, sir, not at all."

"Well, Look, Olsen, about that cactus…"

You mean the one you stole the file on, Olsen thought. He said: "The cristate?"

"Right. How's the investigation going?"

"We're tracking it down now. Deputy Fillmore and me," Olsen said.

"Good, good, because I got a call from the governor. He got a call from Larrabee. And Larrabee is worried about that cactus. He doesn't want it falling into the wrong hands."

"Well, sir, I think it already has."

"No, they mean ... If you find the cactus, make sure you don't disturb the nest, or let anybody else disturb it."

"The nest?"

"The woodpecker hole."

"The woodpecker hole."

"That's what the governor said. He doesn't want anybody disturbing it."

"Why would anybody do that?"

"Who knows. Now look, it's got nothing to do with any sort of treasure," Ossylmeyer said. His words weren't too slurred, for mid-morning. "That's not it at all. You follow?"

"Doing my best."

"See the hole …"

"The boot."

"Right, the boot. See, it's got something to do with federal wildlife regulations. Might be some birds' eggs in there, or something. So make sure they're not disturbed. And don't look for them either. That's a violation of law right there. Got it?"

"Got it."

Olsen tried to picture birds eggs nestled deep in the cactus. But he couldn't. He kept thinking about what treasure Larrabee had hidden in a cactus boot. Stolen jewelry? Dirty pictures? The formula for Coke?

"Jesus!" Fillmore screamed. "Hang up and drive!"

Chapter Fourteen

Hector McFinney stepped from the cab, stretched his arms and wiggled his legs. Sure as hell were stiff. And who's fault was that? Probably the government, over-regulating the design of truck seats – or something. One thing was sure. He was stiff and somebody would pay.

Edweena was already out, touching up the rouge on her cheeks, using the side mirror. Poor thing, Hector thought: This sun is sure hard on her sensitive skin. The sooner we can get paid for this worthless cactus, the sooner we can get her all fixed up. Or so he believed. Edweena noticed him gazing her way, and put the powder back in the case. She pointed at a trail of dust, rising behind a vehicle coming up the hill on which they were parked.

"Looks like we got a smart shopper," Edweena said.

"Heh, heh, they're gonna be shoppin' in the deli for a knuckle sandwich, huh."

"No, they've already bought what we want," said Edweena, whom Hector agreed looked stunning in her low-cut jeans and white tank top bulging with semi-pro softballs – with lots of belly-button turf in between. "I can tell the type."

"Right."

The truck already blocked the road. Hector planted himself on the side the driver would most likely take, if he tried to go around – though that would be a big mistake. Hector had one hand behind his back, his right. And in his right hand he gripped a .357 Magnum, and it sure felt good when he rubbed his thumb up and down the little bumps on the grip. Ooh, that gave him goose bumps on the back of neck. Out of the dust, the approaching Jeep looked just the type college kids drove all around the desert, ripping up everything in their path. Hector hated it that college kids had all the fun. *The hell of it is,* Hector thought, *they could have gone anywhere they wanted in a fuckin' Jeep.* But they took this road instead. Why? Hector hadn't a clue. But, damn, if that brother of his hadn't called this one! He said, let's go there. And, hell, here they were sitting way up on a hill looking straight down into one damn big hole in the ground. Coulda fit the whole damn town of Ajo in it. Of course, you'd have to haul the whole damn town up the damn hill, on account of that's where the hole was. Shit, as if the whole damn town didn't know about it. The whole damn town and all the people in it *made* this hole. Took them damn near a hundred years. That's a lot of copper. They stopped making the hole when it cost more to dig out that shit than what they could get for it. Geniuses of the business world there.

Now the hole was a tourist draw. People drove all the way up the hill to see it. And even past that, behind another hill, was the Ajo Mineral and Mining Museum. Right there, on that second hill was a big blind spot. Nobody could see you from any direction. And, goddamn! Here they were! And goddamn! Here came the Jeep! Edweena knew it would happen just like this. Talk about genius.

The jeep, all new beneath a bit of dust on the fenders and the big fat tires, slowed after Hector held up his hand.

The people inside had the all-American frat-look — big and well-groomed. The driver clearly looked annoyed. So did his passenger. My lucky day, Hector said to himself. I'll teach them not to get annoyed with me. And I'm blamin' them for my stiff back.

The driver made a point to get out of the jeep, to intimidate Hector with his big, broad size and big, broad muscles.

"Hey, dirt monkey, your dump truck's blocking the road."

Hector showed the twenty-something his right hand, his thumb messaging the grip.

"Well, I got a question for you."

A look of concern, if not outright fear, passed over the kid's face. It was brief. He grinned, shook his head. He held out his hand, apparently expecting Hector to hand over the gun. Hector thought: I should just shoot him right now. But Hector was curious. He had never seen that one before.

"Look again, asshole," the kid said. "You aren't the only one with a gun around here. Show him, Ron."

The kid turned to Ron and saw what Hector McFinney already knew. Edweena had clubbed Ron with the barrel of a large shotgun, and Ron – though not wholly unconscious – was severely stunned. He groaned. Edweena clocked him again. He was out cold.

And now the twenty-something kid indeed looked worried, and it was not a passing emotion. He stayed worried. Edweena stepped from the other side of the jeep. Hector gauged frat-boy's expression, to see if the sight of a Edweena in a softball-enhanced tank top would set the young man's hormones aflame. You'd expect that, Hector thought. After all, my brother sure knew her fashion. She dressed more sexy than all the topless dancers in Wittman.

But no. The kid recoiled. Fancy that, Hector said to himself.

"God who art in heaven, what is it you want?"

"You asked the right question, young man," Edweena said. Hector had always admired, his – her! – way with language. English no less. She knew all kinds of words, and always put them

116

in the right order. But let's face it. Edweena was the first one in the family to go all two years of community college.

Hector pressed the gun to the young man's head.

"We want the thing that tells you where you are."

"What?"

Edweena clarified things: "He means a GPS device, you know, global positioning system?"

"I don't know what you're talking about."

"Hector?"

"Yes, Edweena."

"It looks as if he's not going to tell us anything about the GPS. So, you might as well send him on his way."

"You mean shoot him?"

"Of course."

"Oh, I was hoping you'd say that, however much I'd like one of them GPA systems."

And Hector pressed the gun foursquare against the young man's temple. His hand trembled with excitement.

"It's in the glove compartment!" the young man shouted. "It's an old model … it's … Just don't kill me!"

"Didn't plan to." And Hector let him have it with the gun butt. Probably a little harder than a good knockout punch called for, but the some-bitch did call him a dirt monkey – and that sure came across like an insult.

Edweena retrieved the GPS device and turned it over slowly in her hand. She rubbed her rouged-up cheek with her other hand. Beard stubble poked up through the makeup like new sprouts in spring. She handed the device to Hector. He turned it over, his eyebrows furrowed. Sweat beaded on his forehead, suggesting his brain was overheating.

"Where's the little map? Huh? It's supposed to have a little map."

"Must be broken. It just has numbers," Edweena said. "You'll have to ask somebody how it works."

"Oh, right," Hector said, pursing his lips and scratching his scalp with a gun barrel. "Then we'll know what those numbers mean, the ones we spent all our time coaxing out of Roz and that other Upster."

"You sure know how to coax things out of people," Edweena said.

"I do, I do."

Hector glanced over at the two unconscious college students.

"I guess they had all the coaxing they can handle."

Edweena nodded as she tamped down an unruly false eyelash. Then, with a slow-motion tilt of her head, she gazed at the truck trailer. Hector thought: *Damn, she thinks of everything.*

With a knowing nod, Hector went around the truck and lifted the tarp. Just checking. It was hot out. Standard desert hot, maybe 108. Maybe the freak of a cactus could use some air. They had to keep the damn thing alive till they got to Upchurch. He sold books. He was fucking rolling in the dough. He'd pay big money for this fucker, and Roz Ranker would seal the deal. He buys the cactus or we give her a bruising. It's called salesmanship.

One big payoff to free Edweena from the pain of finding just the right fit. Poor Edweena. She couldn't just walk into a store like a normal woman, and steal her size off the rack. But if she had money, why, she could buy her own store. And stock it with a big-but-feminine line. She would call it: The Woman I Be.

It would make her so happy. And Edweena's happiness was Hector's. She was the best brother he ever had.

What to do? Figure out how to make this GPA thing work, first off. Hector pulled back another section of tarp. Roz Ranker sat against the cab, tied and gagged. Hector tore the duct tape from her mouth and showed her what he had.

"Say, sugar, how do you work this?"

"Shove it up your ass."

"First you tell me how it works."

Edweena spoke up. "I have an idea. Why don't we shove her behind the seats. We can beat the information out of her while we're driving."

"Edweena, you are so fucking smart."

Chapter Fifteen

Rudy Ossylmeyer rubbed a shaky hand through thinning gray hair. Shaky shaky shaky. He reached for the bottle and placed it atop the folder. He had left the folder out last night. Forgot about it. OK, maybe he had had one too many. But somebody had thumbed through the folder, somebody who wasn't supposed to. Ossylmeyer could tell. The page he always kept on top was buried three for four pages deep. The department memo – the one telling all employees that anybody caught drinking on their lunch hour would be fired. Instead, somebody had mixed it up. Now the first page showed a crested saguaro stuck in the desert somewhere northeast of Phoenix. That was crested number forty-three.

The department first cataloged it in 1995. It was reported stolen in 2002.

Speculation had it as a Durstan job. But no leads, really. Cactus gone, untraceable. That was until Durstan stole it again. Then the file on forty-three would show the cactus taken from Larrabee's looked just like the cactus taken from the Mazatzal Mountains five years ago.

So what choice did Ossylmeyer have? He had Sylvia nab the file while Olsen was still at Larrabee's looking at a hole where the crested once stood.

It was all politics. And not politics in a good sense. Russell Larrabee had given Governor Pilt his generous support. And Governor Pilt returned the favor, making sure the theft of the headdress crested couldn't be traced to that first theft, indeed a

Durstan job. Before Durstan joined the cactus cult. Durstan had a rolodex of collectors, and knew Larrabee would pay top dollar for a rare cristate.

Once Durstan showed him a picture, Larrabee had to have it.

Ossylmeyer knew all this because Larrabee told the governor. And the governor told him.

Sure wish he hadn't been told. It was enough to drive a department head to drink. Even more than his usual.

Of course, Olsen knew nothing of this when he arrested Durstan. He had caught Durstan hauling away some run-of-the-mill saguaro. Two years after the Mazatzal job.

Talk about worry. All the time Durstan was in prison, the governor worried. Worried that Durstan might threaten to spill the beans. Demand more from Larrabee than a one-time fee. And maybe even blackmail his way up the food chain. Larrabee, Ossylmeyer, then the governor.

But Durstan never said a word. He stole the cactus. He got paid for it and, it seemed, was satisfied. He didn't backstab. A guy like that had no chance in politics, Ossylmeyer thought with a passing grin.

The grin passed. The mood turned sour. He poured himself a drink. Now this. Durstan stole the cactus back. Now he was dead. Then his killers stole the cactus. Here was the thing, Ossylmeyer thought. *If Olsen learns where that crested came from in the first place, I'm screwed.*

It's best he not find out. Maybe I could hire a private investigator, take Olsen out of the picture. Track down the cactus. Give it back to Larrabee. Get a clap on the back from the governor. And, and job security.

Job security! Is that asking too much?

Ossylmeyer put the memo against drinking back on top. Closed the folder and raised the glass. Shaky shaky shaky.

It was a stupid memo anyway.

All the department heads had to circulate it, by order of the governor. Pilt was Mormon and he wanted to dry up state government as much as the law allowed. Here, the memo covered the coverup, hiding the theft of a protected plant. A coverup ordered from on high, from the governor himself. A favor to a political friend. And major donor.

Ossylmeyer sat back in his chair.

How could he *not* drink on the job?

Pour pour.

"Governor Pilt here to see you," Sylvia said on the intercom. Damn, he doesn't wait to be invited, does he? He's the governor. He just barges in.

Time for the Ossylmeyer drill.

He drained the glass and tossed it and the bottle into separate drawers, each padded to dampen the noise. Then he popped two sticks of Dentyne gum into his mouth. He kept a dozen unwrapped in his top drawer, just in case. Next to the gum, he kept a small stack of half-completed department reports. He fished those out and hunched over them, pen in hand.

Pilt strolled in. His posture was ramrod straight, and he sat ramrod straight in the chair across from Ossylmeyer. Department of Public Safety bodyguards remained standing, taking up positions on either side of Pilt. Like the Department of Agriculture director was going to attack the governor, Ossylmeyer thought.

"You can wait outside," Pilt told the two men.

The DPS muscle gave Ossylmeyer the once-over and – apparently deciding he didn't pose a security risk – marched out.

122

"How's the investigation going, Rudy?"

"Good, governor, good. I've got the best cactus inspector in the department on the job. He's working closely with the sheriff's department on this one."

"The best? How many of our own do we have?"

"Uh, two...well, one active," Ossylmeyer said. "The other was hospitalized. He, um, he suffered some emotional trauma."

"You've got one person responsible for investigating theft and destruction of native plants for the entire state?"

"Well, if you remember, I asked for two more last year, but your budget director ..."

"Hey, somebody's got to hold the line. Anyway, the important thing is, you've got that one inspector working the right case."

Pilt relaxed a bit, draping an arm around the chair back.

"Does he know about the, uh, federal regulation?" Pilt asked.

"I told him not to mess with the woodpecker hole."

"Is that how you put it? Don't mess with the woodpecker hole?"

"Or words to that effect."

The governor leaned forward – serious, earnest. "I understand this cactus has fallen into the hands of a cult of New Age cactus lovers. That could look bad for the state. I thought all the nuts were confined to Sedona."

"Well, I guess a few got out."

"You believe in praying to a cactus, Ossylmeyer?"

"No sir, I'm a Methodist."

"Hmm. Does your investigator know how important that cactus is to Larrabee? Does he know that it's the keystone of his botanical collection?"

"Well, actually ... he's knows all about it."

"You mean he knows everything?"

"No, governor. He's knows … uh, just what he's supposed to know. You know, what he needs know. Not too much, of course … but enough."

"OK, I got it," Pilt said. "Now this is how it works. That cactus is important to Larrabee, and that makes it important to me. He assures me if he gets it back, I'll get his continuing support. And I'll need that support when I run for the Senate next year. It's not just money. He can get out the dollar-store vote. And that's no small number. So remember, Ossylmeyer, my career is your career."

Shaky shaky shaky. Ossylmeyer forced a grin, one he knew leaned toward stupid. He couldn't help it. He said nothing, hoping the governor would leave and go run the state or something. But the governor just sat there making small talk. And all the while Ossylmeyer's brain demanded a drink. The brain got petulant. The brain sent clear signals to the body: "Liquor me up or I'll make you twitch like a toad wired to a car battery."

Chapter Sixteen

William Upchurch stepped back. The cluster of saguaros continued to charge the air with uppermost waves of energy, a cosmic generating station. But the Master's prayers and meditations with the uppermost spirits had run more than six hours. It was time for a snack.

He had traveled far this day. Through spirit cactus he had become spirit traveler. He channeled cosmic Beings. And they channeled him. In a galaxy east of our own, he appeared to the people of Xoroxican as a god and told them to stop fighting. And they obeyed. They put down their plutonium-powered ray guns and held hands and danced, as he had directed. But that was only one planet. He had traveled to many planets, and brought peace. Yes, the energy field was strong, but strong enough only for a piecemeal peace. A little peace here, a little peace there. It just wasn't enough. True universal peace awaited the cristate. Then the energy of Carnegiea gigantea would be focused. Concentrated into pure good. He knew from the moment he had seen its picture in a magazine about how the rich live, he knew this was the chosen cactus. He studied the cristate carefully. The top spread into an unbelievably large arc of green flesh and needles, reaching toward the heavens. *What could it be but a transmitter of peace, powered by energies untold, to galaxies unknown, and a receiver of wisdom untapped from spirits unleashed?* Here was the way to true universal peace, the uppermost peace attainable. And when word got out where all this peace came from, people would flock to his church – everyday people looking for answers – not just a few misguided souls showing up now and then.

But, oh, what a stroke of luck when one of those misguided souls turned out to be the very man who had stolen the cristate for the rich man.

Randall Durstan had written from prison. He said he was a man of cactus, a bad man at that. He wanted desperately to change his ways, and he thought how righteous it would be to meditate on saguaros, and their energy fields, instead of stealing them. Uppermost cosmic awareness, he wrote, might be just the path to set him straight. If he cleaned up his act, his wife would take him back and make him pork chops all the days of his life.

So Upchurch brought Durstan into the fold upon his release from prison. And he gave Durstan an important title: Liberator of Cactus Most Holy. He would liberate saguaros – and maybe a few barrel cactus – from those who had ripped them from their natural desert homes.

"Are you sure it's not stealing?" Durstan had asked. "I'm a changed man."

"No, you are freeing these poor saguaros from their confinement in gravel-strewn freeway medians and shopping mall landscaping. At the sanctuary, they will be reunited with nature. And they will create energy fields of peace."

"Well, OK," Durstan said. "I probably stole most of them in the first place."

The cactus Upchurch had just finished meditating before stood on a sharply sloping hill. It was among some fifty saguaros Durstan had liberated. They were arranged in concentric semi-circles, spread out across the hillside. Here, they focused bursts of cosmic energy like a giant lens. A quantum leap beyond even the most powerful crystals. Yes, Upchurch still used crystals, on occasion. But he was moving away from them, outgrowing them – just as he had outgrown Sedona with its New Age flimflam. Besides, there were no saguaros in Sedona. Too high in elevation. He had to journey to the lower desert and start anew. And here, in a desert most remote, he had established his own personal retreat. Here, he would get not just answers – but *the* answer. And when it's time, write a whole other book about it. The first book led the way. The second book would be the way.

He looked around at his large green friends, each filled with a spirit connection to all the universe and its cosmic center. Some still bore gaudy white flowers on the tips of their great arms. The rest had gone to seed, flush with pods that stuck out like big green thumbs. The newcomers – liberated by Durstan – had been planted to grow in harmony with those already here. Here, the freshly planted saguaros saluted the old-timers who been living on this hill from the time Lindbergh crossed the Atlantic. They had lived through scores of blistering summers, where days between rain could fill pages on a calendar. But the cactus could take it. They stored up whatever rain came their way. And they carried within them the water of life, which in turn fed the universal spirits within.

The hill was his shrine. He chose it, however, as much for the cholla as the saguaros. The cholla governed the lowered half. If the sun hit them just right, they had a festive look about them, a cloak of needles. Incandescent. Brilliant. They dotted the hillside by the hundreds, each cactus a dense tangle of arms. Each arm a cluster of detachable limbs little bigger than golf balls. Each ball shrouded in needles, and each needle barbed to catch the flesh of passers-by and hang on with a bone-penetrating pain.

The cholla kept unbelievers from the shrine atop. That and the retreat's sheer isolation. Upchurch strolled down the hill toward his bath. As always, he wore a Gandhi-style loincloth. Like Gandhi he was a skinny man, weighing perhaps 125 pounds. It was part low-carb, vegetarian diet and part marathon meditation. As he neared the bottom of the hill, dozens of cholla balls clung to his legs. A few rode high on his inner thigh. He stepped on carpets of fallen cholla balls without expression. Without a misstep. Without a limp. Did he feel pain? Why wouldn't he? But keep in mind, he was the Supreme Master. Pain was but another path to self-realization. Pain was the path to inner peace and outer revelation. Pain was the path to the secrets of nature. Damn right it hurt, but so much the better.

At the bottom, near a mesquite tree, William Upchurch knocked the cholla balls off with a stick. Then he dipped a towel into a water tank. He cooled himself, first patting his face, then working his way down to the bleeding sores left by the cholla. The moisture gave a sheen to skin that was otherwise brown and shriveled. It looked like old skin, much older than Upchurch's forty-nine years. Upchurch didn't believe in sunscreen. He spent every day outdoors soaking up the full spectrum of the sun's divine light, including a good dose of the ultraviolet. As Uppermost Master, Upchurch knew this: He could not get skin cancer. The cosmic God of All-in-One told him as much during a particularly revelatory trance five years ago.

That spot on his forearm must have been something else.

The open tank had been set out for wildlife by the Arizona Game and Fish Department. Coyotes, javelina, deer and rare pronghorn antelope roamed the land. In times of drought, they made their way to it. Upchurch respected that. He did not adulterate the water with his sweat and blood, however divine they might be. He ladled out the water and rinsed the towel over a rock.

He was allowed this much. He was the Master.

Lo unto any other being who dipped water from the sacred spring.

Upchurch sat for moment, in peace and harmony, then thought about food.

He went to the mesquite tree, some fifteen away, and hung his towel on a low branch. From another branch, he retrieved his baseball cap. It was an official Major League Chicago Cubs baseball cap. He had worn a Boston Red Sox cap, until the Sox became World Series winners. Winners don't need answers. They know what they're about. But the people he led needed answers. They did not have answers, only years of failure and disappointment. They had much in common with the Cubs.

Upchurch settled into a beach chair and picked up the magazine on the rock next to him. It was Substitute World, the magazine for substitute teachers. The cover showed a smiling man in a white shirt and tie, mid-thirties, pointing to a name on the blackboard.: Mr. Reston. Below that, in perfect cursive, were the titles of featured stories: *Five Ways to Deflect Insults from Eighth-Graders, How To Say "Shut Up" Like You Mean It, Virulent New Strain of Mucus Found in Kindergartners* and *Playground Duty: Promotion Or Punishment?*

Upchurch kept in touch with his old life, perhaps thinking it would be nice to have something to fall back on if the church ever … well, he refused to believe the church would ever fail. He never let himself forget, though. How could he forget? The church had been founded on the rock of substitute teaching. Upchurch remembered the days, so long ago. He could see himself – once again – walking through the front door, following seven hours of taunting, incessant talking, runny noses – the ongoing assault to his senses. His young wife, the lawyer, would ask him how his day went.

He always answered: Bad. I need to get away. So one day, he did. He told his wife he was going out for more No. 2 lead pencils – the kids were always losing them – and headed for Sedona. Here was the center of cosmic consciousness – the land of red rocks and vortexes and magic crystals. Here was the place where anybody who was conscious could always achieve a higher consciousness. And so Upchurch channeled and chanted under the tutelage of Sedona's wisest and best New Age priests. They were good. You could tell. They drove the best cars. Lived in fancy manors on scenic hillsides. The older women kept company with young well-toned twenty-something men. The older men married women a third their age. It was all written in the stars, the crystals and their bank accounts.

But the higher consciousness they achieved only got them half the way there. Upchurch soon went beyond that, all the way to Uppermost Consciousness. Upchurch went beyond the vortexes of the dead soil and found energy from the living inhabitants rooted in it. He talked to his spirit brothers in the prickly pear and the oaks along Oak Creek. And the neophytes noticed. He began to attract a following. He could afford a new Saturn Ion. But, despite these trappings of wealth, he made a point to show his disdain for it. He had already begun wearing a simple wrap around his loins, and nothing more.

Then he discovered new energy fields. They had been under his nose all along, in the Sonoran Desert he had abandoned for Sedona. Here, the giant saguaros pulsed with positive energy and, pointing skyward, reached out to channel Maxokkoa and Remondo and Jopagori – and beyond to the One-In-All, Rilukku. Yes, there was much untapped Uppermost Consciousness. He first felt it when he drove back down to Phoenix to consult his lawyer-wife's lawyer, about her pending divorce suit. The desert-dwelling saguaros had cosmic fields stronger than any legal demands for half of all those unnecessary material goods he acquired through Uppermost Consciousness. And what luck! Just outside the small law office, framed by a large picture window, stood a green, three-armed giant. Unbeknownst to his wife and the lawyer, the saguaro shot him with all the energy he needed to resist signing all those legal papers. Ommmm, no!

But the poor cactus was fat, overwatered. It needed freedom. It needed a place in the desert where it could grow into its full potential, and raise universal consciousness. And so it happened that Upchurch moved back to the desert and started his own church of the Uppermost Consciousness. The spirits of saguaros – many begging to be liberated – would connect him and his followers to truths never before revealed.

He had said as much in his self-published book, a copy of which he gave to the Sedona library. His last copy, before things began looking up. The same copy he later checked out, autographed and sent to one Randall Durstan, who – upon reading it – found his calling. The liberation of cactuses great and small. He brought them back to nature. To the desert sanctuary. A holy ground of joyous and free saguaro spirits crackling with energy.

The Master sighed.

Opening his magazine to page thirty-seven, Upchurch noted the brief article on the high suicide rate among substitute teachers. It didn't have to be, he thought. There were answers.

Something crawled across his foot. He put the magazine aside and spotted a fat beady lizard with a tail shaped like an Italian sausage. The Gila monster was hungry. Upchurch reached into a paper bag on the ground beside him. He pulled out a fistful of dried flies.

"Bon appetite, Mr. Bitey," he said. He dropped the flies into a little pile. The Gila monster lapped them up with a slow but sure tongue. Then Upchurch laid out the cool, moist towel on a rock. Mr. Bitey's towel really. The beady lizard crawled under it, and slept the sleep of a Gila monster.

Upchurch leaned back in his chair and, crossing his arms, scanned the eastern horizon. The mountains danced a slow hula in the shimmer of heat waves. He saw nothing. No dust. No approaching truck. No sign of Durstan.

"What's keeping him? Where's the cristate most holy? It should have been here a half-hour ago."

Chapter Seventeen

Olsen flipped his phone open and took the call from Ronnie Clark, then thought: *What's that tree doing in the passing lane?* Then: *Oh, shit.* With a jerk of the wheel, he brought the pickup back onto the highway – and across the pavement to the other side. The truck cleared a small irrigation ditch. It flew into a field and harvested a row of corn, stalks and all. *A real bumper crop*, Olsen thought. He chuckled, glanced over at Fillmore. She glared back at him. She had a death grip on the door handle. He decided to keep the joke to himself.

He was still holding the phone.

"Uh, Ronnie, I'll call you later." He hung up and ran over more corn until he reached a farm road. He turned right and found the highway. He checked the rearview mirror. No hopping mad farmer. If somebody complained, the Arizona Department of Agriculture could make up the losses. All part of their friendly service.

About noon, they rolled into Ajo, where houses on hillsides overlooked a small town square. Shops surrounded the square on three sides. From here, Olsen and Fillmore would head into the desert in search of Upchurch, using the GPS coordinates found in Durstan's book and his bloody shirt pocket. Those numbers placed Upchurch in the Cabeza Prieta National Wildlife Refuge, an area big enough for a crazed cultist to escape the attention of the proper authorities.

"Hungry?" Fillmore asked, a little more composed.

"Always," Olsen said. "The town square has a diner."

"And we need supplies and water."

"I've got everything we need for camping in the truck."

"Two sleeping bags?"

"Four."

"Why four?" Fillmore asked.

"Well, if I zip two together, that's one for me."

"But why four?"

"You know, in case you want to make up a double bed."

Fillmore shook her head, apparently out of sympathy for a man whose size took him to the edge of all three dimensions.

Olsen turned left off the highway onto a street that defined the town square, about an acre of neatly mowed grass. At the Copper Pan Diner, he parked behind an ambulance with a broken taillight and peeling paint. The Copper Pan faced west, looking out across the highway toward a grand Spanish neocolonial-style building that was once the town high school. The mining company built the school, not to mention the entire town. But when the mine shut down, there was no money to support the school, and no kids to fill it. The school closed, and Ajo dried up – but did not blow away. Retirees and artists began to move in and snap up the quaint, but sturdy, houses once occupied by miners and their families. The old school became an artist colony.

Olsen and Fillmore took a booth by the front window. The air conditioning was set at full arctic blast and felt good. Olsen glanced over at a nearby table. He was drawn to the neon-yellow vests worn by a pair of diners. A man and woman seated across from each other. The ambulance crew, Olsen guessed. Paramedics. The woman was in her thirties, heavyset. The man looked to be pushing sixty, his gray hair pulled into a ponytail. They ate hamburgers and chatted amiably.

Once in a while, a new diner would come in and the older hippie-type would ask: "How ya doin', man?"

And the new arrival would always says: "Oh, god, Leo, never felt better. Honest!"

One older man even went so far as to bend over and touch his toes. "See?"

The yellow-vested hippie grinned, shook his head.

"I don't know, Mr. Butterfield. You do look a little pale. You sure you don't need ..."

Before Leo could finish his sentence, Mr. Butterfield turned and ran from the restaurant.

The things you see in small towns, Olsen thought.

After he and Fillmore had a few minutes to study the menu, the waitress approached with pad and pencil. She looked to be twenty-five, with a bushel of wavy auburn hair tied back into a frizzy pony tail. Olsen noticed her hands stained with paint, marking her as a member of the arts community.

"What can I get you?" She first smiled broadly at Fillmore, then turned to Olsen. She kept smiling, but it wasn't the same. This smile went from sincere to forced. Olsen forced a smile back, knowing once again he was being judged by his appearance. What was it now? His fat hands? The stomach pushing on the table's edge? Or just the overall picture of largeness? He glanced across the table at Fillmore. She didn't seem to care one way or the other. She simply set down her menu, ready to order.

"I'll have the chicken salad."

"One Copper Pan chicken salad. Anything to drink?" the waitress said, with the sincere smile.

"Ice tea."

The waitress turned back to Olsen.

"I'm trying to watch my weight," he said. "Number three. I'll have three."

"A tuna sandwich," she said.

"Well, three. Three tuna sandwiches."

The waitress made a face like she had just taken an order for the Donner party.

"Anything to drink?"

"Large chocolate milkshake, but, uh, with two percent skim milk. You know, watching my weight."

She bit her lower lip, dutifully logged the order and headed for the kitchen.

"I like healthy foods, like fish" Olsen said to Fillmore. "You know, fish fits right in with my heritage, my people."

"I didn't know Pimas were big on fish. They're not exactly a sea-going people."

"I'm half Pima, half Norwegian. The Norwegian part likes fish. The Pima part likes fry bread."

"So what's your favorite food? Sardines on fry bread?"

Olsen gazed at Fillmore, startled.

"Who told you?"

She laughed, shaking her head.

Olsen sighed. He always felt it necessary to correct the record.

"I wasn't always, know you, ample. I used to be in good shape, real good shape. Back when I played professional baseball."

"You mean like the Yankees?" Fillmore asked, half impressed and half incredulous.

"More like the Dodgers. I was a top prospect, still in the minors, then I injured my arm in a brawl. Well, somebody injured it for me. You, um, look athletic yourself."

"I was the captain of my college volleyball squad, at Arizona State. Our best year, we went to the second round, got beat by Stanford. They went on to take the national championship."

"You must have been good."

"I was the set up person for Karina ... Karina Foley. She could jump a mile high and she had fists of fury. She had the hardest kill shots I'd ever seen."

"And why you'd go into law enforcement?"

"It just seemed physical, without being menial. I didn't want to sit at a desk. And, besides, there's lots of driving in this job. And I like to drive."

"So does Mario Andretti, but he uses a race track."

Fillmore pursed her lips, narrowed her eyes. Olsen felt the back of his skull to see if Fillmore's stare had drilled all the way through.

"Look, I might drive a little fast, but I pay attention. I don't casually drift off the highway while my mind is lost in the magical land of cellphone chat."

Olsen looked at his watch. Time to shut up.

The waitress set an ice tea in front of Jane Fillmore. She returned a minute later, weaving around the lunch crowd balancing four plates. She placed three in front of Olsen, and one in front of Fillmore. Olsen started with the sandwich on his left. Good tuna. Three bites later, he noticed a tall, wiry man running across the square. He burst into the Copper Pan. Gasping for air, he leaned his hands on thighs and took in about five big breaths.

"Leo, Lucy ..." The two paramedics turned to the man. He was taking in air by the gallon.

"There's somebody in the pit. Tour guide saw the whole thing. Says this kid got beat up by a girl. Real big girl." He paused for breath. "Down in the pit. He's gotta be in real bad shape. Needs an ambulance. Dispatch tried to reach you."

Leo turned to Lucy. Both looked stumped, totally stumped about something. Leo unclipped a big walkie-talkie from his belt. He pounded it on the table, then put it up to his ear.

"Nothing," he said to Lucy.

"You try the switch, Leo?" she said.

"Switch?"

"Yeah, that little on-off knob."

"Oh, that one." Leo turned a small knob and tuned in some static. It was soon interrupted by a distress call.

"Emergency Unit Three! This is dispatch! We have a man down, I mean really far down – in the pit!"

Leo, his face a landscape of crags and stubble, looked alarmed.

"You hear that, Lucy! Man down – far down in the pit!"

The gasping man stood up straight. "That's what I've been trying to tell you."

Lucy shook her head. "Sure, but now it's official." She stared for a moment at the messenger. "What about you, Lester? You look like you could use an ambulance."

"Never felt better!" Lester shouted. His face was ashen.

"Well, we do have that guy in the mine pit," Lucy said, as if making a choice.

Leo cocked his head sideways, his display of alarm even more intense.

"What do we do, Lucy?"

She chewed on her burger, grinding it down thoroughly like a cow working on cud. She swallowed, then shouted: "The ambulance!"

"Damn, let's hurry!" Leo cried. "Wait!" He, too, had a hamburger to eat. He finished it off and carefully wiped the mustard off his chin. He leaped from his seat, yanked the napkin out from his collar and tossed it on the table like he meant business. "There's a dude who needs our help!" Brushing past the messenger, Leo pushed his way out the door and sprinted for ambulance, identified by a magnetic sign attached to the side. It read Your Lucky Day Ambulance Co. Lucy was already waiting. Olsen watched from the window as Leo fumbled to find his keys.

"Let's follow them," Olsen said. "The McFinneys and assault victims go together like ham and cheese."

"Right. And the kid was beat up by a large girl."

"You picked up on that."

"Come on, Billy."

Billy Olsen slapped three tens on the table. They scrambled for the door and across the parking lot. Fillmore ran ahead and jumped in the passenger side. Olsen reached the truck, and paused. He put his hands on his knees, out of breath.

"Just give me … a minute," Olsen said. A few breaths more, he stood up and fished the keys from his pocket.

"Better," he said. He swung the door open, eased in and cranked the engine. Then waited for Lucy and Leo to make their move.

Olsen checked the mirror. No hurry, as it turned out.

The two EMTs were still outside the ambulance as Leo sorted through a large ring of keys, trying one than the other on the door lock.

"It's that one," Lucy said.

"No, that's the one to my aunt's house."

"And that?"

"Goes to my Kia."

Leo scratched at his chin in reflection, then snapped his fingers.

"Now I remember. I had it on a separate key chain. I bet ..."

He pulled on the handle. The door was unlocked. It swung open. Leo peered inside.

"Yep, still in the ignition. Right where I left them."

Leo started to hoist himself into the driver's seat, but Lucy caught of his arm and pulled him back, nearly throwing him to the ground,.

"Hey, it's my turn to drive!"

"You sure, Lucy?"

"Come on, Leo, think. What day is it?"

"Monday?"

"No, it's Tuesday!" she yelled.

Leo cast a sidelong glance, eyes narrowed, then he seemed to get it.

"You're right. It's Tuesday and ..."

Lucy pushed him out of the way and clambered into the ambulance.

"Damn right I'm right," she said, turning the key and coaxing a reluctant engine to turn over.

Leo jumped in. With a tailpipe blowing smoke, the ambulance jerked out into the street. It listed to one side, and Olsen noted the back right tire was one of those undersized spares, a doughnut. It was bald. He fell in line behind the ambulance, which crossed the main highway and headed up the hill, past the old high school. The siren sounded like it needed repair. Olsen soon noted why. Leo, his head out the window, was shouting: "Woooo! Out of our way Dudes and Dudettes!" Woooooo!"

The back of the ambulance had an array of red and yellow lights. They should have been flashing. But only one of them so much as flickered, like it was about to burn out. The emergency lights on top rotated at varying speeds, depending on how fast or slow the ambulance was going. As the vehicle neared the crest, the emergency lights slowed almost to a stop. Any slower and everybody would have had to get out and push.

The ambulance hovered between going forward or rolling backward. Lucy gunned the motor. The tailpipe blew out a fog of white exhaust, and the ambulance lurched forward, clearing the hill and dropping out of sight. Olsen stepped on the gas, sped over the hill and spotted the ambulance careening toward a parking lot and, beyond that, a mammoth hole in the ground. The emergency lights were spinning out of control. Lucy swerved and just missed hitting the visitor's center, where tourists could learn about the big hole just in front of them. An older couple, headed for their car, looked up and froze. They had just crossed paths with a man waving at the ambulance, apparently trying to direct it. The ambulance was not to be directed. Now powered by gravity, the vehicle bore down on all three. Leo screamed: "Wooooooo!"

The couple flung themselves behind a car. The waving man jumped and rolled clear as the ambulance flew past and crashed through a chain-link fence. Brakes were applied. The vehicle spun around on loose gravel, three times, stopping five feet from the pit's edge. Olsen drove through the new gap in the fence, skidding to a stop alongside the ambulance. He lowered himself from the truck, nearly choking on the smell of burning brakes. Smoke billowed out from under the hood.

Olsen took baby steps to the edge of the pit. Fillmore followed. They gazed down. *Hell of a hole*, he thought. You could fit Monaco in it, and still have room for Liechtenstein. A woman, already there, stood next to him. Perhaps eighty, she wore an ID tag that read: Senior Volunteer, Ajo Pit Crew. She pointed into the pit, at a body. Olsen estimated it was about two hundred feet

141

below, on a wide ledge, part of a roadway that spiraled to the bottom, another eight hundred feet down.

Fillmore got out a pair of binoculars.

"He's moving," she said. "Still alive, and waving for help."

"Let me see," Billy Olsen replied, reaching to take the binoculars. She pulled them away.

"I'm not through with them yet."

The ambulance attendants walked up. Leo peered over the edge.

"Bummer," he said. "That guy's never going to get out of there."

Fillmore lowered the glasses, turned to Leo.

"You're supposed to rescue him."

Lucy looked back at the ambulance. The smoke was beginning to clear. The burning-brake smell had abated, somewhat. She handed the keys to Leo.

"Hey, it's your turn to drive."

142

Chapter Eighteen

Binoculars in hand, Olsen watched the rescue from up top. Leo and Lucy spent about ten minutes figuring out how the gurney straps tied down. The patient began to slide off the first time they lifted it, so they set it down and started over. They finally just tied the straps into knots, lifted the gurney and pushed it into the back of the ambulance. After another five minutes, Leo found the keys he had dropped on the ground. He slid behind the wheel. Lucy went in the back with the patient, and the ambulance began winding its way back up the pit. It did three wide slow circles – each a mile in diameter – shaking like a old school bus and belching smoke. With all the speed of a moonrise, it rose up over the ledge and chugged into the parking lot.

Billy Olsen hailed the ambulance, and Leo pulled up beside him.

"Hey, dude, we got no more room back there. Especially for you."

Between thumb and forefinger, Olsen lifted the official native-plant investigator patch for the driver's inspection.

"State native-plant investigator. We're tracking two guys who stole a rare saguaro."

"Hey, man, I'd like to help, but we got an injured man here. And if we don't get him to the hospital ... Hey, Lucy, how long do you think he's got?

Lucy spoke from the back. "He's losing some blood, Leo. Maybe we should give him some plasma."

"Ah, Lucy, I wish I'da thought of that."

"Stay cool, Leo. I got it."

Olsen heard the ripping of a package. Leo, hand on his chin, turned back to Olsen.

"Plant police? I don't see what that's got to do with ..."

An arm was thrust forward, a real cop badge in hand.

"Jane Fillmore, Maricopa County deputy sheriff. I'm investigating a murder. And the man in your ambulance might have information critical to that investigation."

"Wow," Leo said. "He's way beyond critical. Sheesh, I think he's in a coma."

The scream came from the back of the ambulance.

"Ow, stop poking me!"

"Hold still, Phil!" Lucy barked. "I'm trying to save your life!"

Billy Olsen and Jane Fillmore ran to the back and swung open the doors. A young man, strapped to the gurney, squirmed and yelled as Lucy, the much bigger person, struggled to work in an IV needle.

"Excuse us," Olsen said, with enough force to get the attention of both patient and abuser. "Two guys beat you up?"

"One guy and one really tough girl."

"Wasn't a girl," Olsen said. "He dresses like one, and – from I hear – aspires to be one, but ... Uh, they're brothers."

"I saw a family resemblance – ow!"

"Hold still!" Lucy the tech shouted. "I'm looking for a vein!"

"Why'd they attack you?" Olsen asked. "Did you say something to them? They're touchy, you know. It doesn't take much to set them off."

"Didn't say anything. We wanted to see the big pit ... and, and the museum ... we were on our way up the hill, when this big

144

truck, a big flatbed, blocked our path. The mean one came up and told us to hand over our GPS system."

"You had one?" Fillmore asked.

"Oh, sure. Tells your coordinates. Longitude, latitude, altitude. The map part doesn't work."

Fillmore looked back at the young patient, puzzled.

"You said 'we.' Was there somebody else with you?"

The fraternity kid sat up, lost in thought. The nurse tech hit home with an IV needle sliding into a bulging vessel in his right forearm. He made no sound. He stared at the newly inserted IV as blood seeped out around the point of insertion. He fainted.

"Uh oh," Lucy said to Leo. "We're losing him. Better get him to Level One trauma."

"Level One? Level One? Holy Jesus, that sounds serious! Level One!" Leo was panicked. "What a mind-blower! What do we do, man, what do we do?"

Lucy sat back on the bench and stared up at the ceiling.

"Let me think," she said.

Olsen and Fillmore backed away. Olsen wanted no part of this rolling liability factory, and, no doubt, Fillmore felt the same. At the sound of feet on gravel, he turned to see an elderly woman race-walking toward them. The woman was the same mine-pit tour guide who first spotted the frat kid in the pit. She waved a hand frantically as she reached the back of the ambulance and looked in at Lucy.

"Wait, there's somebody else," she said between deep breaths. "Near the bottom … of the pit."

"How do you know?" Lucy asked.

"He called his mother on his cellphone."

"From down there? Lucy asked.

"Must have held his phone up, you know, got a hot spot."

"Must have."

"Anyway, she called the town clerk, and the town clerk called us and asked us to check it out. I got out the binoculars again and, by golly, there he was."

Lucy climbed out of the ambulance and placed her hands on hips, giving her perhaps a more serious demeanor than she had a right to exhibit. She pursed her lips. A bead of sweat rolled down the right side of her head. With her fingertips, she took care of the sweat and a wisp of unruly hair with one swipe, then planted the hand back on her hip. She squinted at the volunteer.

"A second one, down in the pit. You sure about that, Liz?"

The volunteer, ninety-five pounds and frail, couldn't hold her ground. She took a step back.

"Well, I'm pretty sure, Lucy. I had my good binoculars."

Lucy let out a deep breath.

"Well, how'd *he* get down there?"

Liz blinked

and scratched her chin.

"I don't ..."

A voice came from the ambulance. It wasn't Leo.

"They stole my Jeep. They worked us over and threw us in the back."

Olsen turned to the open doors at the back, looked in at the college kid, speaking from behind an array of tubes and hanging bags of saline solution.

"Who?" He knew the answer but he asked anyway.

"Those brothers you talked about."

"The McFinneys."

"Yeah, they stole my jeep, busted through the fence and began driving down into the pit. Not halfway in, the girlie one says, 'Here's a good place.' And the mean one says something like,

146

'Shit, you are so smart.' Then he pushes me over the side, and they continue on down into the hole."

Fillmore crossed her arms, perhaps her answer to Lucy's hand on the hips. But she faced Liz.

"You didn't see any of this?"

"I was on my lunch break. We shut down for lunch, an hour and a half. Of course, we all looked down there, but nobody saw the other kid. You know, way at the bottom and all."

The ambulance patient cleared his throat. Olsen saw an arm push through the tubing and part it open.

"Phil needs help," he said.

Lucy the EMT looked in on her patient, then slapped his hand, forcing it back behind the curtain of tubes.

"You're in no condition to talk," she said, scolding him. "We have to get you to a Level One trauma unit, and fast. You don't have any blood pressure." Leaning in, she read a dial affixed to a metal box that looked like an instrument panel on a Cessna. "Wait, that's a heart monitor. It's worse than I thought."

"Um, uh, what about the poor young man in the pit?" the senior volunteer said.

"Leo!" Lucy shouted.

Leo stepped out of the ambulance. His head bobbing like he had a spring in his neck, he came around to the back, where everybody else had gathered.

"Whoa, I got up too fast. What a rush, man."

"Say, check out the pit and tell me if you see somebody down there, will you?"

He made for the ambulance.

"Wait. Liz, can he use your binoculars?"

"Oh, OK!"

Leo took the binoculars, crossed through the torn meshing in the chain-link fence and went up the pit's edge. Olsen would have followed, but he felt this was a job for the EMT experts. And he had already had enough of staring down into a thousand-foot hole for one day. Though the view didn't rise to the level of a phobia, it made him nervous.

Leo fiddled with the focus knob and scanned the pit. After a minute or so, he lowered the binoculars, then walked back with no particular urgency, like he was out for a stroll in the park.

Handing the glasses back to Liz, he said: "Hey, you were right. There's a dude down there. But he's OK."

"How can you tell?" Olsen asked.

"He's crawling out now."

"I got an idea," Lucy said. "We'll get this first guy to the hospital, and then swing back for number two. He should be out by the time we get back from Tucson. We'll toss him in the back, and rush *him* to the hospital."

"What level trauma unit?" Leo asked.

"Won't know till he gets here, Leo."

"Oh, yeah."

"Come on. Phil could go any minute. We'd better head out."

"Right you are, dude."

Lucy climbed into the back with the patient. Leo patted his pockets down for the keys.

"Bummer," he muttered. Then he snapped his fingers.

"Oh, yeah," he said to himself. "Still in the ignition."

He got in and took off down the hill toward town, as he craned his head out the window and made siren noises. Another siren – a real one – drew Olsen's attention to an SUV coming from the other direction, flying down the hill from the mining museum. It was a cop-tricked Ford Explorer. Emergency lights flashed from top to bumper. The siren was set to jetliner decibels. The SUV, bearing the seal of the Pima County Sheriff's Office, skidded to a stop next to Billy Olsen's official Department of Agriculture motor pool pickup. When the deputy switched off the siren, a veil of pain was lifted from Olsen's eardrums.

The radio was still going, set to full blast. It was the only way to hear it over the siren. The man on the radio shouted: "This is all-Christian radio on your FM dial! It's the most Jesus you'll get on any station. Why, if you don't hear us praise Jesus a hundred times an hour, then you just aren't listening!"

"Amen!" the deputy said. He switched off the radio and got out. The deputy looked to be about thirty. His light brown hair was combed neatly back and his moustache was trimmed to perfection. His khaki uniform had a crispness to it that suggested his laundry was in the hands of a loving Christian wife.

"Can you believe it? I pick up that signal all the way from El Paso."

"It's a miracle," Olsen said.

"Has to be. Has to be," the deputy replied, before eyeing the pit. "Uh, I just heard from dispatch about a young man who called from the bottom of that hole. How is he?"

"He's crawling out now," Fillmore said. Cop-to-cop, she introduced herself. "Jane Fillmore, Maricopa County deputy sheriff."

As if noticing her for the first time, he drew in a breath and his stomach. It was already flatter than any stomach Olsen could have made.

"Deputy Woolsy, Mark Woolsy, Pima County sheriff's office." Olsen could tell what the man was thinking. He was thinking: When you see a creation like Jane Fillmore, it proves there's a

God. On the other hand, Olsen hardly regarded his own body as the work of an all-loving creator.

Olsen made his own introduction. "Billy Olsen. Native plant investigation, Arizona Department of Agriculture."

The Pima County deputy regarded him with the usual indifference. After all, Billy Olsen wasn't a real cop, was he?

"We're looking for the guys who did this. The McFinneys. They beat up the frat kids and stole their jeep," Olsen said.

"Somebody found the jeep, up by the historical museum," Woolsy said.

"Museum?" Fillmore asked.

"Yeah, it's up over the hill. Used to be a Catholic mission, built for Indians who worked in the mine."

Olsen and Fillmore drove up the hill. They met two older men seated on the porch. One was holding an ice pack atop his head. Olsen got out.

"I don't need an ambulance. I'm good."

"What happened?"

"The two guys pulled up. One driving a jeep, the other a big flatbed truck. The left the jeep, took the truck. Headed down a backroad."

"One was big and hairy? Wore a skirt? And the other was kind of mean."

"Yeah, real mean. He tried to make me siphon gas from jeep for the truck. It was kind-a-like smashed in the front. I gave him my best fuck-you look and said no. Big mistake. The mean one clocked me a good one. He asked Ernie, the other museum volunteer, if he was available. And of course he said yes."

Ernie nodded. "I siphoned off six gallons."

"See a big cactus in the back?"

"Part of it, what wasn't under a tarp."

"Part of it?"

"Yeah, it was all gnarly, fanned out. Kind of ugly, if you know what I mean."

"Not really," Olsen said. "Anything else?"

"Hmm, well, I heard some muffled sounds. Saw something squirming in the back of the cab, behind the seats. But I thought it best not to point it out."

"How long ago did they leave?" Olsen asked.

"Maybe a half hour," Ernie said.

"Well, now, they've got a GPS device and a truck that can handle the desert, if it doesn't' fall apart first." Olsen said. "We gotta catch up to them, because it won't take them long to find Upchurch."

The first volunteer looked up.

"Better hide, Ernie. I think I hear the ambulance."

Chapter Nineteen

Olsen swung the truck west off Highway 85, onto a gravel road that took them past a mountain range of mining wastes. A jagged peak rose on their left. The map pegged it as Black Mountain.

The sun had begun its long slow slide toward the western horizon. The shadows were long. And the day got hotter. That's just the way things worked in the desert.

Wind rushing through the open windows felt like the breath of a fevered dog. The windows didn't have to be open. The air-conditioning worked. Cold air could be had at the push of a button. But Jane Fillmore thought it more important to save gas. They were headed toward Cabeza Prieta National Wildlife Refuge, which offered no refuge at all for visitors who ran out of water. Many people who figured to be just passing through never made out it. Conquistadors looking for gold, settlers looking for California, illegal immigrants looking for the jobs nobody else wanted.

Fillmore said she didn't want to end up another bone-dry body on the desert floor. She wanted to make sure they didn't run out of gas before they ran out of water. Olsen objected at first, saying they'd be better off with air conditioning. They'd lose less water to sweat. And they could hear the radio better, although he dropped that argument when all he could get was the Totally Jesus station out of El Paso.

Olsen passed a sleeve across his forehead, mopping up what the wind missed.

Not that he couldn't handle Sonoran Desert summers. He grew up in and around Phoenix. And he still remembered the summers at his grandma's house, listening to her stories on the front porch. It had offered shade, but the thermometer still read a hundred-ten – and often higher. He didn't complain about the heat, not back then. Summers came and summers went, and Olsen weathered them the way most Pimas did. He simply sweated them out. He never saw snow until he was nine. His uncle took him to the White Mountains, on the Apache reservation. They visited the ski resort, packed with snow and Anglos. His mother wanted his uncle to take him skiing, though he really didn't want to go. He had heard of white men hitting trees and dying. But his uncle, who would one day hit a tree and die – only in a car – pushed him into the ski lift. Olsen's mother had given Uncle Ivan a hundred dollars to get little Billy Olsen in skis. She had a notion that Billy's Norwegian half would come alive on the slopes. After all, his father had been a top amateur skier in a country of skiers. So Billy went skiing. He missed the tree, but fell and sprained his ankle. He cried halfway home and never skied again. The following summer Billy Olsen took up Little League baseball.

Olsen stole a glimpse at Fillmore. She was reading a police manual of some sort. The rushing air whipped the few strands of hair that had escaped the binding for a ponytail. She didn't look too uncomfortable in the heat. Still, Olsen made the case for air conditioning, again.

"Hey, I got plenty of water. In the back, with the other stuff. Five five-gallon jugs."

"Hmm."

"We don't have to worry about water."

Three shots. Crack, crack, crack from behind. Olsen fixated on the rearview mirror. The top of a water jug flew off. The one next to it jumped and was drained dry in seconds. The third jug blew apart like a water bomb. Crack. Crack. Crack. More shots. Bullets hit the bed of the truck. Olsen hit the gas pedal. The truck lurched forward as he scanned the mirror for the shooter. He spotted a head popping up from a behind a mound of rocks. Maybe a few hundred feet back. Olsen stopped the truck. He grabbed the binoculars from the dash and swiveled to face the rear window. He focused in on the rocks. He spotted the shooter. He could make out the shoulder straps on what looked to be a halter top. And the lips, purple with the latest in lipstick hues. And even the eyeliner encircling the eye looking down the barrel. The eye stared back at him.

"Duck!" Olsen screamed.

He ducked. Fillmore ducked. The back window shattered.

Olsen raised his head and the binoculars. He spotted Edweena McFinney, still staring down a rifle barrel. Olsen ducked again as Fillmore flipped the door handle and jumped to the ground. With one clean move, she had her service pistol out of her holster and was ejecting shells as fast as she could pull the trigger. Olsen followed the bullets' assumed path. Bits of granite flew off around Edweena McFinney's outstretched head. McFinney retreated behind a bigger rock.

My turn, Olsen thought. Pawing underneath the seat, he grabbed his environmentally friendly .38. It didn't litter the ground with spent shells. He rolled out of the truck, the open door at his back. He ran around the door, to use it as a screen. Fillmore nodded at him from other the side of the cab.

He scanned the mountain. Edweena McFinney appeared to be on her own. Olsen thought: *Where the hell is the other one.* He turned. Right in front of them, it happened. And armed. Olsen hit the dirt. A shotgun blast peppered the door and shattered the window. A pellet found his left shoulder. *Missed me, mostly* Olsen thought. Reflexively, he slapped his right hand over the newest hole in his body. Not so bad. He could handle another three or four of those before passing out.

"Cactus cop, leave us alone! Or I'll put you on the shotgun diet and blow your fat ass off!"

It was Hector.

Olsen did his best to shrug off the fat jokes. Or comments about his weight. They began filtering in after his baseball career ended. That's when he stopped taking care of his body. He stopped physical training. He ate what he liked. Greasy, carb-laden, fatty foods. Tepary Bean Girl would not approve. Still, he wouldn't let Hector McFinney off lightly for his insult. *If I catch you, you're in big trouble*, Olsen thought. *I'm going to tell the probation officer what you said when he writes his sentencing report. Could mean an extra month, on top of life without parole.*

Hector was hectoring him from atop the stolen flatbed, some fifty feet away. He had pulled the truck out of hiding. Easy enough while Edweena provided the distraction.

Olsen faced the back of the flatbed. The tarp had partially blown free of the cristate. The crown rested atop the carpet-shrouded wooden cradle.

Olsen knew of the crested from photos. But this, up close and personal, was different. He could see why Upsters regarded it as some sort of needle-bearing spirit. The crown rose from the saguaro's fluted trunk and spread out into a thick broad fan of intricate folds. A span of some five feet. Something special.

Then there was the hole in the center of the crown. Carved out by a woodpecker. Harboring a boot. Maybe a treasure.

Hector snorted with laughter.

"Why don't you shoot me, needle cop? 'Fraid you might hurt the poor little cactus, huh?"

Hector McFinney raised the shotgun. He happened to be right. Olsen hesitated to put any more holes in one of nature's finest works. Not if he couldn't get a clear shot at Hector McFinney. Fillmore had no such qualms. She spun around, her shoes pressing on gravel, raised her pistol – standard-issue Glock – and fired off three rounds easy as pie. Two of them hit the top of the cab, over Ranker and just left of the crown. The third removed McFinney's baseball cap.

"Damn!" he shouted and jumped to the ground. He climbed into the cab as a bundle bound in rope tried to escape through the passenger window. Grabbing a cord, McFinney tried to yank the bundle back inside. The bundle fought back, squirming and grunting, until McFinney calmed it down with a gun butt.

"Must be Ranker," Fillmore said.

"Yeah, that bundle's got a temper," Olsen replied.

"He won't go far. I'll put out a tire." Fillmore ran forward about ten steps, positioned herself cop-style with a straight-armed two-handed grip on the Glock. Her form was good. Her timing wasn't. Hector McFinney punched the pedal before she pulled the trigger. The tires spun in place as the truck, for a moment, appeared to be going nowhere. Grit, pebbles and dust flew out as the tread fought for traction. The truck bolted forward. A rear tire spit out a golf-ball-sized rock. Same principle as a pitching machine. Olsen followed the rock to Fillmore's forehead. Down she went. Olsen ran to her. With some difficulty, he kneeled beside her. She was bleeding, but awake.

"I'm OK," she said.

Hector turned the truck around and came at them. Olsen aimed at the cab, in the area of McFinney's head. The revolver clicked. *Damn, no bullets. Right, still in the glove box.*

OK, now what? There was the option favored by every B-Western desperado who ran out of bullets. Throw the gun. But Olsen saw something better. The stone that took down Fillmore had settled at his feet. He picked up it, stood and threw. It was less like a pitch than a play at the plate, a quick release in a desperate attempt to stop a run – or, in this case, save a couple of lives. It was a wild throw to the backstop. The rock missed the truck by ten feet. Olsen felt a pain run up his arm, from just below the elbow to his left shoulder, up to the spot where he had been wounded.

That'll do, Olsen thought. He slumped to his knees. Through all the pain, he knew one thing. They were dead now.

Hector McFinney chose not to run them over. The flatbed skidded to a stop beside the pair. Olsen, on his knees, waited for the shotgun blast that would remove the top of his head. It didn't come. Instead, McFinney, his arm resting on the window frame, said: "My brother and I, we're just finishing the deal, that's all. The deal Randall had."

Edweena came out of hiding.

"That's right. We're completing a transaction," she said. Folding up her skirt, she opened the passenger door and hopped in.

"That cactus is protected," Olsen said. "You don't have a tag."

"Screw your tag. Leave us alone, or next time I won't be so kind," Hector said.

Then, as if for the first time, he noticed Fillmore. That is, he noticed – even as she lay half-conscious with a gash in her head – that she was worth a second look.

"Man, I should dump the load I got now, and take you. You are somethin.'"

Jane Fillmore, covered in dust – dust that had begun to stick to her wound – rolled her eyes toward the truck. With some effort, she unpinned the badge on her shirt and showed it to McFinney.

"You're under arrest for the murder of Randall Patrick Durstan," she said.

"Didn't do it, lady. I hated the fucker, but Aunt Babs, you know, she'd a really gotten on our case if we' a-killed him."

"How'd you get the cactus?"

"Well, we just got back from our morning beer. Aunt Babs weren't there. Probably visiting our saintly mother, then checking out pork chop sales in half the stores from here to Arizona City. Let's see. Oh yeah, Randy was there, without no head. We didn't bother looking for it. Not our business. But there was that big cactus. So we just decided to take our share. And Randy's, too, while we were at it."

Hector smiled at Fillmore. He had most of his teeth.

"Hey, we'd take you with us so we can talk about this some more, and why am I so hot for you, exceptin' we ain't got room. And we need to hang on to the Ranker chick until we get where we're goin.' I got to make sure she gave us a good number to find that cactus-lovin' guru. See, we got two long finder numbers that we had to beat out of her and some loser. And we don't trust her. She might be lying. So we're keeping her to make sure she ain't shittin' us. And now, now we got this box that tells us how to find that Upchurch guru with those very same numbers. It's complicated, but Ranker is going to help us, on penalty of lots of pain. And when we find Mr. Guru Master, we got a cactus to sell him. One he wants so bad he can taste it. He'll pay big money for this one, and, goddamn, if he ain't loaded – head of a worldwide

158

church and all. This guy gets checks by the freight-load from poor suckers looking for miracles. Anyway, after he buys that cactus back there, my brother will have a real wardrobe. No more bad-fitting crap from K-Mart."

Olsen nodded. He understood, somewhat.

"And then a sex-change operation?" Olsen asked.

"For your information, it's called gender reassortment. And Frankly, that ain't Edweena. She's comfortable in her balls, but she likes to dress well. She's a damn good dresser, too. But I feel so sad for her. She's hurt every time she picks up a fashion magazine and sees what real fashion is."

"And what is that?"

"All that shit we can't afford."

Hector McFinney, scratched his dirty two-day growth of beard. He stepped out of the truck, gripped the barrel of the shotgun and swung the stock into the back of Olsen's head.

Oh, the pain would return. But for now, it was lights out.

Chapter Twenty

Olsen came to at the siren call of the ambulance. Or rather the imitation of the siren call as performed by Leo the EMT. Olsen lay next to Fillmore. Her foot, resting on Olsen's stomach, twitched. Then it jerked up and plopped down, knocking a bit of wind out of him. As the ambulance slid to a stop on the hard-packed dirt, Fillmore groaned. She lifted her head as Olsen placed her foot on the ground and slowly rose to his feet. Two things came to his attention. One, they had been out cold on a hot desert floor for an hour or so. Two, his head felt like a train wreck. Following his lead, Fillmore stood, holding the back of her own head. Hector McFinney had rung her noodle as well.

Leo and Lucy emerged from the ambulance.

"Get the stretcher, Leo," Lucy said as she hitched up her rayon EMT-style pants. "These two look close to critical."

"Wow, on their feet, *and* in critical condition, man. They need some bodacious help."

Billy Olsen looked at Fillmore and saw in her green eyes the same fear she must have seen in his. Fear that they'd end up in that medical chamber of horrors. And the realization they couldn't shoot their way out of this one. The McFinneys had taken their guns.

"How'd you find us?" Fillmore asked.

"Some guy named Horace called 911," Lucy said. "Or was it Hector? Anyhow, let's get you sorted out."

Olsen and Fillmore took a step toward the truck. They kept their eyes on the EMTs.

Leo opened the back doors to the ambulance, in search of a stretcher.

"How many we need?"

"Better make it two," Lucy replied. "We got a big one here."

"OK ... oh, crap."

"What?"

"You know that college kid we had to wait for, you know, while he crawled out of the mine pit."

"What about him?"

"He got away."

"He got away!" Lucy shook her head, the frizzled ends standing out against the dim light on the western horizon. "I thought I told you to lock the doors when we stopped off at Dairy Queen."

"I had the munchies. I could just taste that coconut-crunch sundae. Man, that stuff's heavy."

Lucy went up to Leo. He was a skinny, aging hippy. She was thirty years younger and built like a Zamboni. The difference in girth appeared to play a big part in determining who was boss. Lucy punched Leo on the shoulder. Not so hard he'd fall down or even feel threatened. But more than a playful tap.

"Come on, Leo. We're professionals. That's the third time this week. You know he needed emergency treatment, as soon as we could get him to get a hospital " Lucy palmed the back of her neck. She was thinking. "OK, let's rescue these two first and then we'll cruise for frat boy number two. He couldn't have gotten too far."

Leo shook his head in a big side-to-side swoop, with a big grin to match.

"You just blow me away. You have an answer for everything." There was no irony here. Just straight out praise for perceived genius.

"Well, we live in a golden era, Leo, where initiative is rewarded."

"And why's that?"

"Deregulation."

Lucy spit on her right hand and patted an unruly curl back into place. She glanced at Leo. "Come on, let's rescue these guys. They need treatment, and we get six hundred big ones for every delivery."

Leo pulled out a stretcher. As he stepped aside, Olsen could see a body laid out flat on a bed, surrounded by tubes and bags. Hadn't that kid escaped? Unless ... they hadn't bothered to drop off the first college student, the one they had actually bothered to rescue from inside the mine pit. Jesus, Olsen thought, they doubled back to the mine pit and waited for number two, who – having crawled all the way out – still had the strength to escape. Number one wasn't so lucky. Right now, he looked like a botched experiment.

"All righty" Lucy said, with a cheery smile. "Let's go with the big guy. It'll be easier to fit him in first."

Olsen took another step back.

"I'm fine," he said. "Really, I feel great." And, in a way, that was true. His dread of the ambulance had overshadowed any awareness of injury.

"Man, come on, dude. You'll thank us in the morning," Leo said. They stepped closer, but his words didn't close the sale. Fillmore excitedly grabbed Olsen's left arm, pressing the bicep where he once had muscle. She squeezed him till it hurt. Olsen took that as a good sign. She, too, feared for her life.

"Ready?" Olsen said, looking down at her.

"Ready."

"Now!" They turned and ran for the truck, both reaching the same door and grabbing for the same handle.

"My turn to drive!" Fillmore yelled.

"Not now!" Olsen replied, trying to squeeze his hand in. She slapped it away. Then she edged inside of him, opened the door and slipped behind the wheel, yanking the door closed. Through the open window, she shouted.

"Go around to ... but watch out!"

A hand reached around his torso, a thick strong hand.

"Gotcha!" Lucy screamed in his ear. "Get the tie-downs ready, Leo!"

Lucy shuffled backward, prying Olsen's grip from the door handle. She had the strength of ten EMTs. But his foot got tangled with hers as he lost his grip. They stumbled backward and Olsen sandwiched Lucy between himself and the ground. She said: "Ooof!" With a grunt, Olsen got to one knee and, took two deep breaths, then hoisted himself upright. Dashing around the back of the truck, he jumped in the passenger's seat.

He slipped on his seatbelt, turned to Jane Fillmore.

"OK, Deputy Fillmore, let's go. With you, I'm just taking a big chance. With them, I'm a goner!"

She frowned. Held out her right hand.

"Key?"

Billy Olsen patted his pockets and came up empty. The McFinneys had shaken him down, all the way to his last penny.

Lucy was at Fillmore's open window. She said: "You're in no condition to drive, honey."

Fillmore locked the door. Lucy reached in through a shattered window with a bleeding arm and, like a zombie feeling around for her next victim, grabbed Fillmore by the elbow. Fillmore struggled but Lucy held on and tightened her grip.

"Come on, we can help you."

"We're, like, the best in town, man," Leo said as he reached through the window and fished for the other arm. He pulled it from the steering wheel. He helped draw Fillmore toward Lucy, who could now wrap a forearm around her neck.

Olsen ran his hand beneath the dash. Somewhere down there was a spare key on a magnet. *Got it.* He popped the key loose, just as the EMTs had managed to work Fillmore's head out the window. She screamed. Leo and Lucy were unfazed. They kept pulling.

Olsen slipped the key in the ignition. But he didn't dare drive off.

"OK! OK!" he shouted. "I'll go first. That's want you wanted."

Lucy let go Fillmore's of head as Leo released her arm. She fell back into the seat, looking paler than usual. The EMTs picked up the stretcher. Lucy shook her head.

"Finally, a patient who understands how the medical system works," she said. "First we load them up, then we get their insurance information."

Maybe it was one move. Maybe two. Certainly, no more than three. Olsen jammed the key into the ignition, turned over the motor, wrapped his arm around Fillmore and grabbed the wheel. He slipped the shifter into drive and punched the gas. The truck fishtailed, then sped off. Olsen glanced in the rearview mirror. The ambulance and its crew were in the dust. Fillmore's head rested against him. She seemed content. Olsen smiled. He was content, even as he sped down a dirt road at sixty-five, one hand on the wheel.

Contentment was short-lived. Fillmore opened her eyes, took a quick look at Olsen and pushed him aside. She grabbed the wheel. The truck fishtailed again. She pulled out of it with ease.

"What the hell are you doing?'"

"Uh, saving us."

"Like hell."

Olsen shrugged.

Fillmore floored it. They rocketed down the unimproved road and into the wildlife refuge. The desert passed by in a blur.

Olsen gripped the door handle with his right hand. He unfolded a map with his left. The map was the work of the U.S. Geological Survey, the best available. Olsen had marked on it, using the coordinates scribbled in Durstan's book. That would get them to Upchurch's retreat. That and Olsen's passing familiarity with the Cabeza Prieta Wildlife Refuge, having tracked down a cactus thief or two here.

On the other hand, he thought, a little technology wouldn't hurt.

"Maybe if had we your GPS device …"

"In my backpack," Fillmore said. "Standard sheriff's office issue, but it's accurate. It'll put us within twenty feet of Upchurch."

"Where's your backpack."

"Behind the seat."

Olsen checked. He pulled out the backpack. It had a bullet hole in it. He fished out the GPS device. It had a bullet hole in it. He handed it over to Fillmore.

She turned it over. It had an exit wound. Half the electronics had been blown out.

"What are the odds of that?" she said.

She tossed it behind the seat, as something caught her attention. Something in the mirror. She shuddered. Olsen adjusted the mirror. He saw emergency lights, spinning like quasars as the ambulance gained on them.

Chapter Twenty-One

Somewhere in the Valley of the Ajo, Fillmore lost the ambulance. She drove like vampires were after them, letting up only after they were well into the heart of Cabeza Prieta National Wildlife Refuge. As the sun slipped below the horizon, Fillmore flipped on the headlights. The beams caught saguaros with arms raised in the act of surrender. And organ pipe cacti looking like their namesake, clusters of green fluted pipes ready to belt out a Bach fugue in D minor.

Fillmore slowed as the road narrowed and grew more rutted. Olsen relaxed his grip on the door rest. He preferred ruts over speed. A hot and dry June air greeted him through the shattered window. The Arizona monsoon season was a month away. That would be different. Humid and stormy. But still hot.

"You have the time?" Fillmore asked.

Olsen pressed a button to light up his watch.

"Eight, almost eight-thirty."

She nodded.

"I'm not sure I can find my way around this place in the dark," Olsen said. "There's a half-moon. Not much to go on." He pictured himself stumbling around the desert, blind to landmarks and rattlesnakes. And his shoulder wasn't doing him any favors. It still ached from the buckshot pellet. He'd like to give that a night's rest.

"Maybe we ought to make camp until first light."

"Sounds like something out of a Western."

"Could be."

Fillmore glanced at Olsen.

"And whose side were you on? The Indians or the Norwegians?"

Chapter Twenty-Two

The saguaros were spread out over the hillside, some still ready to receive the gift of life from the lesser long-nosed bat. Maybe to the bat it was just a meal, a tongue full of nectar lapped up from the saguaro blossom. But to the saguaros, it was sex, kinky sex involving bats, as they flew from flower to flower and impregnated them with fresh pollen.

The flowers – big and gaudy – made sure they were easy to find, even by blind bats. As Billy Olsen rested against a boulder, he could make out perhaps a half dozen saguaro blooms by the spare light of the half moon. And where there were flowers, he figured there must have been a few bats still flying up from Mexico to fondle them. There was one now. Olsen rummaged about the sleeping bag he was sitting on and found his binoculars. He saw the form of the bat plunging headlong into a banquet of pollen and nectar.

Lowering the binoculars, Olsen looked across the small clearing of their camp, gazing at the form of Jane Fillmore. Even poorly lit, she looked good. She sat cross-legged on the extra sleeping bag he had packed. She munched on some dried fruit and nuts he had also packed. Catching cactus thieves often meant nights of surveillance on the desert. Olsen came prepared.

Fillmore looked up, noticed Olsen watching her. He looked away, trying not to let on.

"Do you think the McFinneys did it?" she asked.

The question gave Olsen permission to look again.

"Did what?"

"Killed Durstan."

"You have some doubt?" Olsen asked.

"Well, they struck me as mean ..."

"They're certainly mean."

"Especially, the ... uh ... normal one," Jane Fillmore said. "OK, not normal, but the one who doesn't wear dresses. He was a real ..."

"Bastard."

"Yes, a real bastard. But they didn't strike me as ... well, literally they struck me ... but figuratively, they didn't strike me as someone who would bother to take a man's head off. Do you see ..."

"Yes, I think so," Olsen said. "The McFinneys are cruel but lazy. They'd love to shoot someone. Beat them to a pulp with fists and bats, but removing ..."

"Too much work," Fillmore answered.

"Maybe," Olsen said. He turned the matter over in his mind several times, like looking at different sides of a cube. "But maybe it was more than a robbery, stealing cactus from a cactus thief. Maybe there some revenge to it, getting back at Durstan for cheating on their aunt."

"Durstan had other people who didn't like him. You said he was a smooth operator."

"Too smooth for his own good."

Fillmore leaned back on her own rock, sipped water from a bottle. She replied: "Durstan talked Roz Ranker into becoming an Upster."

"But she was ready for it," Olsen said. "He told her about his new-found religion, but she seemed to take to it all on her own. You know, some people look for new answers, whether it's through cactus or crystals, to forget about the past. Finding God in a big green plant – or anywhere else, for that matter – can wipe out all the bad memories. I think you can make a case that she became an Upster, not because she wanted to join him in communing with saguaro spirits, but because she wanted to forget him."

"And forget about what *she* did, testifying against him, to save her own skin."

"He helped to erase that guilt when he got out of prison. He converted her, then rejected her, for his wife," Olsen said. "And the pork chops."

"OK, there's a motive. But what about the wife?"

"Durstan's wife?"

"Babs never accepted his New Age religion, did she?"

"But she didn't hate it." Olsen said. "She just took no interest in it. All she wanted to do was make sure Randall had a clean pair of socks and a plate full of pork chops. This all came out in the trial. And she played no part, zip, in his cactus-hauling business. It just didn't interest her, with one exception."

"What was that?" Fillmore asked.

"She wanted Durstan to hire her nephews, her older sister's reprobate kids," he said. "Nobody else would hire them."

And so it was back to the McFinneys. And, here, the conversation stalled. Hefting himself up, Olsen stepped over to the truck-bed and fished a beer out of the cooler. It would help wash down the beef jerky and chips. Slowly, he lowered himself to the ground, still feeling like he'd been hit by a truck – which he had. He popped open a can of beer and he drank a good half of it in one go. With a woman in camp, he'd keep to a one-beer limit. Not that it mattered. When he was in the field, one was his limit anyway. At least he had some self-control.

He looked away, toward the sky. The half-moon slipped nearer the horizon and the desert slipped nearer to complete darkness. Striking a match, Olsen fired up the Coleman lantern. He set it between the two of them. In the glare, Fillmore's face beamed with the intensity of a firefly – at least in the way that Olsen remembered fireflies. He hadn't seen one since he left North Platte with a shattered arm. Nebraska had fireflies. Not so Arizona.

Fillmore gazed back at Olsen, though clearly not with the same longing he had felt and tried his best to suppress.

"So you know a lot of Pima mythology stories – Coyote and the like."

"No, not really. My grandmother told me a few. One or two of them stuck, like the story of Tepary Bean Girl."

"You told me, already. Well, started to …"

"Well, my grandmother made her up, to teach me about the foods of our culture."

"Your grandmother taught you all about your culture, didn't she?"

"She tried, but I was very young when she had me all to herself. And sometimes in summer, after I turned five. But even then I didn't pay much attention. I wanted to play sports, well, actually just baseball. I was big, but athletic. OK, I had a little baby fat, but nothing like …" He didn't want to dwell on that, so he moved on: "My grandmother knew all the creation stories."

"Like Tepary Bean Girl," Fillmore said.

172

"Well, that's not part of Pima lore. I only ever heard it from Grandma Rosa. But I like the story."

"What's the story?"

"Tepary Bean Girl was like the Johnny Appleseed of the desert. She went all around placing tepary beans in the hollowed-out boots of saguaros. One bean per boot."

"That's a lot of saguaros."

"Well, she did not have time for all of them. And then there was Crow. He would come out every full moon to look for the beans she had hidden. He'd eat whatever he found."

"Uh huh," Fillmore said with a nod.

"So Tepary Bean Girl had to choose wisely, selecting saguaros guarded by Coyote."

"Coyote?"

"Well, he'd direct Crow to the wrong saguaro. You know, Coyote the Trickster."

"OK, but why? Why did Tepary Bean Girl run around plopping beans in a cactus? Are they magic beans?"

"In a way. Tepary beans are a native Pima food. They are rich in protein and complex carbs, the good kind, and low in fat. But they have fallen out of favor with the Pima. When the Pima lost their culture, they lost the tepary bean."

"The whites slaughtered the Pima and took their culture?"

"No, no, not all. The Pimas and the Anglos have always been at peace. But still the whites set up two reservations for the Pima and their adopted cousins, the Maricopa tribe. And the white farmers diverted the water that once flowed from the Gila and Salt rivers into Pima soil. Tepary beans, squash and corn were replaced by handouts of starchy, high-fat foods. We now have much of our water back, thanks to settlements in long-running legal battles. But maybe it's too late. Big Macs

173

are now a staple of the Pima diet. Look around. Obesity is everywhere. Diabetes is more common than baldness."

"I've not seen any bald Pimas."

"Well," Olsen said, "there you go."

"So what's all that have to do with Tepary Bean Girl."

"She foresaw the time that the Pimas would forsake their culture, and their foods. But she told the saguaros to hold onto the beans, and keep them safe, until they are rediscovered by her people."

"So saguaros are full of beans."

"So my Grandmother says."

Olsen took another sip of his beer. Fillmore adjusted herself, turning half away from the light. Half a firefly.

"Anyway, the culture's on life support, but not dead. Some members, like Anna Stewart, have unearthed a lot about our people in the old days, before Columbus and, well, the Norwegians. Anna's a professor at Arizona State University. One of the smartest people I know."

"Anna Stewart, is she Pima?"

"She prefers to call herself Akimel O'odham – that's Pima for people of the river. The word Pima itself came about through something of a misunderstanding. The Spanish explorers, when they first met our people, asked – in Spanish – what we called ourselves. 'Pima,' we said. Roughly translated, it means, 'don't understand.' "

Jane Fillmore chuckled, then caught herself. The lit half of a her face grew red, briefly.

"I'm sorry. I didn't mean to …"

"That's OK," Olsen said with a shrug. "It's just something we got stuck with. Anyway, Akimel O'odham is the tribe's official name now, and one that many, like Anna Stewart, prefer."

"She must be smart, Anna Stewart."

"Smart and … pretty."

"You and her? Are you...?"

I wish, Olsen thought. He said: "No, she runs in a different circle. I'm a cop with an arm patch. She's a professor who writes law-journal articles on tribal sovereignty. And she's been seeing a federal district court judge, Navajo. First Indian on the federal bench. Besides, she's leaving for South America on a Fulbright Scholarship, to study indigenous political structures, or something like that."

Fillmore smiled, as she took off her official deputy-sheriff ball-cap and shook out her hair. Olsen smiled weakly, and – he figured – stupidly. The hair fell to frame her face and make her look even prettier than she did in her official capacity.

He reciprocated the question.

"You and the medical examiner?" he asked.

"Just friends, so far," Jane Fillmore said. "We play a lot of tennis together. He's a good athlete. And keeps himself in shape. That's important to me. Somebody who thinks enough of himself to stay fit."

Billy Olsen began fiddling with the binoculars, still in his right hand. He held them up, not quite at arm's length and appeared to take an interest in the focus wheel, rolling it around in his fingertips. Of course, he had something else on his mind altogether. Now he knew. Jane Fillmore liked men who were fit and trim. Anna Stewart liked men who could engage her intellectually. He calculated the odds of becoming romantically involved with either one of them: about the same as a doughnut becoming pope. Still, here he was, in the field with a fellow officer. There was the advantage to be gained by having a captive audience. He could show Fillmore that – despite appearances – he still had the athleticism of his playing days. Maybe she thinks, just by looking at him, he's somebody who has let himself go. Now, as the evening lingered, he had plenty time to come through with a second impression.

"Sure, it's important to be fit," Olsen said. "When I played ball in high school and professionally, I was in great shape myself. I was even cast for a TV commercial, you know, for a local Ford dealer in Lincoln. Then that hothead smashed my arm. Never quite recovered."

"I bet you were, something."

"Well, yeah .... and I still have some of that old agility. I haven't lost it all. I'm in a lot better shape than I look. Watch ... "

Getting to his feet, Olsen picked up a golf-ball sized rock near his sleeping bag and gave it a soft toss her way. "Throw this right at my feet, hard as you can. You have to get up to do it."

"I don't see the point."

"I was the best fielding pitcher in the Central Prairie League. Balls drilled right back to the mound, at my feet. I never missed one. Lightning quick reflexes. Throw it at my feet."

Jane Fillmore fired the rock. Olsen noticed something about her delivery. She didn't throw like a girl. She had a damn good arm and launched the rock with a force of slingshot. Olsen bent down and noticed something about himself. He couldn't reach his feet anymore. This shouldn't have been news, but – as he couldn't even see his feet – he hadn't given it much thought lately. And even if he could reach them, it wouldn't have mattered. His reflexes had lost a step or two. He couldn't beat a sloth in a game of ping pong.

The stone skipped up and hit him the stomach, then fell quietly to the ground. Olsen thought: *No harm there*. He had plenty of padding, and he didn't feel much of anything. But *damn, his back*. It had locked in place, freezing him into a forty-five degree stoop. Sure, he could force himself to stand up straight, but he'd pay a big price: unbelievable pain.

He'd save that for tomorrow.

Olsen titled his head, looking up at Fillmore. By her expression, he could tell. She felt his pain, if not his humiliation. "I'm sorry," she said. "I threw it too hard, didn't I? I had a good arm in high school, but I couldn't hit."

"Should've been a pitcher," Olsen said as he turned like a statue granted the gift of mobility, from the waist down. "Guess I'll call it a night. Could you get the lamp before you go to sleep?"

Without bothering to crawl inside the bag – that would have been a killer – or even take off his hiking boots, Olsen lay atop the bag on his side and wondered if he would be able to stand up in the morning. Or sit. Or play bagpipes in a parade. It was hard to imagine. Movement was agony. So he just lay very still, stiff as a frozen French fry, as he drifted off to sleep, drifting until he felt the ground beneath him move. It felt like a snake. And rattled like one, too.

Chapter Twenty-Three

The McFinneys caught some shuteye in the cab. They took turns. One of them had to stay up to keep an eye on Roz Ranker.

Then they hit the road early, predawn. They didn't have a clue where they were or where they were going. Edweena was at the wheel, having given Hector the job of trying to figure out the numbers on the GPS device. His leg hurt, sure. But thinking hard made him nearly forget all about it. He scratched his head. He saw long strings of numbers that had something to do with their place in the universe.

"I know right where we are, exactly where we are, unless this damn thing's not working. And if it ain't, I'm gonna beat the hell out of the jerk I stole it from."

"You already did," offered Edweena.

"Hell, you're right! You are so right. Jeesh, I can't believe I'm the brother of a god-damned genius."

Hector went back to the device, about the size of a fat wallet. Then he looked out the window, as saguaros, cholla cactus and mesquite passed into and out of the high beams. Setting the device on his lap, Hector McFinney removed his sweat-stained ball cap and scratched a head of hair washed with bars of Dial soap.

"Where are the goddamn signs."

"Signs?" asked Edweena McFinney, her mini-skirt rising high up a hairy thigh.

"Yeah, the road signs with the numbers on it. So you can tell if you're at the right number."

Hector looked down at the GPS, furrowed his brows.

"Turn right, here."

Edweena swung the big flatbed to the right, running the truck off a one-foot ledge and down a ravine. Hitting large rocks and running over creosote and other assorted bushes, the truck and bounced like a carnival ride all the way to the bottom, where it finally stopped.

"Jesus H, that was some ride," Hector McFinney said.

He opened the door and stepped into the sandy wash. He held up the GPS monitor.

"Well, hell, now we're getting somewhere. Look, Edweena, the numbers finally changed."

Edweena got out, straightened out her skirt and grabbed the flashlight they had stolen off the frat boys. She walked around the truck and looked at the device.

"Finally, after all that driving around, you got it to work," Edweena said. "That's why I put you in charge of that thing."

"Hell, I'll show Ranker," Hector said. "Yeah, I'll show her just how much I don't need her to tell me how to work this damn thing."

Hector took the flashlight and went back to the cab. He reached behind the seat and pulled Ranker out by the binding. He pushed her against the truck and untied her – somewhat roughly, lest she got the idea he was, at heart, a nice guy. She still had the gag in her mouth – the sock he had worn for a week without washing. He removed the sock.

He knew what would come next.

"You assholes! You two are as ugly as you are stupid. And you are as stupid as you are cruel!" Then she had a word for each of the McFinneys individually. First Edweena: "You are the worst cross-dresser west of Albuquerque! Look at those shoes, and that blouse, and those softballs. That's a match made in Hell!" Second, Hector: "And you, you have the brain of a baboon, except baboons smell better!"

Hector smiled, and maybe blushed a little. He didn't expect the compliment from the mouth of Roz Ranker. But, damn, she said it. He's a baboon – the king of the jungle! Shit, wait till he told his old bar friends back in Wittman, after he beat them all up. But he wasn't entirely happy with what Roz Ranker said about his brother. Well, at least, he had his doubts.

"Edweena, what's a cross-dresser?" Hector asked.

Edweena drew a big bony hand across her whiskered cheeks. She looked reflective, but that was to be expected. She was just so damn smart. Hector nodded knowingly: First person in the family to take sex education at the college level.

Edweena said: "It's a person who wears crosses with Jesus on them, for a fashion statement. I read that somewhere."

"You sure do read a lot," Hector said, shaking head in amazement.

"Well, anyway, as you can see, I don't go for that sort of thing. So, I guess I'm not the world's best cross-dresser."

Hector, however, just couldn't figure out this Roz Ranker chick. She made a face like they didn't know what the hell she was talking about – but his brother knew damn well just about everything. She was one smart brother. Ranker, though, seem to stop paying attention. She was looking around in the dark and trying to figure something out.

She spoke. "That was one hell of a bumpy ride. Where the hell are we, anyway?"

180

Hector grinned. He knew it was his best smart-ass you-don't-know-shit grin.

"Well, for your information, Gabby Abby ..."

"That's not my name, idiot."

"Well, Gabby ... Ranker ...for your information, I figured this damn machine out. Figured it all out. See, we were at number 1158. Now we're at 1065."

He showed her. Damn, if he didn't know high-tech like the back of his hand. He took a quick look at his hand.

"You dimwit!" Ranker snapped. "That's the elevation. We just dropped ninety-three feet because you drove the truck down into a goddamned canyon."

"Elevation? What do you know about elevation. Edweena, what does she know about elevation?"

Edweena picked up the flashlight. She ran the beam up the wash they had just come down, following a trail of crushed plants. She set the flashlight upright on the edge of the flatbed. The beam caught her in something of a glancing blow. Half-illuminated, Edweena crossed her arms so that each hand lay on its opposite shoulder, a pose a super-model might strike. Hector realized she had worn just the right blouse, a pink rayon number that buttoned up the side. You didn't notice the sweat stains in the armpits, really, Hector thought.

"Well, it all depends on what she means by elevation," Edweena said. "She could be making another fashion statement. Maybe it's about my shoes. I don't see anything wrong with heels on a desert soar-bay."

Hector glanced over at Roz Ranker and smirked. He smirked like he'd never smirked in his life.

"Soar-bay," he said. "She knows all those fancy words."

"God help us," Ranker said. "I need to meditate, draw on the energy of the cactus spirits ... I need to cleanse myself now of all my impure thoughts."

Hector snickered.

"You got a dirty mind."

"I'm not talking to you," Ranker said. "You're an idiot. I'm talking to your brother. And why does your leg have a hole in it?"

"Forget about the leg. I have. And nobody talks to my brother without permission. You need an appointment to talk to my brother. Not just anybody can come up and talk to my brother. Just who the hell do you think you are!"

Shit, Hector said to himself. That's just the kind of thing that made him want to go and beat the crap out of people. Things like just coming up and talking to his brother. *Don't people got no sense?*

"It's OK, Hector. I'm all ears," and Edweena made a point to show how well appointed these ears were – tilting his head side to the side and stepping fully into the flashlight beam. Nobody could miss the earring with cut red glass the size of a walnut.

"I have to meditate. I need, the spirit-in-cactus. Unless you got a crystal on you. It's a poor substitute, but right now, it'll do," Ranker said. "I need to raise my consciousness before I meet the Master. You two idiots have all but dragged it into the gutter."

"You sound as loopy as Randy," Edweena said.

"I don't want to hear about him. I'm experiencing a spiritual crisis right now. Can't you tell?"

Edweena shrugged her shoulders, her arms still folded in a most feminine way. Hector couldn't get over how well his brother filled out the mini-skirts. Six-feet, 180 pounds, all full of body hair – and yet – so poised.

"There's a cactus. You can get high on that," Edweena said, pointing to the crested on the flatbed.

"Not get high. Get to a higher consciousness."

"I don't see the difference."

"That is only for the Master, anyway. He's the only one qualified to tap its energy field, and give all of us the answer we've been waiting for. I could find myself in big trouble, if I tapped an energy field I wasn't supposed to – like those Nigerians cutting holes in pipelines to get the gasoline. They're not qualified, and they blow themselves up. I'm ready for higher consciousness, but not that high. Energy field in a saguaro like that could knock me right off my feet. I could go insane, or even be killed."

"Hell," Hector said, "we'll probably drive you crazy or kill you anyway."

"I cannot meditate myself into Upper Consciousness on this crested. Only the Master can."

Hector couldn't believe what he just heard. He thought at least she had common sense. Shit, a cactus is a friggin' cactus. You tapped the energy on one, why you've tapped them all.

"Too much energy field," he said, with as much sarcasm as his intellect would permit. "I'll show you how much energy field the goddamned cactus has."

Raising his right leg over the edge of the flatbed, Hector clambered aboard, stood over the cristate – prone in its cradle – and raised his hands.

"Sweet Jesus in the cactus. Raise my consciousness with your energy! And heal my leg!"

The brakes slipped and the truck lurched down the wash. The truck hit bottom and jerked to a stop. Hector flipped off the flatbed, landing on his back, atop a prickly pear cactus.

"Ow! Shit! Ow! Too much energy!"

Hector rolled off the prickly pear onto his face. He felt the energy flow through like a thousand points of pain. He waited for Jesus or God or somebody to come and take him to a better place. He waited for the Red Cross. He waited for the doctor carrying a big bag of morphine. He waited and waited, but there was no relief in sight. Even his brother remained in some distant place. Now he, too, wished he could be somewhere else. He wanted to go back to that moment before he stood and raised his arms to get the energy and become more conscious. If he could go back to that moment, he would do everything differently. He would not seek to tap into the vast energy of the cactus, in hopes of being propelled into a higher consciousness. He would set his life on a different course. He would pistol whip the broad for making him think about doing something that stupid in the first place.

Hector heard voices.

"He's the dumbest piece of meat on the planet," Roz Ranker said.

"That's an unfair thing to say," Edweena said. "He's never had the educational opportunities I had. He couldn't get into the college of his choice, because of a prejudice against people with assault convictions."

"Yeah, he's not hard to read. But you, what's your story? You dress like a woman, but you're still hairy and smelly like a man. Why don't you make up your mind?"

Hector rolled over onto his back, away from the prickly pear. Raising his head, he spoke.

"He's conflicted."

With that, he dropped his head back to the ground. It bounced off a small pebble, but that was nothing. What were a few fired-up neurons in a boundless universe of energy? He floated on waves of energy – beyond pain into some other world where the sun shone ever more brilliantly, where the moon was ever so big and white, like an albino pizza; where starlight shot through his body like a billion laser beams. Where ... where ... *oh, damn. Oh, damn. I feel like I'm some kind of higher consciousness. Well, the hell with that!*

Hector didn't want to lose his edge, which he had acquired through years of delivering bodily harm to others. And hurting people was something Upsters just didn't do. So, after a brief internal debate, he mentally stomped his inner-Upster and slowly got to his feet. Confronting Roz Ranker, he uncaged his inner jerk, metaphorically speaking.

"You're just the kind of smart-ass broad I'd love to teach a lesson."

"You try anything, and you'll be pulling your teeth out of your butt."

That just didn't make any sense. Hector tried to figure out just how his teeth would get there in the first place. Then he felt anger and resentment toward Roz Ranker. She was supposed to be begging for mercy, and she never did. She just didn't get it, did she?

"You don't see, do you? Edweena needs help. Expensive help."

"Psychiatric help?"

"No! What're you talkin' about?" Hector rolled his eyes, shook his head and frowned. "She needs help setting up her new line of clothes. A whole line for big-and-tall men who dress like women."

"Clothes for big-and-tall cross-dressers."

"You said it." Hector punched his fist into his open palm. "But we need capital. It's a free enterprise system and we need capital." He nodded toward the cristate. "That's why we're taking this baby to Upchurch. He was gonna pay Durstan a ton a' money for it. Now it's our ton a' money, see?"

Hector then leaned in closer to Roz Ranker. In the beam of the flashlight, deep shadows crossed her weathered face. He lowered his face for emphasis.

"Don't forget, we tried you first. You had a chance to buy the finest saguaro in the entire world, and you refused. You know, we were even thinkin' about cutting you in, making you a partner in 'Edweena's big and tall clothes for men who like dresses.'"

Hell, there she goes again, Hector thought. Looking at him like he was so full of shit he just might explode. Then she did the unexpected. She reached out and touched his face, then slid her hand gently across his cheek. She smiled, halfway.

"Not my type," she said.

Chapter Twenty-Four

Billy Olsen rolled off the lump under the sleeping bag. He opened his eyes. A few stars still dotted the sky, but a faint glow from the east foretold the sunrise. A pack of coyotes not a hundred yards away made noises like yipping pups. They must have caught a rabbit. It let out a piercing wail, then went quiet.

He smelled coffee. Time to get up and find Upchurch. And if they were lucky, get there before the McFinneys. And nab the cactus. They couldn't have been far from the guru's camp. Olsen just needed to figure out which way to turn.

Bats flew overhead.

They came from a sharp ridge just to the west. They came by the hundreds, flying like the air was boiling, heading south to their daytime roosts. They had spent the night feasting. They had found a place that must have been thick with blossoming saguaros.

Olsen started to sit up. His back told him to go slow, or it might have to hurt him. As did the bruises from the assault by truck. The hole from the pellet of buckshot. And the once-battered pitching arm, usually throbbing from sunup to his first cup of coffee. Up he rose. Slowly, slowly. In the span of three minutes, he was sitting up. Fillmore was already awake and heating coffee on a Coleman stove.

He pointed to the ridge, and the bats.

"They found a saguaro garden. Upchurch's. Matches the coordinates I marked on the map."

"We're closing in," Fillmore said, smiling. She had probably awoken just before Olsen, but she needed no time to clear her head and limber up. She arose pre-perked. True, her khaki shorts and shirt were a bit wrinkled. She had slept in them. And maybe her eyes still were a bit puffy. But she still had the glow of youth and the shapely health of a fitness-magazine model. Olsen sighed, feeling out of place beside her.

Fillmore seemed not to notice.

"Have some coffee," she said.

She poured two cups, sat one on a rock and took a sip from the other. She wasn't going to bring his coffee to him. He'd have to get it himself.

Heeding the threat of painful blowback from his body, Olsen got to his feet slowly and carefully. Then he remembered. Bending down, he tossed aside the sleeping bag to see what that lump was that kept him half-awake through the night.

Dead rattlesnake.

Crushed by his weight. Two thoughts came to mind. The first was one that would have come to anyone: He was lucky he didn't get bitten. Two: He felt bad for the snake. He felt bad whenever he killed an animal. Thanks to his grandmother, he came to appreciate all the animals of the desert as something like kindred spirits. He wasn't an animist really. There was nothing magical about coyotes and turtles and rabbits in his mind. But he sensed they were part of a natural order that was disappearing in a cloud of human activity. Just the same, he thought, better the snake than him.

"What is it?" Fillmore asked.

"Nothing, just a stick."

With all the speed of a drawbridge, Olsen stood up and went to his coffee. Usually, he liked to sweeten it with a bit of sugar – two, three teaspoons. This time, he settled for black. Not bad. It had caffeine either way. A half-cup later, his arm stopped hurting and his appetite began to compete for attention. Not that there was much to satisfy it. The McFinneys had stolen the other cooler, the one packed with eggs, bacon and waffles ready to heat and eat. He grabbed his backpack, filled with trail mix, dried fruit and nuts.

A few fistfuls and another cup of coffee made for breakfast. They cleaned up and raced each other for the driver's side. Olsen won, having anticipated the scramble to see who'd drive.

He bounded into the cab like the Olsen of old. Olsen the Athlete. But he still hurt like Olsen the Afflicted. He grimaced and did his best to disguise it. Smile through the pain. Cranking the engine, he pulled back out onto the stretch of road known as El Camino del Diablo – the Devil's Highway. It got the name from the luckless travelers of old, who – using this as a route to California – died of heat exhaustion or thirst on the way. They probably would have been OK if they had made their way in, say, January, instead of June or July.

It's tough way to learn about the desert ecosystem, at least in summer. If you're not prepared for it, it'll kill you. It's a lesson still being learned. Immigrants from Mexico see the Cabeza Prieta as a clear shot to Phoenix. There's nothing here to stop them, or so they're told by their human smugglers, the coyotes. See? Just unbroken stretches of open desert. What they don't see is enough water, a need measured in gallons.

They certainly don't see shade when the ground is broiling at 140 degrees. They learn about the desert the hard way.

Just now, the morning was pleasant. Bearable anyway. That would change when the sun cleared the horizon.

The road ran parallel to a ridge, on their left. A half-hour later, the sun showed up. The wind blew hot.

Olsen knew this much. He couldn't drive all over Cabeza Prieta hoping to luck into William Upchurch, only to run out of gas in a place where people on foot measure life expectancy in minutes. The gas hog of a pickup was already down to less than a quarter tank. There was a spare can in the back. But the McFinneys shot a hole in it. On the bright side, it didn't blow up.

And that ridge on the left. Something was wrong.

Olsen slowed to a stop. He brought out the map.

"Shit."

"What," Fillmore said.

Olsen pointed. "That ridge, to our left. That's where Upchurch is."

"You have some eyesight."

"No, he's on the other side. I've got it marked on the map. We must have missed a turn, but I can't go back and look for it. We don't have enough gas."

"How'd you miss that?"

"I don't know. I, uh …"

"Now what?"

Olsen grabbed the binoculars off the dash.

"I see a way over. A narrow pass. It's not one we can drive. We'll have to hike. Shouldn't take but a few hours."

"And if we die?"

"Nobody will ever find us."

Olsen folded up the map. He caught Fillmore looking him over. He knew what she was thinking: That he was in no shape to hike up mountains, especially in hellish heat. And, damn, she was probably right. But he chose not to dwell on the probabilities, though it was definitely a long shot.

Olsen turned toward the ridge. He'd get as close as he could to the foothills. They'd hike the rest of the way. Truly off-road now, the truck bumped along an uneven terrain of rocks and assorted desert flora. Olsen didn't like tearing across undisturbed wilderness. Sometimes the job called for it. Sometimes he had no choice. It was drive across the wilderness or watch the cactus thieves leave him in the dust. Then again, maybe this time they could have walked the extra mile.

As it happened, they walked most of it anyway. The desert made sure of that. Not five-hundred feet from the road, the pickup sailed off an unseen outcropping and crash-landed on a rock the size of a Galapagos turtle. Something important broke on the underside. Perhaps a crankshaft. Olsen could only guess. The truck was a goner.

"You should've let me drive," Fillmore said.

"You don't know this country like I do," Olsen replied.

Fillmore said nothing. Instead, she sighed.

Olsen reached over and popped open the glove box. He grabbed a fistful of bullets, on the off chance he'd be reunited with his gun.

He stepped out of the cab. He hoisted the remaining five gallons of water from the truck bed. The other canisters, shot full of holes, were empty. He pulled out five one-gallon milk jugs and filled them with the water. He fit three into a large backpack, then lifted the whole thing up high enough to slip his arms through the straps. His back protested, but that was the price for staving off thirst.

Fillmore packed the other two jugs, and slung the pack over her shoulders like it was filled with foam peanuts.

"Ready?" Olsen asked, knowing *he* wasn't.

"Let's go!" Fillmore said cheerfully.

She made scaling an eight-hundred-foot ridge in the rising heat sound like a brisk workout. Olsen wasn't even sure about making it to the foothills, a mile hike in itself. It wasn't the struggle of lugging all that water, so much as the burden of his own weight.

Chapter Twenty-Five

Olsen slipped on loose rock. He hit the slope stomach-first and slid down like a felled redwood. Fifteen painful feet later, he stopped.

"Oh my god!" Fillmore came half-running, half-sliding down the slope. She kneeled beside Olsen. "Are you OK?"

Olsen took inventory: Legs probably bleeding, though he couldn't really see them. Arms, the same. He could barely open his eyes for the all dirt in them, and a few tiny pebbles. His breathing was heavy and labored, through raw lips. His shirt was drenched in sweat, sticking to his body like a warm dishrag. His chin must have hit a rock. It had a gash.

"I'm fine."

Olsen rolled onto his back and got to his feet, then sat on a nearby rock, rubbing his eyes with a shirt-sleeve. He thought: I'm finished. Here he was a desert rat. He had the blood of desert people running through him. He had hiked the desert in worse heat than this, tracking down cactus haulers in temperatures approaching a hundred twenty degrees. He could handle it, at one time. Now ... now it seemed like a good idea just to sit here and wait for the heart attack. Or the stroke. Or nothing at all. Anything sounded better than going on. He was on empty. He was tired. He was lifeless. And he had a rock in his shoe.

Fillmore's shadow fell across his face.

"You don't look fine."

"Just give me a minute."

Glancing up the mountain, Fillmore said: "We don't have far to go. We should top the ridge in about an hour, once we get past some loose rubble." She looked back at Olsen. "Maybe two."

Olsen got a water jug from his backpack, took a long drink. The water ran down his cheek and dribbled on his shirt, so soaked with sweat it couldn't get any wetter.

"Maybe it's your diet," she said. "You need more fiber."

"I need to give up waffles."

"Waffles, doughnuts, Big Macs, burritos supreme, fries, soda, shakes, white bread, fudge-nut ice cream, fried chicken, Lorna Doones, American cheese, beer foreign and domestic, wine, breadsticks, potato chips ..."

Billy Olsen held up his hand. "One thing at a time, though a beer sounds pretty good about now."

Water would do. He handed the jug to Fillmore. "Drink up. No point in dying of thirst before you run out."

They passed the jug back and forth and slaked their thirst, leaving some for later. They found a spot of weak shade under a paloverde tree. After a rest, Olsen rose to his feet. Refreshed. Recharged. Like the lame throwing away their crutches at a tent revival, he could walk again! He pushed past the rocky debris and worked his way up to more solid ground. They had no trails to follow, but took advantage of natural formations that suggested a zigzag path to the top. Things weren't so bad now. Frequents sips of water and standing rest stops every hundred feet or so set a pace he could handle. Fillmore seemed to grow impatient at times. She could have sprinted up the mountainside, if she wanted. He could manage one foot in front of the other.

194

By noon, they had reached the ridgeline. It offered a view in three directions. The valley they had just climbed out of. The valley on the opposite side of the mountain. And the valley to the east, which the ridge ran toward and dropped off until it disappeared altogether. That's where Olsen saw the dust trailing a vehicle. The dust rose like a tornado was passing over the landscape, picking up and scattering everything in the way. That was one fast truck, carrying two mean cactus thieves and a hostage. They'd found the passage. Ranker knew the way, Olsen figured, and the McFinneys got her to talk.

It came down to this. He and Fillmore had to reach Upchurch before the McFinneys. And they would, with any luck.

Just one question. Where the hell was Upchurch? His camp? It should have been right below them. Looking down the slope – opposite the side they came up – he couldn't see anything. A lower range blocked the view. He and Jane Fillmore started down, walking, stumbling and sliding, careful not to fall.

Reaching the valley, they climbed up the lower range to the crest. The slope drained into a broad basin a few hundred feet below. Olsen could make out a low mound planted with hundreds of saguaros, arranged in circles. The cactus in the inner circles appeared bigger. Olsen raised his binoculars and saw something of a reddish brown stain on the ground near the circle's center. He panned the area, until he spotted a large mesquite tree.

A man was seated beneath it, judging by the bare skinny legs sticking out from under the tree's canopy.

Chapter Twenty-Six

The skinny man wearing a Cubs cap and sitting in a beach chair did not stir at the approach of Olsen and Fillmore. He continued to read a magazine even as the very large cactus cop and the very fit deputy got close enough to touch him.

They didn't. Instead, Olsen said: "William Upchurch?"

The skinny man tossed the magazine on the dirt, annoyed, as though he had just been bumped from the last flight out of Barstow. Now Olsen got a full look at him. He was a skeleton in a loin-cloth wrapped in scabs.

"Where's Durstan? Where's the sacred cristate?" Upchurch asked.

"Durstan's dead," Olsen said without emotion.

"He has become universally conscious," Upchurch said.

"We just told you. He's dead," Fillmore replied.

"But his spirit lives on. Somewhere. Next time I meditate, I'll get his address."

"About the cactus," Olsen said. "It's headed this way now."

Upchurch followed Olsen's gaze across the basin, to the truck outrunning its own dust.

"Oh, spirit of a million watts, I welcome it with open arms."

"I wouldn't," Olsen said. "The men in that truck are dangerous. And they have one of your followers hostage. And second ..."

"I've heard enough," Upchurch said. He stood, went to a creosote bush a few feet away, reached into it and pulled out a small-bore rifle – a .22.

"Look, you don't know the McFinney brothers. They're bad. They're cruel. And …"

"They're wanted for murder," Fillmore said.

She reached out to Upchurch. "Better hand me the rifle."

"You are standing on holy ground. There are no weapons allowed, except for the one I hold in my hand. And only because I am the Master do I have the Universal Spirit of Spirit's blessing to use it."

"You sure you didn't just make that up?" Olsen asked.

Upchurch pumped the rifle, putting a round in the chamber. It looked like something a twelve-year-old would take rabbit hunting, but Olsen didn't mistake it for a toy. A well placed hollow-point could still clean out a good portion of his cranium.

Upchurch's face reddened through the layers of spiritual bliss. It looked a lot like rage. "Don't mock me, or I will leave you out of my plans for universal peace. Or maybe just shoot you."

The truck was several hundred yards away, and Olsen was getting nervous. In less than a minute, the McFinneys would arrive and begin their routine of assault and battery. For a fleeting moment, Olsen thought of rushing the skinny man and grabbing the rifle. He must have outweighed the guy two-and-a-half to one. But he decided against it. After several beatings, crashes and other near-death experiences, he didn't want to get shot again on top of it.

And besides, Upchurch was a deeply religious man. He'd have no problem pulling the trigger in the name of all that is holy.

The truck slid to a stop. Upchurch shot out the two front tires and put a bullet through the windshield.

"Get out, you spiritual deadbeats. Before I end your earthly travails."

"Stop shooting, you crazy bastard!" Hector McFinney screamed. He and Edweena jumped from the truck. A bumping sound came from behind the cab, along with screams muffled by a gag.

"What's that?" Upchurch asked.

"Upster," Hector said, though he didn't say it with contempt, as Olsen had heard him say before. His voice showed a reverence for the term. Odd. "I'd say she has a lot to learn, though," Hector added.

"Get her down."

Climbing up behind the cab, onto the flatbed, Hector dragged out Roz Ranker, bound and gagged. She thrashed. And grunted like an angry ape.

"You want I should untie her?"

Upchurch took a long look at her. She was squirming to go full throttle.

"No, not now." Then he turned his attention to the truck, and the cactus. He circled around and stepped back a good ten yards, so he could better see the cristate. And perhaps have more time to react should the McFinneys decide to jump him.

"Oh, holy, holy, holy divine cactus spirit. It is magnificent. With this, I shall traverse the universe. I shall connect with the Spirit of oneness that dwells at its center, and learn the secret to universal peace. I shall bring this peace to everyone,

198

everywhere. Now, you two, plant this crested on top of the hill. I must meditate and pray soon."

Hector took a half step toward Upchurch.

"Hey, wait a minute. Can't you see my brother has a feminine quality about her? She's delicate. And besides, she's wearing casual dress, the way you might dress for a day at the beach. Not for planting cactus."

"There are no beaches here in the holy shrine of Uppermost Consciousness and ..."

'If you're to go on about tapping into some big energy field on that mutant cactus, forget it. I already done it. And it knocked me off my damn feet," Hector said, still sore from falling on a cactus.

"What do you mean? Only the Master can tap that kind of energy. You didn't … you didn't get the answer, did you?"

"Maybe I did. And maybe I didn't."

"And maybe it won't matter," Upchurch said.

"You're not going to shoot me, are you?"

The Master slipped a skinny finger under the trigger guard.

"I don't know."

Edweena clasped her brother's shoulder. Her large and sun-burned wrist was tastefully framed by a pink ruffled sleeve, something more suited to a French countess than a thug.

"It was an accident," Edweena said. "Hector was only trying to tighten the cactus down, and he slipped and fell into a trancelike state. It just looked like meditation, but … I don't think he achieved oneness or anything like that. I'm just glad it wasn't me. All that spiritual energy would have melted my eyeliner."

Hector McFinney scratched his head through a hole in his cap.

"It weren't an accident."

"Yes, it was," Edweena said. She pushed up a drooping softball. "Don't you remember? Don't you remember that the Master had first dibs on the cristate? And he who has otherwise tapped its spiritual energy has committed a sacrilege and would experience the wrath of the divine bullet?

"What?"

"You made a mistake. You meditated on the wrong energy field. You channeled some trash spirit from that prickly pear you fell on. That's all. So there's no reason for the Master to drill you, right?"

Hector McFinney glanced up at Edweena, then to the rifle and back to Edweena, squinting as though his brain were in labor. Then his eyes popped wide open, with the birth of a live thought.

"You are so smart, Edweena. Of course, of course. It was an accident. 'Cause otherwise, I get plugged." He turned to Upchurch. "Honest to holy Jesus, it was an accident. I didn't do no meditation on that damn cactus. I slipped and fell off the truck it were on. That's why my back's all a bleedin.' I fell on a cactus of a lesser spirit."

Upchurch's finger snaked around the trigger.

"P-l-e-s-e," Hector said, spelling out please, as best he could. "Shit, we'll plant the cactus for you. And we won't charge you extra."

"Well, I am anxious to tap the energy field and get the answer to world peace and reducing credit-card debt," Upchurch said. He placed his finger, once more, in front of the trigger guard, as a gesture of goodwill. "Get going."

Edweena motioned a frilly-sleeved arm to the truck.

"The tires are flat. We can't very well drive on the rims."

"Drive to the base of the hill. Plant the cactus there. Close to the energy field, close enough to focus all the energy of all those spirits. It will come down the hill in a torrent, and through the cristate, lift me to the edge of the universe. Or maybe the center. Whichever is greater," Upchurch said.

Hector nodded. "That's good. You will be one transported son-a-bitch."

"Cut the small talk. Just show me your hands at all times. If I don't see your hands, I won't ask what you're doing with them. I'll just assume you're reaching for a gun – and shoot you."

Upchurch waggled the rifle barrel toward the truck. It was the universal gesture of go over there or get shot. The McFinneys complied. They drove the truck to the base of the hill, the rims leaving ruts in the desert floor. Getting out, Hector seemed to have a joy in his step, as though he obeyed out of love and not because he had to. And he whistled, though Olsen couldn't make out any particular tune. It was just the whistle of somebody happy in his work. Somebody who had had a profound spiritual experience. Edweena McFinney followed behind, her ankles occasionally collapsing as a high heel buckled on a rock or sank into a soft spot on the desert floor.

Hector climbed up on the flatbed and began unlashing the wood-frame cradle holding the crested.

Olsen thought: *Good time to explain my presence*. He took a tentative step toward the holy man. But the Master took a deliberate step back and raised the rifle.

"Close enough. Any closer would be a sacrilege."

Olsen smiled and folded his arms, presenting the picture of a big, harmless, affable kind of guy – which for the most part, he was. He tilted his head toward Fillmore, who was taking a drink from her last water bottle.

"She's a Maricopa County deputy sheriff, and she's here to arrest those men on the truck. The McFinneys."

"For what?"

"The murder of Randall Durstan."

Olsen thought he saw Upchurch blink. Maybe the corner of his mouth twitched. Otherwise, he showed no sign he could be bothered by the fate of anybody stuck here on Planet Doom.

"You're saying they killed him?"

Fillmore wiped her lips.

"They're suspects," she said. "They wanted the cristate for themselves. They saw a chance for big money. They killed Durstan for it, so they could sell it. They figured you for a ready buyer."

"There's no money here. Durstan brought me saguaros because he was a follower. He wanted to atone for stealing cactus, and to seek enlightenment."

"Well," Olsen said, rubbing the back of his neck. "That's why I'm here. I'm an agent for the state Agriculture Department ..."

"What are you doing out here? Aren't you supposed to be inspecting grapefruit for aphids?"

"No, I track down stolen cactus – like that one."

"Oh."

Olsen nodded.

"I think you should reconsider taking it off the truck. I have to take it back, after I arrest the McFinney brothers for stealing it, on top for their arrest for murder. And, well, um, you're under arrest, too."

"You can't arrest me. I'm saintly. And I've got a gun."

"You conspired to steal the crested," Olsen said. "If you come with us quietly, I'll put in a good word for you with the prosecutors."

"Mr. ..."

"Olsen, Billy Olsen."

"Mr. Billy Olsen, I'm above that sort of thing. You can't arrest me, anymore than you could arrest Jesus, Buddha, Mohammed or God, for that matter. Now, stand there quietly while the Brothers Stupidov plant the holiest of the holy cactus, or I'll introduce you to the spirit world. And not in a good way."

Upchurch made his way toward the truck, sliding barefoot through the needle-laden prickly pear and chollas. Olsen and Fillmore followed, watching their step. Roz Ranker, gagged and hands bound, stomped along behind everybody else.

"Just one thing," Olsen said, just above a whisper.

"Better be good."

"Durstan lifted the crested from the estate of Russell Larrabee ..."

"It didn't belong there," Upchurch snapped.

"Point well taken, but I thought I should mention the cactus holds something valuable. Something within."

"I know. I intend to tap into it."

"It's not just that. Larrabee placed something in the boot, sometime back. Coins. Gold coins. A lot of them, I'm told. His security against a world financial collapse. And what could be more secure than the middle of a giant cactus."

"In the boot."

"A cavity, first dug out by a woodpecker for a nest. Long abandoned."

"I know what a boot is," Upchurch said, annoyed.

"It's a big boot."

Billy Olsen gestured toward the hole halfway up the crested's spreading crown.

"Big enough to fit a couple of small poodles," Olsen said. "Or a small fortune."

"A treasure?" Upchurch asked. He sounded skeptical.

"That's my understanding." Olsen nodded. In truth, he had no idea what Larrabee had hidden in the cactus. But apparently it was something of value. If only he could get Upchurch to buy into it. That seemed a fair trade to Olsen: A treasure hunt for Upchurch, and a little more time for him.

Upchurch replied, in the calm all-knowing voice of the Master: "I don't believe you."

"Have one of the McFinneys check it out, before they bother to unload the cactus."

"No," Upchurch said in a scold, his baked-complexion showing a flash of red. So that was that. Olsen was out of bargaining chips. He had nothing to buy more time. Another word and Upchurch would begin drilling him with small-caliber slugs. They reached the truck.

Saddling the crested's trunk atop the flatbed, Hector shouted down: "Hey, Mr. Master! You got any support beams?"

"Over there." Upchurch pointed out a pile of two-by-four planks, near an old Saturn sedan, the Master's car. The planks would hold up the newly planted cactus.

"Thanks." Hector said, staring off somewhere in the direction of the planks, apparently awaiting further instructions from his brain.

"Hurry up!" Upchurch said, with a gun waggle. The McFinneys went back to work, untying the ropes that held the cradle to the flatbed.

"Uh oh, snag!" Edweena piped up, frowning at a pantyhose caught on a needle.

The wardrobe malfunction was a definite attention-getter, giving Fillmore the chance to slip unnoticed into the truck's cab. Unnoticed by all but Olsen. She quietly emerged with their guns – her Glock and his own .38 Smith and Wesson.

She mouthed the word, "Catch." Then threw the .38 for a strike.

Olsen snagged it with his right hand, and twirled around to meet the stock of Upchurch's .22 rifle. The Master had swung for the fences and smacked a high hard one, Olsen's forehead. There was no pain, just a shockwave that ran through his skull. Olsen went to his knees. Though he stayed conscious, the world appeared a distant planet. The blow had spun him back around to face Fillmore. Just as no one paid her any attention, so too did Roz Ranker go unnoticed. She had managed to remove her gag and bindings, then she overpowered Fillmore, wresting the Glock out her hand. It flew ten feet, hitting the ground with an authoritative thud.

Olsen understood Ranker's attack. An enemy of Upchurch was an enemy of hers. The women wrestled around in the dirt, until Upchurch went up to them and told them to stop. He did the gun waggle.

They complied.

The McFinneys stopped to watch, perhaps wondering if they should make a move themselves. But Upchurch gave them the gun waggle, and they went back to work.

"Good work, for an acolyte," Upchurch said.

"I've reached my third level of consciousness."

"What's your name, child?"

"Ranker. Roz Ranker."

"Hmm. Sounds familiar. OK, Ranker of the third rank, tie them up."

Roz Ranker picked up the same ropes the McFinneys had bound her with, tying Fillmore's hands behind her back. As Olsen stared blankly at the ground, a thought appeared out of the fog of concussion. He plucked the .38 off the ground and slipped it into his back pocket. Nobody noticed. The old hidden-ball trick. Finished with Fillmore, Ranker bound Olsen's hands and led him to the mesquite tree. She sat him down next to Fillmore and tied their feet together.

At least now they had shade.

Upchurch told the McFinneys to pick up the pace. Which they did.

With a red-faced grunt, they slid the cradle and the root end of the crested over the edge of the flatbed. They went slowly, feeling for the fulcrum.

"Hold it!" Edweena shouted.

The top end of the cradle began to levitate. Edweena jumped off the truck bed. She managed a two-point landing with her heels. Hector gently pushed the top of the cradle. Edweena nudged the cradle down toward the ground. The cactus pivoted on its fulcrum until the roots met with the shallow hole Hector had dug. The crown rose steadily like a brilliant sun of green, before stopping somewhere close to late morning. Though on terra firma, the cristate still listed about ten degrees off center. Hector got behind the wheel and slowly backed up the truck, following Edweena's hand signals in the side mirror and pushing the cristate toward the vertical. With a wave of her frilly sleeve, Edweena signaled stop. Leaping out, Hector ran back around to help Edweena secure the cristate with two-by-fours. They angled the beams into the trunk, bracing it on four sides.

Hector pulled the truck forward. The cradle fell away. The saguaro stood.

"Shit," Olsen said. "Amazing what the McFinneys can do when they've got a gun to their heads."

Olsen stood in awe. He repeated to himself: *It's so much more magnificent than anything captured in a photograph.* The crest spread out from the trunk like a giant chair back, bulging with tucks and rolls, and scalloped edges.

"First a ritual cleansing," Upchurch said.

He dabbed a bit of water on the shriveled skin of his shrunken frame. Then he kneeled before the great crested and chanted something Olsen couldn't make out. Arising, Upchurch spread his arms out, approached the cristate and reached his arms out and cried.

"Great cosmic vibrations, I do not have the answer. I'm not getting the answer! What must I do? That? But … That's asking a lot."

Olsen heard one side of a running conversation. A Bob Newhart routine with cosmic consciousness on the other end.

"Well, if that's how I get the answer, so be it."

Upchurch stepped up to the crested and pressed his flesh against the needles, a dense array of a thousand little lances. He wrapped his arms about the cactus and squeezed.

The Master said nothing. He just pulled himself into the needles, and through the pain. Olsen realized now that Upchurch had raised his consciousness to a whole new level. A level of insanity.

Upchurch shrieked.

"What's the answer? All that pain! I suffered! I channeled seven saints and John Lennon, but I didn't get the answer!"

Blood pooled at his feet.

In the meantime, the McFinneys overpowered Roz Ranker. They tied her up and tossed her into the shade next to Olsen and Fillmore, making sure to gag her again. Edweena hefted the Glock.

Upchurch paid no attention. He backed away from the cactus and turned around. He had more holes in him than a kindergarten corkboard. Hector and Edweena trained guns on him, but he was too numb with pain to notice. Padding barefoot across the scorching desert floor, he made his way to the watering tank and began a ritual cleansing. He daubed away the blood of a thousand pinpricks. And his mood appeared to lighten – from dispirited to hopeful.

Upchurch raised his arms.

"My followers! The world expects an answer. I will deliver it, now that I have found how to unlock the energy field. And inject it directly into my bloodstream."

Then he nodded. "Yes, that's the way."

Apparently, Hector agreed. He flung his rifle to the ground and shouted, "I'm way ahead of you, guru man!"

Stripping down to his underwear, he dashed to the cactus and slammed into it standing up, knocking a two-by-four loose. The saguaro titled from the impact and began to list. Hector held on tight, straining to keep it from falling over.

Hector shouted: "Help me, Jesus!"

Chapter Twenty-Seven

"Help me, somebody! It hurts now! I'm not looking for the answer no more!"

Hector's cries were a bit muffled by the carpet of needles pressing into the side of his face. Edweena ran around waving Fillmore's Glock in the air, yelling: "Let go! Let go!"

"I can't! It's sacred!"

Of those who watched, perhaps Upchurch and Roz Ranker shared the same sentiment – that the cristate was sacred. They didn't scream, "Let go!" – knowing if he did, the cactus would fall and likely break apart. Instead, they prayed for the cactus spirit. Billy Olsen and Jane Fillmore didn't wanted to see the cactus fall either. Not so much out of reverence for the cactus spirit. They just didn't want to lose a rare wonder of nature.

Edweena pleaded with Upchurch, Hector's new spiritual adviser.

"Cactus guru, tell him to let go! Or I'll kill you!"

Olsen, for one, had never seen Edweena so worked up. Usually, she left the craziness to Hector. But, of course, he was preoccupied.

"That can't be done," Upchurch said, patting himself with a fresh, dampened rag. "It will bring down a terrible curse on all of us if he drops the cactus. The spirit of all cactus spirits will smite us like the bad children we are."

"If he doesn't let go," Edweena pleaded, "that damn cactus is still going to fall, but he'll be underneath it."

"Help!" The cristate leaned another inch.

"Untie me and I'll help," Olsen said.

"OK, OK, you're big enough. Maybe you *can* help," Edweena said, waving around the Glock with something of a flourish, like a socialite with a cigarette. "But don't try anything stupid, or I'll kill you and put you out for the coyotes."

Olsen nodded without expression.

Edweena loosened the binding, then stepped away – getting out of fist range while staying well within bullet range. Olsen rubbed the circulation back into his hands as he stood and stretched. The man struggling to keep the cristate upright was some fifty feet away. Olsen did not sprint the distance. He moved at a deliberate pace, hoping Edweena did not notice the bulge in his back pocket. She didn't. All she could think about was Olsen helping out. The big man sacrificing his body to save a cactus, and her brother.

Olsen stepped past Hector, who was starting to look a bit pale. He stepped around to the exposed spines, rows of crisscross patterns, nails tapering to needle-points lit up by the sun. They would harm him only if he violated the space they were meant to protect. He did not. Instead, Olsen picked up the loose two-by-four and propped it against the side of the cactus closest to the ground. The cristate stopped moving.

"Should hold, for now," Olsen said.

The trunk listed maybe five, ten degrees off vertical. Any more and Hector would have lost it.

Edweena said softly. "You can let go now."

And Hector pulled first his arms, then his body, off the needles. He took three steps and turned. He offered up a thousand rivulets of blood. As he walked, he left of a trail of it, a broad brushstroke of red.

"I saw things no man has seen before. Or woman. I saw the big guy. The leader of all the universe, you know, Mr. Universe, except not so many muscles as you think."

"Over here, lad, for your cleansing bath of untreated water. Just don't debase it."

The skinny prophet had his .22 back. Hector went up to him, pushed aside the rifle and decked him.

"Screw that. I'll take a shower at the motel, when we find one."

He helped the Master off the ground, then picked up the rifle. Hector glanced over at Edweena, who busied herself wiping dirt off her pink silky blouse. The whole blouse was covered in dirt, but this one spot got all the attention. She looked on as Hector spoke.

"Mr. Universe gave me a revelation. He said we take the money Upchurch had agreed to pay Durstan for the cactus. But we take the cactus and, when the heat's off, sell it again, to some other sucker. So it is written, except I didn't actually see it written down anywhere. That's just what Mr. Universe told me."

Edweena scratched a sweat-stained armpit.

"You know, Hector, that revelation sounds a lot like our original plan."

"That *is* a miracle."

Hector poked Upchurch with the rifle.

"Give us all your money, as revealed to me by Mr. Universe."

"Ow, that hurts," Upchurch said, rubbing a bruise on his shoulder. "Anyway, I have no money. All my worldly wealth goes back into the church, and student loans."

"You're lying. You can't fool me or Mr. Universe."

"I have no money, but I have a treasure."

"Where?"

"In the cristate. In the boot."

"The woodpecker hole?" Edweena asked.

"You are full of shit," Hector said.

"How can that be? We are now brothers in spiritual pain. I cannot lie to you."

"What kind of treasure."

"A sizable treasure, I am told. If you recover it, you can keep it."

"How come you didn't tell us this sooner, when we could have just reached in?" Hector asked.

"I just learned of it, on achieving oneness with the great spirit of the needles. And when the cop told me."

"All true," Olsen said. "There's a treasure in the boot."

"Boot?" Hector asked. "What boot?"

"The woodpecker hole."

Hector gazed up at the crested.

"Treasure, huh?"

"We sure could use some treasure," Edweena said.

"Who couldn't?" Olsen added. "Of course, you might sleep better if you answer for your crimes first. Then you can enjoy your treasures, your conscience free and clear."

Hector snickered. It sounded like marbles rattling around his sinus cavities.

"I got no conscience. Anyway, I talked to Mr. Universe. He said I could do any fucking thing I wanted, as long as I balanced it out with something good. You know, like beating up a lawyer."

Then he gave a Olsen a second look.

"Get over there by the girlie cop. And shut up."

Olsen sat down under the mesquite tree next to Fillmore. And quietly began working to loosen her bindings.

Turning to Upchurch, Hector poked a rib with the rifle barrel.

"OK, I'll make you a deal. You go get the treasure and I won't break your legs."

"That's fine. I enjoy being close to the Universal Spirit, joined as it is to the saguaro most holy."

"Hell, if you put it like that … get out of my way. I'll do it."

Hector stepped forward, then turned his gaze upward.

"That goddamn hole's at least ten feet up. I can't reach that."

Fillmore nodded toward the flatbed. "Maybe if you pulled the truck up, you could stand on that."

Hector turned to Fillmore.

"Did I tell you to shut up yet?"

"Not yet."

"OK then. Good idea."

Edweena watched as Hector pivoted toward the truck.

"Be careful!" she shouted.

Fillmore shucked off the now-loose ropes. She and Olsen would wait for the right moment. Olsen figured about five minutes into the future.

Hector maneuvered the truck up to the cactus while Edweena fanned herself with her fingertips. It did little to stop her from sweating. Her blouse was saturated and clung to her like a wet T-shirt, revealing the titillating outline of her bosoms. Two softballs. No nipples, just stitching.

Hector got out of the truck and clambered up the flatbed. Then atop the cab. Keeping his balance, he slowly reached into the hole. He blindly began to feel about the cavity, then abruptly pulled his hand out.

Hector McFinney shouted down to Upchurch.

"Hey! How do I know you didn't sneak a rattlesnake or somethin' in there? Huh?"

"Well, I didn't a have chance to, anymore than I had a chance to sneak a gun in there"

Hector sneered at the pastor of pain, then chuckled.

"So you did sneak the gun in here," Hector said. "You want me to think it's a rattlesnake, so I can make you come up here, instead of me. So you can grab the gun, and kill us. Maybe I'm not so smart as my brother, who's like a sister to me, but I'm a step ahead you, dude."

Turning to the crested, Hector reinserted his hand and began push it down the cavity. He made faces as he worked his arm further in. It was a tight fit and, every so often, a needle near the opening would find his flesh. He cursed, alternating between two common vulgarities. This was not a revelatory pain, Olsen guessed. It was a nuisance pain. Once it ceased, Hector pushed his arm in a little more.

"I got something! I got something!"

"What is it?" Upchurch asked.

"Ain't no rattlesnake. Wait, there are two things. One kinda feels like a box. A box of something valuable…"

Hector McFinney withdrew his hand, with the box. Small and lacquered, like a jewelry box. Shifting it to his left hand, he reached back inside the crested and felt around.

"I think it's a nugget. A gold nugget, like it was supposed to be in the box but ...Got it!"

Hector McFinney grinned and glanced down at Edweena.

"This is gonna be good! We'll get you fixed up. No more cheap crap from Costmo or Mallmart."

He brought out a pebble, or something the size of a pebble. Holding it to his face, Hector McFinney studied one side, then the other. He was not pleased.

"A goddamn bean."

He flung the bean over his shoulder. It bounced off a rock and stopped a foot short of Olsen, still seated beneath the mesquite tree. He slowly picked up the bean. He rolled it over in his fingers and examined it closely. No doubt about it. A tepary bean.

Chapter Twenty-Eight

Billy Olsen tucked the bean in a shirt pocket, and waited. But he already knew the answer. Tepary Bean Girl was not going to save him. Not today. So he made his move. Reaching into his back pocket, he tugged on the gun. But he couldn't budge the damn thing. His shorts were too tight. If he could stand up ... no, that wouldn't work. Edweena would notice him before he could free the pistol. He'd be shot before he could shoot back. So Olsen wrestled with himself. He jammed his hand deeper in the pocket and struggled to work the gun free. He didn't struggle long. The cramp hit his thigh and he fell sideways to the ground. Tears ran from his eyes, as he went fetal. Edweena glanced at him, showed no pity and turned back to Hector.

Olsen took his hand from his back pocket and rubbed his thigh, messaging out the cramp.

And he thought: The absence of pain can be such a treat.

Flat on the ground, Billy Olsen looked up at the cristate. That's one hell of a saguaro, he thought. Then he spotted Hector holding the small lacquered box. He picked himself up for a better look.

"The gold! The gold!" Hector shouted, waving it above his head as stood atop the truck cab.

"Toss it to me! Carefully!" Upchurch shouted. "That is sacred treasure. I will it keep safe."

"Screw you, Upman."

"Upchurch."

"Up yours."

"I don't like the tone of your voice. You're not a true Upster. You're a thug."

"I'm ambidexidrene."

"You mean ..."

Edweena shoved the Glock into the Master's ribs. They weren't hard to find. "Quiet. You're distracting him."

Hector snorted in laughter, shaking his head.

"'Distracting.' Holy Pee. Wish I'da thought of that. You are smart. Jesus, you are smart."

Through a two-day growth of whiskers, Edweena's face blushed Crayola crayon red.

"Yeah," Hector said. "That ought to shut-up Mr. Holy Moly for a while. This here's *our* gold. I'll just take me a look-see."

Hector turned the box over, wondering how it opened.

"Got it!" he said.

He gripped the box with both hands and tried to force it open, in something of a one-man tug-of-war. All he got for his trouble was a face flush from the strain. Between his teeth, he choked out the mantra for hard-to-open things: "Son-of-a-bitch!" Pulling harder and growing redder, Hector's arms fought with each other for possession of the box. They swung wildly back and forth, and up and down – until he threw himself from the truck.

Brother Edweena covered her eyes as Hector bounced off the desert floor.

"Hector, watch out! That dirt doesn't come out!"

The box popped open on impact and a dozen or so coins flew out, three or four rolling off in different directions.

218

Getting dirty wasn't on Hector McFinney's mind. He jumped to his feet and scrambled to pick up the money, leaping from piece to piece.

"Don't worry, Edweena, I got it all! I got it all! All …"

The coins rested in his open right hand. He stirred them around with his left index finger. "All ninety-seven cents."

Edweena peeked through her fingers.

"How much?"

Hector flung the coins into the desert. Quarters, dimes, nickels and pennies. "Not enough for a roll of cheap toilet paper."

Edweena shook her head. She put her face in hand.

"Poor Hector. And you were so brave."

Olsen glanced back at Fillmore. She nodded. She knew. They made a dash for Edweena.

Startled by the sound of advancing feet, Edweena turned – leading with the Glock. Olsen slipped and fell. Fillmore broadsided her with a shoulder, then struggled to wrestle her to the ground. Edweena dropped the gun, but she wouldn't go down. She had Fillmore by a good seventy pounds. Fillmore went to Plan B. She slipped around behind Edweena and grabbed her arms by the elbows and held on.

But it was like wrestling an alligator. Fillmore was losing her grip.

"Billy!"

Olsen got off the dirt and lunged at Edweena. He tore at her blouse. Buttons popped off, revealing big softballs about to bust out of a too-small bra.

"Don't touch those!" Edweena cried.

Olsen pulled the bra back and grabbed one. It was bigger than expected. Bigger than the baseballs of his playing days.

He fumbled it. It bounced off the ground, leaving a small crater. Edweena screamed and squirmed.

"Do something!" Fillmore cried.

Olsen reached for the remaining softball. He managed a three-fingered grip and, with a wheelhouse swing, brought the ball down on top of Edweena's head. She slumped to the ground.

Olsen saw Fillmore staring at the ball in his hand.

"They're not as soft as a lot of people think," he said.

Click. A distinctive sound. A round being loaded into a chamber.

"I'm through with assault and battery!" Hector shouted. "This time, I'm turning to hommyside."

At a hundred yards, someone's Olsen's size would have been an easy target. But at sixty feet, it was like shooting a barn. Hector raised the pistol – a big caliber – and squared it with Olsen's head.

Upchurch had gone unnoticed. He had been shuffling down the wash, and now was some twenty feet from Hector McFinney. "Sacred coins, at one with the spirit world of the desert. And of the universe. I will put them on display, alongside cosmic cactus crystals. And I will ask all my members to follow the path of the cosmic creator of all and donate ninety-seven cents each time they seek enlightenment at the Chapel of the Cactus Spirit. That's a pretty good deal. Most churches ask for a dollar."

Hector rolled his eyes, smirked.

"Crazy bastard," he said, snickering.

As he looked back, finger tightening on the trigger, Olsen was at the release point of his windup. He snapped the ball off his left hand. The pitch was high and wide to the left – by a foot, maybe a foot and a half. The grin on Hector's face was bigger than Howdy Doody's.

"Nice ..."

It was meant to be a mocking comment. Like "nice try." Or "nice pitch." or "nice one."

But the words couldn't beat an 82-mile-an-hour curve ball, which broke right and down and caromed off Hector's forehead. The gun fell to the ground. He staggered off toward the water tank.

Olsen couldn't believe the man was still conscious. He himself had fallen to his knees, doing all he could to keep sight of Hector. And doing his best to hide the pain that shot from his wrist to his shoulder, and down his back.

Upchurch walked into his field of vision and picked up a coin. His face lit up at the discovery. "It's not just a nickel!" He dropped it in the box he had just picked up. He started to move on, but a splash caught his attention. He turned to see Hector washing himself in the tank. The water turned dark, a mixture of mud and blood.

Upchurch snapped. "You're fouling sacred waters!"

Looking up, staring somewhat stupidly through glazed eyes, Hector said: "Shut up, or I'll beat the crap out of you."

After a few more splashes, Hector staggered over to the mesquite tree and fell back in the lawn chair. Eyes closed, he reached for the towel on the rock. It had a lump. He held it by the lump.

"Has a little pillow," Hector said.

"No! No! You can't do that!" Upchurch yelled.

"Go back to your coin collection, Uphole."

Tilting his head back, like a customer in a barber chair, Hector dropped the towel over his face and a spread it open. Then he screamed. He jumped up and the towel fell away.

Mr. Bitey the Gila monster was hanging from his nose.

Chapter Twenty-Nine

Hector yanked on Mr. Bitey. That was a mistake. The more he tugged on Mr. Bitey, the harder Mr. Bitey bit down. And when Mr. Bitey wasn't preoccupied with maintaining his grip, he casually chewed on Hector's nose, working in the poison from a gland in its mouth.

Hector hurled to himself to the ground, rolling around and thrashing his arms.

Scooping up her Glock, Fillmore followed Hector around, unable to get a clear shot.

"Hold still!" she snapped. "I'll take care of it."

"The smell!" he yelled. "It's killing me!"

The poison had an effect, too. In a few minutes, Hector stopped moving. He lay on his back, breathing heavily through his mouth, making farty noises on the lizard's belly.

"I'll just separate the head from the body with a clean shot," Fillmore said.

"Better not." Olsen said. "That's a protected species. I've got a better idea."

He pushed himself up on his right arm, the one that didn't feel like it had received occupational therapy from well-meaning gorillas.

"Take his feet." Fillmore lifted the feet, an ankle in each hand. With his good arm, Olsen raised Hector's torso and – together – they worked him toward the water tank.

"Dunk him," Olsen said.

"No! No! No!" Upchurch screamed. "That's an abomination. That water is holy!"

Upchurch hopped around and rattled his sacred money like a medicine man with fire ants.

"Sorry," Olsen said. "It's the only way."

He and Fillmore heaved Hector headfirst into the tank, and Mr. Bitey floated to the top.

"You've had experience with these creatures," Fillmore said. "I'm impressed."

"Well, I read something in a magazine. I don't know all that much about Gila monsters in the wild. I've only seen one outside a zoo, before this. They're kinda shy."

Fillmore nodded. She was no longer so impressed. On-the-job desert smarts seemed to impress her. Magazine smarts didn't. She liked the physical world, and Olsen came up short in that category in any number of ways. Maybe he just should have lied, made up some incredible Gila monster tale. *Yeah, I know Gila monsters. I once stepped out of my sleeping bag with a dozen of them hanging on me like leaches. They crawled in to get warm. Anyway, I knew what to do.*

Except Olsen was a poor liar. So he kept quiet. Failing to make an impression, he figured, was better than making a complete ass of himself.

Wrapping the towel around Mr. Bitey, Billy Olsen fished the creature out and set it on a rock. Then he and Fillmore hoisted Hector from the tank and laid out him on the desert floor. Olsen forced some water from the lungs. Hector cleared the rest himself with a coughing fit.

If Fillmore didn't fall head over heels for Olsen, at least she could be counted on to cover his ass. He could see her glancing about, never losing sight of the other three. Edweena groaned, flat in her back. Roz Ranker was still tied up, still gagged. Upchurch continued to jump around like a madman. He had been leaping in the direction of his .22 rifle and bending down to pick it up when Fillmore yelled: "Freeze!"

She showed her Glock.

Olsen had his .38, still wedged in his back pocket. Now that he had the time, he worked it loose, slipped in some bullets and looked around for somebody to train it on. *Let's see. Hector, nearly comatose. Edweena, half conscious – or half unconscious. Roz Ranker, bound and gagged. Upchurch, getting nuttier by the minute.*

Olsen pushed the gun back in his pocket.

A calm had settled over the scene, and matters once pushed to the side now came to his attention. For one thing, he noticed just how hot it was. Mid-afternoon and a hundred-and-ten. The other thing: His hunger. He glanced about the camp. Judging by the 120-pound man who ran the place, there probably wasn't much real food to be had. Some dried fruit, maybe. Then Olsen remembered. He found his backpack under the mesquite tree and pulled out several pounds of trail mix. He poured out a handful of raisins, nuts and M&Ms, and pressed them into his mouth – as fast as they'd fit.

He shook the bag, to loosen up the second fistful, then paused. He felt something in his shirt pocket – the bean. The tepary bean. He thought of his grandmother's story, the story of Tepary Bean Girl. He didn't believe it was a real Pima tale, a page out of Pima mythology. But he sensed it. He sensed she was somewhere up there, giving him dirty looks for pigging out on salty snacks.

Rolling up the bag, Billy Olsen returned the trail mix to the backpack.   Upchurch was still dancing around. Olsen went to him and placed a hand on his shoulder, a hand too large to be ignored. Upchurch stopped shaking his coins and muttering about the desecration of the sacred water, gazing up at the man behind the big hand.

Now that Olsen had his attention, he said: "You're under arrest for theft of a protected native plant. You have the right to …"

"I didn't steal it. It was a gift."

"I think you're mistaken," Edweena said, casually swatting at flies attracted to her eyeliner. She was sitting up, massaging a lump you could see from a blimp. "That cactus was ours, and we offered to sell it to you. It was no gift."

"Hey," Olsen said. "Let's not get into that. It doesn't matter. You and your brother are under arrest for theft, too."

"And murder," Fillmore added. "Let's not forget murder. You also have …"

"But we didn't kill anybody," Edweena said. "And we didn't steal that cactus. Uncle Randy was the real thief. Then he died and, left us the cactus as part of our inheritance."

Edweena stood and saw her brother stretched out on the ground, unconscious. She ran over and bent down beside him.

"What happened to him? His nose looks .... chewed on,." Edweena said.

"He disrespected Mr. Bitey," Upchurch answered.

Edweena scooped a handful of water from the water tank and splashed his brother. Hector came to with a symphony of groans. The spray washed away more blood. Hector's nose, to Olsen's surprise, hadn't been chewed to mush. True, it was inflated to the size of a small melon, but the swelling would go down – in time. And, yes, a few of Mr. Bitey's teeth had broken off and become embedded in the tissue. But those could be removed – by a skilled surgeon.

Once he got some medical attention, he'd be OK.

Moving him to the shade would be a good start. Olsen glanced over at the mesquite tree, but something else caught his eye – dust rising from the east. It came from the pass through which the McFinneys drove. Through the dust emerged a van, emergency lights spinning in a blur. A long-haired hippie was leaning halfway out the driver's side window, wailing like a ghost in a cheap movie, faking the siren.

A minute later, the ambulance skidded to a stop, nearly knocking over Upchurch.

"Hey, watch it!" Upchurch shouted.

Leo and Lucy leaped from the ambulance. They scrambled over to Upchurch, each grabbing an elbow.

"You all right? You look kind of scabby, dude," Leo said.

Upchurch shook them off.

"I'm fine."

Lucy and Leo looked the man up and down, as though they didn't believe him. They appeared ready to render treatment, when Upchurch pointed to Hector.

"He was bitten a by a Gila monster. He needs help badly."

They turned to Hector, lying on the ground, largely insensate. Olsen could see Lucy's eyes widen in acknowledgment of their good fortune.

"He's in the worst possible shape, Leo. We've got to move on this one."

As they broke for Hector, Leo spotted Olsen and stopped. He gave Olsen a long, hard look.

In turn, Olsen was consumed by dread. His breathing became more labored. He felt as though his kidneys might shut down. He felt his body failing him. And the worse he felt, the worse he looked. The EMT driver slowly looked him over, head to toe. And back up again. A full body scan.

"Hey," Leo said, "you don't look so good."

"How did you, how the hell did you find us?" Olsen asked, trying to mask the panic in his voice.

"You know, man, illegals cut through here all the time and, dude, is it hot in the summer. They forget their freakin' water bottles, and man, do they get sick," Leo said. "So, you know, we're just out here trying to drum up some business, when we heard someone scream."

"That's the guy you want." Olsen pointed to Hector.

He had mixed feelings about offering up Hector, but if the ambulance crew made a move on him, he'd have to shoot them.

Lucy, who had stopped alongside Leo, glanced from Olsen to Hector.

"He's right. This guy over here could be dying. Get the gurney."

Leo cocked his head, giving Lucy a sidelong glance.

"You sure we didn't like leave it at the hospital, when we had the college kid?"

"The hospital? We didn't take him to the hospital."

"We didn't? But ..."

Lucy's eyes darted from horizon to horizon, as if to see who might be listening in.

"No, remember? He .... you know."

Slapping his head, Leo chuckled.

"Oh right. That was a bummer, huh? But it happens."

As Leo ambled back to the ambulance, Lucy examined the patient. She shined a little flashlight in eyes, in his mouth, in his ears. Olsen approached.

"You might have noticed his nose has been chewed on."

She examined the top of the nose with the little flashlight, although in the full summer sun, it didn't illuminate anything that wasn't already illuminated.

"Let me guess," she said. "Um, um, um..."

"Gila monster bit him."

"Oh, right," Lucy said.

Leo returned with a spinal board and laid it alongside Hector.

"Look," she said. "You remember our training. If we lift him, we could paralyze him for life."

"You're right, man. We'd better roll him."

Lucy and Leo knelt down and rolled Hector over once, face down. Then a second time, face up on the board. His nose, still oozing, was now covered in dirt. Lucy and Leo, satisfied, nodded their heads in tandem.

But Lucy brought her hand to the uppermost of her chins. She thought out loud.

"Better cover his face up, keep it out of the sun while we load up the board. You know how long that can take."

"Sure, I'll just grab this lumpy towel."

Chapter Thirty

Billy Olsen met Jane Fillmore in the Needles Arizona parking lot. He lingered in the shade of a large well-trimmed mesquite as she pulled up next to him in her SUV deputy cruiser. The tires made tracks in asphalt turned syrupy by the mid-afternoon heat. The timing was Olsen's choice. He figured a murder suspect would be less likely to run if the thermometer topped one-twelve, as it did now.

Fillmore sported a pair of light denim slacks and a white cotton blouse. Over that, she wore a shoulder holster, fully stocked. Cop in plain clothes. Of course, there was nothing plain about the cop inside them.

Olsen should have figured it out sooner, but a week later – it came to him. He called Fillmore and she agreed to meet him here. But before he laid out his suspicions, she had to agree on one other thing: A low-key arrest without an army of uniforms. For some people, the more it looks like everybody's out to get them, more upset they get. This was one person you didn't want to upset.

They entered the nursery, through the overhanging mesquites and onto a brick patio, surrounded by large and decorative cactus plants. The office, to the left, overlooked the patio through a small sliding window. Olsen could make out the top of Roz Ranker's head. The flaming red hair was a giveaway. Out past the patio, out past the rows of potted barrel cactus, Olsen saw the hired help – Victor Rodriguez –

sprucing up an ash with a pruning saw. They made their way through the rows of cactus. Rodriguez spotted them and stepped down from the ladder.

He cradled the saw in his arms. He was perhaps sixty, with a rough, acne-riddled complexion.

Rodriguez once had pulled a few jobs with Durstan. Not many, just enough to get to know the guy. Just enough to know he liked the man, but he hated the job. Rodriguez couldn't stand the idea of ending up in prison, again. He'd already done five years for manslaughter – justifiable manslaughter, Rodriguez liked to say. He caught the man with his wife and stabbed him and stabbed him and stabbed him. Every stab was justifiable, he'd say.

He nodded as Olsen stepped in front of him. Olsen had told him he'd be here, and why. Rodriguez was only too glad to cooperate. He considered a Durstan a friend. And maybe an inspiration. What Olsen thought was a birthmark on his neck, now looked to be a small green tattoo of a cactus.

"He's in the greenhouse," Rodriguez said.

The greenhouse was a large bit of framework wrapped in plastic. It was just north of a few boxed paloverde trees. Olsen and Fillmore entered from the eastside, slipping into a world made calm and cool by big exotic cactuses and the breeze of big window-mounted swamp cooler. At the center, a slab of plywood on sawhorses made do as a tabletop, about five feet across. Atop that were baby saguaros planted in baby-size pots, pushed together to form a bumpy green blanket of needles.

How cute, Olsen thought. But he wouldn't want to have to burp them.

Ted Ranker appeared from a side room, an empty planter in one hand and a small gardening spade in the other. He smiled, stretching out the dimple in his chin. His blond hair curled out from beneath a well-stained safari hat. Olsen glanced back at Fillmore. He could see a hint of longing in her eyes. It was just a physical longing – he was pretty sure. At least she never looked at *him* that way.

"Hey, Billy," Ted Ranker said, "sorry about that bar incident. I got a bit worked up, thinking about Roz. But thanks to you, she's back. And, guess what? We're going to church on Sunday. A good Christian church, where everybody who's not there goes to Hell."

Olsen smiled back. It was forced smile. He fished a couple of pebbles out of his shirt pocket. He held them out, one in each hand.

"These two pebbles came from the same place. Randall Durstan's driveway. They're stained with the same grease. It's spread all over the driveway."

Ted Ranker shrugged and cocked his head.

"Yeah?"

Olsen gestured with his right hand, then his left.

"This pebble came from my shoe, and this ... this came from yours. It's a got a bloodstain on it. Durstan's blood."

Folding his arms, Ranker squinted at the pea-size stone. He frowned.

"How do you know whose shoe that came from?"

"You gave it to me at the bar. Remember? You dug it out of your shoe."

The smile returned to his ruggedly handsome face, and he waved off Olsen with the hand holding the spade.

"Oh, well, hell," Ranker said. "Of course, I'd been over at Durstan's a time or two. But that was a long time ago, back before he went to prison. We'd agreed to, uh, market some of his product." He paused. Took a deep breath. "And hell, Durstan was always bleeding. It happens when you're life is stealing cactus."

"Oh, he never bled like that before. No, you picked this up the day Durstan was killed. And who knows? Maybe you got another pebble or two still stuck in those tractor treads that pass for soles. How about a look?"

"No, no. Not now. I'm busy. I've got to repot all these little fellers. They're outgrowing their cribs."

"Really, I insist." Olsen looked back at Fillmore. He wanted to be sure she was on the same page. "We insist?"

Fillmore nodded and patted her holster.

"We insist," Fillmore said. "See, We have evidence you killed Durstan. The rock you picked up in your shoe. You had a clean shirt when we saw you that afternoon at the nursery. You wouldn't change shirts midday just because you got a little dirty. But a bloody shirt, sure. And that scene in the bar provided the motive. Durstan turned Roz away from Jesus, and into an Upster. You're a captive of that old-time religion. You couldn't stand the thought of Roz worshipping cactus spirits, instead of kneeling at a pew."

Olsen glanced at Fillmore, shaking his head. In his mind, he was screaming: *Not now with the motive. Let's ease into it.*

Aloud, Olsen said: "We don't know everything that went on, you know, with Roz."

"But you said..." Fillmore cocked her head.

No, Olsen didn't say rub Ted Ranker's nose in his wife's fall from grace.

233

"We can talk about that later," Olsen said. "For now, just forget what the deputy said, come along peacefully, and we'll make sure you have full access to the prison chaplain. Not some wimpy Episcopalian priest, but an honest-to-goodness, Jesus-fearing Bible-thumping preacher."

Slowly, Ted Ranker shook his head. His face seemed to go blank. His arms went limp, and the pot and spade fell from his grip. He hands, now empty, shook like leaves.

"Excuse me, I'll be right back. I just have to get my good hat."

Ranker ducked into the side room, and emerged with a chainsaw. He yanked the chain and smoke spewed out as the motor sputtered and settled into a tinny roar. The chain became a blur.

"OK, you got me. I hated that Durstan turned her from Jesus. But I didn't kill him for that. You know why I killed him?"

Olsen and Fillmore shook their heads. They said nothing.

"Because he screwed her."

"And you went to his house," Olsen said.

"I overheard Roz on the phone, with Durstan, early that morning. I happened to be watering a Chilean mesquite. I was standing behind it and I heard every fucking word she said. 'You have something for the Master? Why can't you tell me? Of course, I still love you ... but ... yes, I'll tap the saguaro spirits and send you all my energy. And I'll wait ... until ... what? Until the coast is clear? Sure, Randy.' Then she began to cry into the phone. 'Good god, Randy, I'm still pissed you chose pork chops over me. And ... and I'm sorry I got scared and turned state's evidence against you. But we're one in spirit, and I do miss that big organ pipe a' yours.' That was all I needed. Hearing that in her voice. Hearing her go all ga-ga for the man she put in jail. I figured enough was enough. I tossed the chainsaw in the truck drove out to Durstan's. His big truck was still there, with that cristate he just stole. Didn't care about that. I wanted him. I found him in his garage. I told him it was bad enough he turned My Roz from Jesus. But I could never forgive him for screwing her in the biblical sense. He told me it was over. I said, 'Yes, it is. Over and off.'

Ranker lifted the spinning chainsaw.

"And now it's your turn."

He swung the saw back and forth, as if to clear out some invisible forest. He missed Fillmore's neck by inches. She stumbled backward, catching her heel on a large decorative boulder. She fell. Her head glanced off the edge of the plywood table, as Olsen dived for her the way he would a sinking line drive. It was a clean catch, saving Fillmore's head from a bad hop off a concrete floor. But the table had knocked her unconscious and Olsen had no time to drag her clear of Ranker, and his chainsaw. Easing Fillmore down, Olsen dove across the greenhouse, crashing through cactus and potted trees with all the subtlety of a train derailment.

He rose to his knees, worked the revolver from his back pocket.

Olsen's commando move went unnoticed. Ted Ranker stood over Fillmore.

"Stop!" Olsen shouted.

Ranker ignored him. He raised the chainsaw. It whirred away, feet from Fillmore's neck.

Not a good time to shoot, Olsen thought.

Better to talk. Distract him. Make him angry. Draw him away for a better target. Like Olsen himself.

235

"Hey, cowboy," he said, making sure to chuckle. "How did it feel when Roz showed up with that tattoo on her neck? You know the one, that cute little cactus tattoo she got from the cactus thief who converted her, then screwed her. Or was it the other way around? Durstan screwed her, then converted her."

Damn, it worked. Ranker let out a profanity – turning from Fillmore – began whipping the saw around like he was swinging a dead cat. Olsen pressed the trigger. The bullet sailed wide, snapped a branch on an ornamental tree and shattered a pot. He fired three more rounds. All missed Ranker and ventilated the greenhouse.

Ranker lowered the saw.

"Why, you can't hit anything. The only target bigger 'n me in here is you."

Olsen held the gun steady in his left hand. He trusted his left hand, for curve balls and guns.

"I didn't want to hurt you!" Olsen said, above the saw's roar. "I'm aiming at the saw! I'm trying to knock it out of your hand. Like the Lone Ranger."

"I'm trying to lop your head off, and you don't want to hurt me? You're more of a wimp than Durstan. He was always going around saying he swore off killing. 'Upsters don't kill,' he was always saying. 'They have uppermost consciousness. They know better.' Well, in my religion, killing's OK by me if it's OK by God. And Durstan offended God by putting my Roz on the path to Satan."

"What'd I do?"

"You pissed me off."

"And so you're going to ...?"

"In the name of the Holy Ghost ..."

Ted Ranker raised the still-churning saw and continued cutting a swath through his imaginary forest.

Olsen fired again, but he couldn't get a fix on the saw, whipping back and forth like a scythe. A barrel cactus absorbed the bullet like a block of foam.

Slashing away, Ranker was two swings from removing Olsen's shirt and a layer of fat, if not his head. Olsen had nowhere to go. He was backed up against an agave, its thick fleshy arms topped with spearpoints that could skewer a hippo.

Olsen had no choice. He had one bullet left. He aimed at Ranker and fired. A small hole appeared high on Ranker's left shoulder, with a smattering of blood. Not a good shot, Olsen thought. He was trying to hit the chest square on. A shot that would stop him. The shoulder wound didn't. It only fueled his rage. Ranker whipped the saw like a lariat – and let it fly. Olsen dived. The saw sailed overhead, into the agave. The chain caught an arm and launched it into Olsen's back. Not too deep, just deep enough to stick. Deep enough to hurt. He reached for the arm. It was an easy reach, if you didn't mind the serrated edges shaped like fishhooks. Olsen grasped the arm, muttered an obscenity, and pulled it free. His hand was throbbing but his back felt better. He stood and dropped the arm, thick and fleshy. It hit the dirt floor of the greenhouse with a soft thud. Other than that, all was quiet. The chainsaw, buried deep into the agave, had become clogged with thick fibers and sputtered to a stop. Olsen looked around. He had lost track of Ted Ranker.

"Behind you, Billy."

Olsen spun around. Ted Ranker must have stepped right over him. He had gone around the agave, making no effort to retrieve the now-silent chainsaw. Instead, he went to a pegboard and picked out something different – a tree saw.

For big trees.

Ranker flipped the saw once in his hand, the way a big leaguer flips a bat, then he stepped around the agave, toward Olsen. With an outstretched arm, he slashed his way through the air. And he smiled with rapture, the rapture of head removal. It was apparently not confined to any one religion.

Olsen shuffled backward, tracking Ranker while glancing around for any more agaves. He backed into the plywood bench top, nudging it back an inch or two. *Right, it's not anchored down. It's just sitting on sawhorses.* He held that thought as Ranker swung the saw like a machete. Olsen ducked. The blade missed by an inch. Maybe it was a centimeter. Close enough for Olsen to realize he had no time to think. Only act.

With a squat, he placed his hand beneath the loose tabletop. With a grunt, he rose and hurled it like Soupy Sales in a pie fight. Ranker, a bit baffled, had lowered the saw to see what was up, leaving himself wide open. The tabletop drilled Ranker with dozens of baby saguaros. The plywood fell to the floor. But the tiny saguaros held fast, clinging to Ranker's face like potted burrs.

"Ow! Ow! Ow! Help me. Somebody help me! It hurts!"

"Hands up, Ranker. You're under arrest"

"Who said that? I can't see! I've got cactus in my eyeballs!"

"Deputy sheriff Jane Fillmore." It was indeed Fillmore. She had gotten to her feet and unholstered her Glock.

"Promise no more trouble," Olsen said.

"I promise. Just help me!"

"OK." Grabbing a little plastic pot with each hand, Olsen plucked baby saguaros out of Ranker's eyes.

"Ow! Damn. Hurts more when you pull them! Do the rest. My face feels like it's on fire!"

"Let's go, Ranker," Fillmore said. "They'll get you fixed up in jail, at the infirmary."

With prodding from her pistol, Ranker shuffled from the greenhouse, past rows of cactus toward the parking lot. Olsen followed, passing Victor Rodriguez as the gardener went from plant to plant with a large watering can. He must have heard the commotion. And he must have figured it wasn't his business to interfere with police work. They passed the office, the red hair glowing in the window. Beneath the hair, a pair of eyes followed the two cops and her husband. The eyes said: Get him out of my sight.

At the patrol car, Fillmore opened the back door and carefully pushed Ted Ranker into the seat.

"Watch your face," she said. "It's full of cactus."

Ranker stared back, peering out from a mask of a little green squares.

"I know. And I'm OK with that. I think I see Jesus."

With that, he passed out.

Epilogue

Billy Olsen's porch had a new view: The Four Peaks mountain range – four jagged spikes reaching for a low black cloud heavy with rain. Settling back in a molded plastic chair, he was still slightly winded from his three-mile walk through the desert. His sweat suit, living up to its name, was soaked.

He took a sip of warm green tea. Even more sweat beaded up on his forehead. It was a good sweat. The well-earned sweat of a workout. Not the sweat of excess weight after a walk up a flight of steps. He looked around. It was a good view. The view of a compromise worked out with his attorney, Ronnie Clark, and Mike Farley, the tribe's lawyer. Olsen gave up the land his grandmother's house sat on, but not the house. The tribe agreed to move the house to the highlands near the reservation's eastern boundary. From here, he could watch the summer storms roll down from the mountains. He could watch bald eagles stoop along the Verde River, talons for fishhooks.

Now that he had the house, he thought the museum that once threatened it was a good idea. When the museum opened, he would visit it often. It was half-completed now, though Olsen couldn't see it from here. Too far away.

Dust rose from a road that curled around a nearby hill. Too soon to tell whose dust it was.

Olsen thought back. It had been three months since pocketing the tepary bean. Three months since he took the hint from Tepary Bean Girl. Three months of good food and exercise, and here he was – fit and healthy at 215 pounds. Well, moving in the right direction anyway. Sure, Tepary Bean Girl was just a story. She wasn't real. Not even real Pima lore.

Still … there was that bean in the crested. It wasn't blown in by the wind.

Of course, his good habits weren't entirely inspired by a bean in a cactus. There was the wake-up call. Shortly after Ted Ranker's arrest, Olsen had chest pains. It was just heartburn, as it turned out. But the doctor ordered more tests, and just as she suspected, Olsen's diabetes was no longer a potential disease. It had become an actuality. Olsen had to get in shape, eat right or face a life of insulin injections and deteriorating health. So he changed his ways. He began regular walks through the desert that surrounded his relocated house. He gave up the pancakes, the waffles, and the greasy burgers and fries. He gave up the beer, mostly. He ate the foods his grandmother told him about. The tepary beans. The squash. Fresh melons. Whole corn. All foods from the ancient ones. And sardines. They went well with the occasional beer.

The car was closer. The dust trailed a Volkswagen Beetle. It was Mary Martinez, coming to join him for another walk. She too had changed her ways. By some standards, she was a still a big girl. But for Olsen, she was one fit Pima. And funny, too. He did not have to read leaden, mind-numbing books to converse with her, as he would with Anna Stewart. He did not have to return to the buff physique of his playing days, as he would with Jane Fillmore. Anyway, she was back to dating the man who sees dead people, the medical examiner.

All that in three months. Of course, there was more.

There was Ted Ranker, the murderer. He got 10 years for second degree murder. Relatively light. His attorneys painted Randall Durstan as an unsympathetic victim, what with bedding the poor man's wife. And some jurors told the press the guy had it coming, however barbaric the means.

As for the magnificent cristate, number forty-three, Durstan had indeed stolen it twice. Once for Larrabee, snatching it from the Mazatzal Wilderness of the Tonto National Forest, northeast of Phoenix. And later, for Upchurch, as a the centerpiece of his Upster retreat in the Cabeza Prieta Wildlife Refuge. And that's where it stayed.

State and federal officials decided against moving the cristate. That would only lessen its chances for survival.

Russell Larrabee was charged with stealing native plants from federal property. He was out on bail awaiting trial. William Upchurch pleaded guilty to receiving stolen protected plants and got six months in state prison.

He continued to believe that the ninety-seven cents he had found in the cristate was sent to him by the twin Universal Spirits, Rilukku and Webster. And he had begun a quest to decipher their real meaning. The authorities knew all about this, as they had monitored his phone calls to his disciples. He asked them to meditate and pray everyday at the shrine, to find the answers. He had so many questions. Was ninety-seven the number of years left before the world was consumed by flaming meteors of cactus? And would only ninety-seven Upsters be spared? Or was the number some kind of cosmic correlation between pain and enlightenment?

Larrabee had a millionaire's sentimental attachment. It spoke to his legacy. The first ninety-seven cents made on the first sale at his first discount dollar store. He just knew, one day, the Smithsonian would come calling. They'd want the coins for their collection. Larrabee imagined them on display, next to Rockefeller's first dollar. So they had to be kept safe. Safe from home invasions and bank robbers. So one day Larrabee propped a ladder against the cristate, climbed up to the fanned crest and pushed a box of coins into the boot. Nobody would ever find them there, or so he thought. Until Durstan stole the whole damn cactus.

Larrabee asked for his ninety-seven cents back. Upchurch refused.

Now it was in the hands of the lawyers. Larrabee sued to recover the loose change – and Upchurch fought back, saying he had the Universal Spirit and even more lawyers on his side. In a few short months, the legal bills over who owned ninety-seven cents topped $100,000.

Rudy Ossylmeyer, ex-director of the Department of Agriculture, did not fare well. As reported by the media, he quit to spend more time with his family. Olsen knew otherwise. The governor told Ossylmeyer to get out or face criminal charges. Joshua Hempf, the fruit inspector who couldn't stand blood, became acting director. As it turned out, despite his phobia, he was a fair and efficient administrator. It took a bit of adjusting, but it was a nice change for Olsen. It was like getting used to the rush of fresh air after years of smog.

As for the governor and Larrabee, they were friends no more. "He might have contributed some to my campaigns, but I barely knew the man, really," the governor said. Anyway, Larrabee now had a rap sheet – not the kind of person a politician wants to be seen with. And, as was quickly becoming apparent, Larrabee's fortune would soon be consumed by his lawyers. The   penniless make the worst campaign contributors.

At last, the McFinneys. Edweena McFinney never could commit herself to womanhood, in the surgical sense. But she always identified herself with the fairer sex, and so took a job as a roller-skating carhop, where she could wear short skirts and show off her legs. She even went so far as to shave them. But she went for a softer feminine touch on top, giving up the softballs for small sandbags. She pleaded guilty to reckless driving, stemming from the time she and Hector drove a large flatbed truck into a sheriff's patrol car. She got probation. It sounded like a slap on the wrist to Olsen. But the prosecutors and the judge agreed that Edweena was good at heart and that her brother was the real troublemaker. Left to herself, she was a danger to no one.

And her brother? It's hard to say. After Hector McFinney was loaded onto the ambulance, he was never seen again. The ambulance drivers, Leo and Lucy, told the police they thought they had dropped him off at St. Mary's Hospital in Tucson, but they couldn't swear to it. Then Leo remembered something, according to police transcripts.

Leo: "Oh, wow, was it my turn to close the door in back?"

Lucy: "You lost the coin toss, remember?"

Leo: "Bummer."

Lucy: "He could be in Mexico."

Lt. Arnoldson: "Mexico?"

Leo: "Oh, like we didn't stop for a Tecate and some tacos on the way back, man."

www.ingramcontent.com/pod-product-compliance
Lightning Source LLC
Chambersburg PA
CBHW071558110726
47908CB00007B/2157